"Everybody has this playboy image of me," David grumbled.

"Don't you see yourself that way?" Susan asked.

"Hell, no."

"Then why do you flirt so much?"

"I don't flirt that much."

"Oh, yes you do, David. Even your—your body language is inviting."

"What's that supposed to mean?"

"You know, those big, dark, bedroom eyes and that deep, sexy voice—"

"You think I have bedroom eyes?" He took a step closer.

"Spare me. You know you do."

"You think my voice is sexy?" He took another step.

She inched back and felt the wall behind her. "Knock it off, David," she said with an attempt at a laugh.

He closed the gap between them and planted a hand on either side of her head. "But you don't even know how good I can be, honey. Yet."

* * * *

For fans of *Wendy Wyoming* (SSE #483), she wasn't the only one with a secret identity. Read on as the mysterious, sexy deejay is unveiled, and her notorious brother, David, attempts to shed his ladies' man reputation....

Dear Reader,

Welcome to the Silhouette **Special Edition**
experience! With your search for consistently
satisfying reading in mind, every month the authors
and editors of Silhouette **Special Edition** aim to offer
you a stimulating blend of deep emotions and high
romance.

The name Silhouette **Special Edition** and the
distinctive arch on the cover represent a
commitment—a commitment to bring you six
sensitive, substantial novels each month. In the
pages of a Silhouette **Special Edition**, compelling
true-to-life characters face riveting emotional
issues—and come out winners. All the authors in the
series strive for depth, vividness and warmth in
writing these stories of living and loving in today's
world.

The result, we hope, is romance you can believe in.
Deeply emotional, richly romantic, infinitely
rewarding—that's the Silhouette **Special Edition**
experience. Come share it with us—six times
a month!

From all the authors and editors of Silhouette
Special Edition,

Best wishes.

MYRNA TEMTE
The Last Good Man Alive

Silhouette Special Edition

Published by Silhouette Books New York

America's Publisher of Contemporary Romance

This book is dedicated to
Debra Sims White,
a kindred spirit from day one.

My sincere thanks to the following people for their assistance in research: Jack Reber, KHQ-TV, Spokane, Washington; Dave Johansen, Cheyenne Frontier Days, Cheyenne, Wyoming; Patty Polsky, University Hospital, Denver, Colorado; Donna Savarese, The Children's Liver Foundation, Sherman Oaks, California; and Jeff Orlowski and Deedee Demane, Colorado Organ Recovery Systems, Denver, Colorado.

SILHOUETTE BOOKS
300 East 42nd St., New York, N.Y. 10017

THE LAST GOOD MAN ALIVE

ISBN: 0-373-09643-7

First Silhouette Books printing January 1991

Printed in the U.S.A.

Books by Myrna Temte

Silhouette Special Edition

Wendy Wyoming #493
Powder River Reunion #572
The Last Good Man Alive #643

MYRNA TEMTE

grew up in Montana and attended college in Wyoming, where she met and married her husband. Marriage didn't necessarily mean settling down for the Temtes—they have lived in six different states, including Washington, where they currently reside. Moving so much is difficult, the author says, but it is also wonderful stimulation for a writer.

Though always a "readaholic," Ms. Temte never dreamed of becoming an author. But while spending time at home to care for her first child, she began to seek an outlet from the never-ending duties of housekeeping and child-rearing. She started reading romances and soon became hooked, both as a reader and a writer.

Now Myrna Temte appreciates the best of all possible worlds—a loving family and a challenging career that lets her set her own hours and turn her imagination loose.

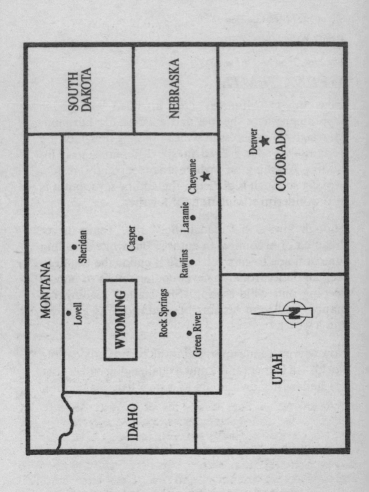

Chapter One

"The ring, please?"

David Hunter blinked in surprise when he realized Rev. Baker was looking at him expectantly. Flushing at the realization he'd been caught daydreaming, David hastily fished the bride's wedding ring out of his pants pocket and smacked it into the minister's outstretched hand. His most important duty as best man accomplished, he exhaled a silent sigh of relief and glanced over at the man standing beside him.

Jason Wakefield had been his best friend since junior high school. There wasn't a man alive David liked better, or one he would rather have marry his little sister Melody. He glanced at her and grinned, remembering the hassles she had given Jason before finally agreeing to marry him.

Poor old Jase had been a wreck, almost worse than David had been himself last January, when his fiancée had thrown her engagement ring back in his face. The memory brought a stab of pain and a quick pang of jealousy toward the couple beside him. David squelched both emotions, reminding himself he was sincerely happy for Jason and Melody. But dammit, he would have been a groom three months ago himself, if only Liz had trusted him.

Well, sooner or later he'd get over the whole darn mess, but he wished he could show as much class in doing so as Jason's last girlfriend, Susan Miller. David knew Susan had been hurt when Jason and Melody got back together, but there she was, about ten pews back, dressed to kill and wearing a smile on her pretty face for everyone to see. Now there was a woman with some pride and guts. Maybe he should try to get to know her better. . . .

"Jason, you may kiss your bride."

Resolutely blinking back tears, Susan Miller drew in a shallow breath and held it while Jason Wakefield beamed an adoring smile down at Melody Hunter, his new wife. *Lord,* she thought frantically as her eyes burned and a lump formed in her throat, *I didn't think it would be this hard to give Jason up. If I hadn't sent him back to Melody, maybe we could have . . .*

Susan bit the inside of her lower lip. Whatever her regrets, it was too late to change anything now. The couple in front of the altar shared a kiss filled with such tenderness and passion, a chorus of sentimental ahhhs swept over the sanctuary. Susan's seven-year-old son, Timmy, punctuated the ahhhs with a loud, digusted, "Oh, gross!"

Chuckles echoed through the church. Heads turned. Timmy's four-year-old brother, Eric, opened his mouth as if to add his agreement. Susan clapped a hand over his lips in time to prevent a second outburst. Both boys subsided into a fidgety silence, and the minister asked the newlyweds to turn and face the congregation.

"Friends, it's my pleasure to present to you, Jason and Melody Wakefield," he announced with a broad smile.

The pride and elation in Jason's eyes hardened the lump in Susan's throat until it felt like a jagged slab of concrete. Damn! She wished she'd never allowed her friends to drag her to the Roadway Inn for a drink last May, wished she hadn't run into Jason, wished she hadn't listened to his sad tale of heartbreak over Melody Hunter.

But she hadn't been out for an evening with adults in months. It had been easier to talk to an old high-school acquaintance like Jason than strike up a conversation with a stranger. Besides, Jason was such an attractive man, she'd been flattered by his attention. Before she'd known what was happening, she'd accepted one date with him, then another and then another.

Though they'd never been lovers, he'd been thoughtful, affectionate and absolutely wonderful with her sons. His friendship had brought laughter and sunshine back into her life, reminded her she was still a woman and restored at least some of the self-esteem she'd lost during her divorce. But she had ended all that four short weeks ago.

So what if he's the last good man alive? she lectured herself. *He didn't love me the way he loves Melody. It just wasn't meant to be.*

The organ blared out the triumphant notes of the recessional. The happy couple swept down the aisle. Susan swallowed hard, squared her shoulders and lifted her chin. No matter how miserable she felt, she was not going to spoil Jason's wedding day. She owed him that much.

Following the boys through the receiving line, she plastered on a bright smile and managed to offer sincere congratulations to the bride and groom. After all, she had known darn well that Jason loved Melody Hunter from the beginning. It wasn't his fault she'd been dumb enough to fall a little in love with him, and she *was* happy for him and for Melody. Unfortunately, at the moment she couldn't help feeling bereft and more than a little sorry for herself.

"Well, I'll just have to get over that," she muttered, ushering the boys out of the church for the short trip to the reception .

Susan had never been inside the Cheyenne Country Club before, but the boys didn't give her much time to inspect the elegant dining room. Eric made a beeline for the refreshment table and stood staring in openmouthed awe at the five-tiered wedding cake. Timmy was equally impressed by the champagne fountain. Recognizing the governor, the mayor of Cheyenne and the president of the University of Wyoming among the guests, Susan experienced a surge of empathy for her sons. Though her ice-blue summer suit was certainly appropriate for the occasion, she felt intensely out of place in such elite company.

Well, what did you expect from the Hunters? she asked herself.

Melody's father, Michael Hunter, owned a TV station and two radio stations. Her mother, Karen, wrote a popular syndicated newspaper column. Her sister, Barbara, was a White House correspondent for one of the major television networks, and her brother, David, had been Denver's most popular disc jockey until he'd come home to start taking over his father's media empire two years ago.

If Cheyenne had a jet set, the Hunters were its star members. They were all good-looking and respected, the kind of people who always wore exactly the right clothes and said exactly the right things. Though they were friendly and welcoming, Susan found them intimidating. They were just so darn ... perfect.

She glanced wistfully toward the exit, but the wedding party arrived then. Resigning herself to an hour's stay, Susan led the boys to a table on the west side of the room and studied Jason's new family to pass the time. Her throat constricted at the sight of him surrounded by so much love and affection.

Waiters passed trays of champagne while the bride and groom cut the cake. Then David Hunter stepped forward to offer the first toast.

"Jason. Melody. This is an exciting day for all of us. We wish you good fortune, wonderful memories and a long lifetime of happiness together." He raised his glass to them. "To the bride and groom."

"To the bride and groom," Susan echoed along with the rest of the guests. She felt utterly alone. The chilled champagne slid down her throat, easing the tight, dry sensation.

"Mom, can I have some cake now?" Eric asked impatiently, tugging on Susan's skirt.

"Oh, sure, honey."

Both boys took off before Susan could collect herself enough to stand up. By the time she made her way through the crowded room and caught up with them, Eric had piled a plate embarrassingly high with cake, nuts and mints, and Timmy was right behind him. Shaking her head in mild exasperation, she intercepted the scamps, grabbing Eric's wobbly plate just in time to prevent an accident. She turned to check on Timmy and immediately reached for his plate, as well.

"Looks like you could use an extra hand," a deep, resonant voice said from behind her.

She twisted around and looked up into David Hunter's brown eyes. Lord, but he was a big, good-looking devil, she thought. Maybe even better looking than Jason. His dark hair was attractively windblown. He had eyelashes and cheekbones a fashion model would kill for. If not for a bold, straight nose and a rugged jaw, he would have been almost pretty. And that warm, sexy smile of his could melt a glacier.

Self-conscious under his amused scrutiny, she smiled, shook her head and held up both plates. "Thanks, but we can make it. I'll get them settled and come back for punch later."

"Go ahead and get it now," he insisted, taking the plates from her hands. He grinned down at the boys. "Show me where you're sitting, guys."

"But . . ."

Without giving her a chance to finish the protest, David followed the boys into the crowd. Susan gazed after his broad-shouldered frame for a moment, then picked up two cups of strawberry punch and a stack of napkins. Eric and Timmy were already attacking their food when she reached the table.

"Eric, don't eat so fast. You'll make yourself sick," she warned, setting a cup in front of each son before giving David a rueful smile. "I do feed them once in a while. Thanks for your help."

He chuckled. "You're welcome." He stepped closer and took her arm. "Let's go get some of that cake for us."

"Look, David, I know you must be busy," Susan began, hustling in her high heels to keep up with his long strides. "You don't need to eat with us."

He stopped walking and smiled down at her. "You wouldn't make me sit all by myself, would you?"

Judging by the envious glances she was receiving from women all over the room, Susan doubted there was any danger of that happening. Nevertheless, that darn sexy smile of his quickened her pulse and dampened her palms.

"Oh, uh, no," she answered, chagrined by her reaction. "Of course not."

"Good."

He escorted her to the refreshment table, putting a hand at the back of her waist. His light touch sent a tingle of awareness shooting the length of her spine. Susan ignored it.

If she were ready for a new relationship with a man— which she most certainly was not—David Hunter would be her last possible choice. Oh, she liked him well enough; he was a charming man, and she had enjoyed a casual acquaintance with him during the months she had dated Jason. But David was the most sought-after bachelor in town and was too sophisticated and much too close to Jason for her ever to become seriously involved with him.

When they had filled their plates and rejoined the boys, Susan soon realized she needn't have worried about developing a relationship with David. He barely had time to taste the wedding cake before Erica Weston, a svelte brunette, stopped beside his chair. She gave Susan and her sons a cool smile, then casually laid a well-manicured hand on David's shoulder.

"Well, hi there, stranger," she said in a low, husky tone.

David looked up at the woman and a broad grin stretched across his mouth. "Good to see you again, Erica."

"Wasn't that just the nicest wedding you've ever seen?" she asked, batting her eyelashes at him.

"Yes, it was," David agreed.

"You haven't been around lately," she said, giving him a pretty little pout. "Have you been working too hard at that old radio station again?"

"I'm over at the television station now," he answered.

Erica's eyes widened. "Oh, that sounds fascinating, David. We'll have to get together so you can tell me all about it. You still have my number, don't you?"

"You bet."

Erica left with such obvious reluctance, Susan quickly patted her mouth with a napkin to hide a smile. David took a bite of his cake, answered a question from Timmy about the TV station, then turned his attention toward Susan. His lips parted as if he were going to ask her a question, but before he could get it out, a tall buxom redhead wearing a tight, sleeveless dress approached David from his left.

David addressed her as Nicole and exchanged polite chit-chat until she left, every bit as reluctantly as Erica had done. A blonde named Becky followed Nicole to David's side, and another redhead, named Debbie, followed Becky. He greeted them all with genuine warmth and interest, made each one feel special for a few moments and sent them on their way without committing himself to a future date with any of them.

Susan found it fascinating to watch and admired David's patience and unfailing courtesy. At the same time, she was utterly grateful she would never be involved with the man herself. The last thing she needed in her life was another smooth operator.

Caught up in her observations, she gasped in dismay when she realized Eric had eaten everything on his own plate and was filching more nuts and mints from Timmy's. Before she could scold him, however, a pretty blond teenager approached the table and invited the boys to come outside for games with the other children. Since her sons had behaved themselves far longer than she normally would have expected, Susan gladly gave them permission.

David turned to watch them leave. "They're really great kids," he said, turning back to her.

"Thanks. I'm proud of them." She glanced away when his warm, admiring smile started doing funny things to her insides despite the scene she'd just witnessed. "Don't you have some best-man duties to take care of?"

He craned his neck until he located Jason and Melody, surrounded by guests near the fountain. "Not for a minute," he answered. He leaned closer, giving her a conspiratorial grin. "Want to help me decorate their car?"

Smiling at his devilish expression, Susan shook her head. "No, thank you."

One of the ushers approached the table then. He nodded and smiled at Susan before turning to David. "Everything's ready."

"All right, Alan," David replied, scooting back his chair.

David introduced her to Dr. Alan Jordan, a local cardiologist, then excused himself and hurried off toward the exit. Susan decided it was time for her to leave, as well. She pushed back her chair and reached for her purse. When she stood up, however, a passing waiter handed her a small, plastic bag filled with rice.

Oh, what the heck? she thought, taking two more for Eric and Timmy. *Might as well see this shindig through to the end.*

The minute she joined the other guests waiting for the bride and groom's departure, the boys ran over to greet her. She winced inwardly at the grass stains on their Sunday-school pants, but smiled at their happy faces.

"Do we getta throw rice now?" Timmy asked eagerly.

"In a few minutes. Don't unwrap it until they come out," Susan instructed, giving each of them a bag.

"Did you and Daddy do all this stuff when you got married, Mom?" Eric asked.

Stroking his tousled, sandy hair off his sweaty forehead, Susan shook her head. "No, we had a very small wedding, honey."

The crunch of tires on gravel announced the arrival of a vehicle. Jumping up and down in excitement, Timmy pointed toward the driveway. "Wow, look at that!"

David Hunter parked Jason's blue Blazer in front of the sidewalk leading into the building. The wedding guests burst into laughter and applause at the helium balloons filling the interior and the clever pictures painted on the vehicle's side windows. David battled his way out of the balloons, slammed the door and bowed to the crowd. A gleaming black Porsche roared up behind the Blazer, followed by a line of other cars in preparation for the newlyweds' send-off caravan.

"Careful with my wheels, Doc," David grumbled as Alan Jordan climbed out of the low-slung sports car.

Barbara Hunter hurried out of the building a moment later. "They're almost ready," she called, holding up her hands for attention. "We need all the unmarried women over to the left of the sidewalk so Melody can throw her bouquet. Everybody else, get your rice ready."

Having no desire to take part in that particular ritual, Susan stayed exactly where she was. Timmy shot her a perplexed look. "You're not married, Mom. Aren't you supposed to go over there, too?" he asked without the slightest effort to keep his voice down.

"Never mind, Timmy."

"But, Mom—"

"Mom, I don't feel good," Eric interrupted, leaning against his mother's legs.

Susan bent down and felt Eric's forehead, telling her older son, "It's not important, Timmy."

David Hunter turned his head at the sound of Timmy's voice and walked over to them. "What's going on?"

"Nothing much," Susan answered, sending Timmy a warning scowl.

Timmy pointed at the group of women across the sidewalk. "Mom won't go over there," he said indignantly.

"Come on, Susan," David coaxed with a broad grin. "You're not superstitious, are you?"

"But Eric's—"

David reached down and swung Eric up into his arms. "I'll watch the boys for you."

"But—"

"Go on." He nudged the small of her back with his free hand. "We'll be just fine. Won't we, guys?"

Both boys nodded vigorously. Susan silently cursed the lessons on honesty she'd drilled into Timmy, then gave in rather than create more of a scene than she already had. Casting a last anxious glance at Eric's flushed face, she turned and stalked off across the sidewalk. She found a spot toward the back of the group, intending to duck if the bouquet came anywhere near her.

"They're coming!" someone near the building shouted.

The newlyweds paused in the doorway while Melody Hunter-Wakefield scanned the women on the left side. Her gaze zeroed in on Susan, and an impish yet determined smile spread across her face. Then she stepped outside and tossed the flowers in a perfect arc, aimed directly at Susan.

Hemmed in on all sides by eager, laughing women, Susan couldn't get out of the way. The bouquet dropped into her hands like a guided missile finding its target. She stared at the collection of pink rosebuds and baby's breath in consternation, barely feeling the congratulatory pats from the other women. A shout went up from the crowd. She looked up in time to see Jason and Melody run past her under a shower of rice.

An instant later her eyes met David Hunter's over the top of a stout woman's enormous, flower-bedecked hat. His intent, contemplative expression gave her the distinct impression that he'd been studying her for some time and raised goose bumps on her arms despite the warmth of the afternoon sunshine. Then his head jerked around at the thunk of the Blazer's door slamming shut. Realizing David wanted to join the caravan, Susan shook off the odd, tingling sensation and hurried toward him to claim her boys.

She dodged around the woman with the hat just in time to hear a horrifyingly familiar sound. The stout woman shrieked and jumped back with surprising agility. Susan caught one glimpse of David's stunned face through the crowd, kicked off her high heels and took off at a dead run.

"Mom, come quick!" Timmy shrieked.

She reached them a moment later and could only stop and stare, aghast at the tall, handsome man holding Eric. David's tan took on a sickly, greenish tinge as the boy retched in his arms and a pinkish flood splashed down the front of his ruffled tuxedo shirt.

Susan handed Timmy her purse and the bouquet. "Oh, David, I'm so sorry," she said, extending her arms to Eric. "Come here, sweetheart."

David instinctively stepped back, holding the boy away from her. "No, Susan. You'll ruin your clothes." He pulled a white handkerchief from his hip pocket and gently wiped off Eric's face. "It's all right, Eric."

"Mommy," Eric wailed, tears streaming down his pale cheeks as he reached for her, struggling against David's hold.

"Everything I own is washable," Susan assured David, taking Eric into her arms. "But be sure to send me your cleaning bill."

"Hunter, come on," Alan Jordan called from the passenger seat of the Porsche. "They're leaving."

David glanced down at his chest and grimaced. "Go ahead without me, Doc," he answered, shooting Susan a lopsided grin.

The newlyweds' car drove off, a long string of tin cans tied to the rear bumper clattering and banging behind it. David inclined his head toward the building and shouted to Susan over the honking horns from the rest of the caravan. "Let's go inside. I'll change while you get Eric cleaned up. Then I'll drive you home."

"Boy, Eric, I can't believe you barfed all over Mr. Hunter like that!" Timmy chided his little brother.

"I couldn't help it," Eric cried.

"That's enough, Tim," Susan warned, hauling Eric into the ladies' room. She set him down on the counter, ran cold water over a handful of paper towels and cleaned him up as best she could. Wanting only to escape before David arrived and prolonged an embarrassing situation, she perched Eric on her hip and hurried back outside.

Timmy ran ahead and brought back her shoes. As she stepped into them, he asked, "What if Eric barfs again, Mom?"

Susan glanced down at her younger son. His normal color had returned, his thumb had found his mouth and his eyelids were drooping. If she could just get him to the car and get out of here, he would probably fall asleep. "He won't, Timmy. Why don't you get the keys out of my purse and open the car door for me?"

While Timmy ran off to obey her request, she boosted Eric up a little higher and headed for her red Subaru wagon. Carefully picking her way across the loose gravel in the parking area, she silently cursed her son's deadweight and the high heels forcing her to slow down. Lord, she hoped it would take David a long time to change his clothes. Fifty feet away the open car door beckoned. She boosted Eric again and trudged faster.

Too late. The door to the building banged open behind her. She heard David call, "Susan, wait," then the sound of feet running in her direction. She kept right on walking. She didn't want to be rude, but it had been a miserable day. She'd had enough of this blasted wedding, enough of the whole darn Hunter family. All she wanted was to go home, put Eric to bed and wallow in some much-deserved self-pity in peace.

David caught up with her a second later and grasped her arm, forcing her to stop. "Hey, why didn't you wait for me?"

Susan shook off his hand and started toward the car again. "I don't need any help. I'm perfectly capable of driving home by myself."

A light frown creased his forehead. "Well, of course you are," he said in a calm, reasonable tone that set her teeth on edge. "But why should you when you don't have to? If Eric gets sick again, it'll be a whole lot easier if you have another adult along."

"Look David, I know you mean well, but—"

"But nothing. It'll only take a few minutes, and I'm happy to do it." He reached out and plucked Eric from her arms as if the forty-five-pound child weighed no more than a piece of paper. Eric snuggled against David's broad chest, his eyelids falling shut as he let out a contented little sigh.

"Are you always this bossy?" Susan asked, struggling to hold on to her patience.

"Only when I'm right," he retorted with an easy grin that charmed Susan in spite of her irritation.

She bit back a grin of her own and silently followed the man and boy to the car. Timmy obligingly tossed David the keys. When they were ready to go, David rolled down the window and drove over to the curb where his sister Barbara stood watching the scene with interest.

"Come pick me up at Susan's when Alan gets back with my car, okay?" he asked.

Barbara Hunter leaned down, smiling at everyone inside. "What's the address?"

Susan explained where she lived, then settled back for the ride across town. Timmy kept up a nonstop monologue from the back seat. Despite the heavy Labor Day weekend traffic, David handled the car with confidence, darting occasional concerned glances toward Susan.

Though she felt each glance, Susan resisted the urge to look back at him. A bone-deep weariness, more emotional than physical, washed over her. A headache throbbed at her temples. She rested her head against the seat and closed her eyes, but within the confines of her small car, she couldn't help but be excruciatingly aware of David's every movement. She didn't like it one bit.

When he parked in her driveway fifteen minutes later, neither of them had spoken more than five words. Timmy bolted from the car, still carrying his mother's purse and the somewhat battered bouquet. Susan stepped out, opened the back door and unfastened Eric's seat belt. Before she could pick him up, however, David nudged her out of the way and handed over her keys.

"Go ahead and open the door," he suggested quietly, reaching for the boy with an ease one might expect from an experienced father. "I'll carry him in for you."

The sight of her small, sleepy son cuddled so trustingly against the big man's chest nearly undid what little was left of Susan's composure. She managed a nod, then whirled around and entered her modest clapboard house. Timmy charged past her and headed for the bathroom, but Susan halted abruptly inside the front door.

In the chaos of trying to get herself and the boys ready for the wedding, she'd foregone her usual Saturday-morning cleaning. Judging from the condition of the living room, her sons had had one heck of a great time while she'd been dithering over what to wear and taking extraordinary pains with her hair and makeup.

Tonka trucks and Legos surrounded a blanket-draped card table. The sofa and chair cushions were propped up against each other on the floor, forming tunnels for the trucks. Fuzzy raisins, peanut fragments and squashed M&Ms littered the exposed sofa bed. Tinkertoys and Transformers decorated the coffee table, and a pair of grungy little socks trailed away from an equally grungy pair of sneakers lying under the TV.

Susan sighed and shook her head. Somehow it hadn't seemed quite this messy when they'd all raced out of the house to go to the church.

"Where do you want him?" David asked.

Susan started at the sound of his voice so close behind her, then flushed and kicked a Matchbox car under the sofa as she led the way to the boys' room. "In here. Just put him on the bottom bunk."

David gently deposited Eric on the rumpled bed. Susan tugged off her son's shoes and removed his stained shirt and pants before pulling the sheet up over him and smoothing his hair back off his forehead. When she straightened away from the bed, she found David watching her from the doorway with the same, intent expression that had given her goose bumps earlier. An involuntary shiver zoomed up her spine, but she covered it with a smile.

"Does he always sleep like a rock?" he asked, nodding towards Eric.

"Usually." She gestured toward the living room and followed David into the hall. "He works pretty hard keeping up with Timmy."

"I imagine he does." He reached down and picked up a car made out of Tinkertoys, a soft, reminiscent grin curving his mouth. "I had some of these when I was a kid."

Susan replaced the furniture cushions and picked up an armload of stuffed animals. David's arm shot out, blocking her path when she would have passed him on her way to the toy chest.

"Don't put the toys away on my account," he said seriously. "I'd rather sit down and talk for a minute before my sister gets here."

"All right." She perched on one end of the sofa and unobtrusively slipped off her shoes while David lowered himself onto the other end. "What did you want to talk about?"

He hesitated for an instant, fiddling with the toy he still held. Then he looked straight at her. "I don't know you very well, Susan, but I wanted to tell you how much I appreciate everything you did for Jason this summer. And what you did for my little sister. I don't know if they would have gotten back together if you hadn't—"

Intensely uncomfortable with his choice of topic, she interrupted him. "Oh, David, please. I...I didn't do anything."

"Yes, you did. You helped Jason through a rough time, and I think you could have held on to him if you'd tried. Most women would have, but you didn't. And your coming to the wedding and being such a good sport . . . well, it really put his mind at ease. Melody's, too."

"We only dated a few months," Susan replied stiffly. "It hadn't gone that far between us."

He raised a skeptical eyebrow at her. "I was around you two enough to know you really cared about him. Jason's such a good guy, it's hard not to care about him. It was pretty unselfish of you—"

"Okay, okay," she interrupted again, fighting a sudden sting of tears at the back of her eyes. If he only knew how many times she'd regretted pushing Jason out of her life! "I was incredibly noble." Her voice cracked, and she had to swallow before she could continue. "But give Jason a little credit. He would have figured out what he wanted sooner or later."

David slid across the sofa until he sat next to her and covered both of the fists clenched in her lap with one of his big hands. "Hey, I'm sorry. I didn't mean to upset you."

Susan sniffed inelegantly and looked out the window behind the sofa, praying for a glimpse of a black Porsche coming down the street. "What did you mean to do?'

"Well, whatever it was, I've sure made a mess of it," he answered, giving her hands an awkward pat before moving away. An agonizing silence stretched between them. "Look, uh, do you want me to wait outside?" he finally asked.

His hurt tone brought a wave of remorse down on Susan. David was only trying to be kind and helpful. She sniffed and looked over at him, giving him a shaky smile. "Don't worry about it. I know I did the right thing. It's nice to know someone else does, too."

"But you still miss him."

Biting the inside of her lower lip, she nodded.

"I know how you feel," he said softly.

Susan shook her head in disbelief, remembering how all the girls had practically swooned in the halls of Central High

School whenever David Hunter walked by. She'd done it herself a time or two. And all those women at the reception this afternoon . . .

"You know how I feel?" she demanded with an incredulous laugh. "You've never been rejected in your life!"

An angry flush darkened his neck and ears. "Oh, yeah?" he shot back. "Tell that to my ex-fiancée. She married some mealymouthed accountant last week."

"I'm sorry," Susan said after a tense moment. "I didn't know you'd ever been engaged."

He shrugged and his expression softened. "It's all right. We broke up last winter, so I've had time to get over it."

"It doesn't sound as if you're quite there yet."

"Maybe not," he admitted, giving her an endearing, abashed grin. "But I'm working on it."

The sound of a powerful engine filtered through the screen door. David glanced over his shoulder, then pushed himself to his feet. "There's my sister."

Oddly reluctant now for him to leave, Susan followed him to the front door. He opened it and called out to Barbara that he'd be there in a minute before turning back to Susan.

"Maybe we could take in a movie or go out for a drink sometime," he suggested. "You know, misery loves company."

Shaking her head, she smiled. "I appreciate the offer, David, but that's how it all started with Jason."

"Oh. Well, I guess I can see how you'd feel that way," he said, his expression sobering. "But if you ever need a friend or someone to talk to, Susan, I'm available."

"Thanks. And thanks for all your help today."

"No problem." He raised his hand and chucked her under her chin. "You keep that chin up, okay?"

"Okay."

She watched him bound gracefully down her front steps and, as far as she was concerned, out of her life. Oh, they might bump into each other out at Frontier Mall or maybe in a fast-food restaurant once in a while. But David would go back to his own busy circle of friends, and she would go back to the quiet, home-centered existence she'd led before Jason had entered her life. Now *there* was a depressing thought.

David lowered himself into the passenger seat and sent her a jaunty wave as the car zipped away from the curb. Susan waved back until the Porsche disappeared around the corner, then turned away from the door.

"Well," she sighed, feeling as devastated inside as her living room looked, "I guess that's that."

Chapter Two

"For God's sake, Barbara, this isn't the Indy 500. Will you slow down?" David demanded when his sister ran a second red light.

Barbara Hunter grinned at him and obligingly lifted her foot from the accelerator. For all of two blocks. "What's the matter, little brother?" she asked. "Won't Susan go out with you?"

"What makes you think I asked her out?" he grumbled, looking away and shoving his hands into his pants pockets.

Her green eyes dancing with mirth, she shrugged. "Oh, nothing much. Just the way you followed her around all afternoon with your tongue hanging out."

"I did not!"

"Well, maybe you weren't quite *that* bad," she conceded with the teasing condescension an older sibling learns early in life. "But don't try to tell me you're not interested in her."

"Gimme me a break. I was just trying to be a nice guy for once."

"Uh-huh."

"Barbara—"

"If you're attracted to Susan," she interrupted, glancing in the rearview mirror, "I'd say your taste in women is improving."

"Oh, yeah?" David asked, resigning himself to a sisterly lecture whether he wanted one or not.

"Yeah. I liked her a lot. She's certainly attractive, and her kids are adorable. And considering how hard it must have been for her to come to the wedding, I thought she handled herself with a lot of class today."

David shrugged. "I like her a lot, too, but she's still hung up on Jason."

"So what? She'll get over him eventually. And when she does, then you can—"

"Move in and be her second choice?" David asked indignantly. "No, thanks."

Barbara rolled her eyes. "Stop competing with Jason and spare me the false modesty. You can charm any woman alive, and I doubt Susan's the exception. Of course, it might help your chances with her if you'd get rid of your harem."

"I don't have a harem."

"Then what was that parade of beauties to your table? I'll say this for you, bro—your taste is certainly eclectic."

"Come on, sis," he muttered. "Those gals are my friends."

Barbara snickered. "Those gals made it pretty obvious they want to be more than friends with you. Are any of them over twenty-one, by the way?"

"What's that got to do with anything?" he demanded. "And what was I supposed to do? Say, 'Go away, I'm trying to hit on Susan'?"

"Of course not. But it might help if you didn't welcome them so warmly. You know, be polite but distant."

"I don't know how to do that without looking like a jerk. Besides, I happen to like women. Why should I be rude?"

"You don't have to be rude, David. But no woman wants to feel she's part of a herd or just another notch on some guy's bedpost. Would you like it if the shoe were on the other foot?"

"No, I don't suppose I would," David answered thoughtfully. Then he smirked at his sister. "And now that you've got my love life all figured out, when are you going to figure out your own?"

"Are you hungry? I could do with a hamburger." Without waiting for an answer or bothering to signal her intentions, Barbara turned off Pershing Boulevard and whipped the sports car up to the drive-in window of an aging fast-food restaurant.

"Don't try to change the subject," David said.

She turned on him with the steady, unblinking gaze that had been known to make a U.S. senator, congressman, even a Pentagon general or two squirm when she conducted an interview. "What do you want to eat?"

David threw back his head and laughed. Oh, boy, had he ever hit a raw nerve. His sister acted tough sometimes, but he knew darn well that the tougher she acted, the more vulnerable she felt. Her nostrils flared, and her eyes threatened to shoot green sparks. "The usual," he answered quickly.

With one last warning glare at him, Barbara turned away and shouted their order into the speaker. When she'd finished, David reached across the gear shift and put his hand on her shoulder.

"You want to talk about it, sis?" he asked quietly.

She stiffened at his touch for a moment, then exhaled a soft sigh and looked at him, a smile curving up the corners of her mouth. "Yeah. I'd like that."

The girl at the window handed out a white paper bag containing their double cheeseburgers, French fries and soft drinks. Barbara passed it over to David and drove to Lions' Park. When they were settled at a picnic table and had taken the edge off their hunger, she confided, "I guess I wasn't expecting to feel so ambivalent about the wedding."

He flashed her a teasing grin. "Feeling bad the squirt beat you to the altar?"

"No," Barbara answered with a scowl. "I'm really happy for Mel and Jason, but seeing them so ecstatic with each other makes my own life seem ... empty."

"I know what you mean," David said, adopting a more sympathetic tone. "I suppose it didn't help having Alan there," he added, referring to her long-term relationship with Alan Jordan, which had ended the previous January.

"Oh, I don't know about that," she drawled thoughtfully. "It was nice seeing him again, but I realized right away that I haven't been missing Alan as much as the idea that I had someone special in my life. Someone to come home to."

"I feel that way, too, sometimes. You know, ever since Liz broke our engagement, I've really been hitting the singles' bars because my apartment seems so blasted lonely."

"If you really want to settle down and get married, David, maybe you need to change your life-style."

"I've thought about it," he admitted.

"Come to any conclusions?"

"Yeah. I'm sick of living in an apartment, for one thing. I've decided to buy a house. I might even ask Jason for one of those ugly pups he's always got running around the ranch."

"You're going to replace Liz with a dog?" Barbara asked, sputtering with laughter.

David threw a French fry at her. "Hardly. I just want to make a real home for myself, wife or no wife. Besides, I can use the tax break. Now, will you stop laughing at me?"

"I'm not laughing at you," she assured him with a fond smile. "In fact, I think it's a good idea. Have you started looking for a house?"

"Not yet. But I don't want anything big or fancy. Just a nice, comfortable little place that's closer to the station."

"Like the ones in Susan's neighborhood?"

David nodded thoughtfully. "Now that you mention it, that wouldn't be a bad location."

"Isn't that a coincidence?"

"What?" David replied, his eyes narrowing at his sister's smug grin.

"The house across the street from Susan's has a For Sale sign in the yard."

"You're really subtle, sis."

Her eyes widened in mock innocence. "You took so long to say goodbye, I couldn't help noticing it."

David gathered up their trash and dumped it into a garbage can. "We'd better get back and see if Mom needs some help."

Barbara followed him to the car, grudgingly passing him the car keys when he held out his hand in silent demand. "Well? Aren't you even going to look at that house?" she asked once they were settled inside.

He shook his head. "Susan made it pretty clear she's not comfortable with me. She'd hate having me for a neighbor."

"She'll get over that. It looked like an awfully nice house, David. At least think about it."

"I think all that wedding stuff pickled your brain," he grumbled.

Barbara laughed. "No, I've decided I'm going to be the old-maid auntie in this family. So it's up to you and Melody to provide me with lots of nieces and nephews to dote on."

David hooted at the idea of his glamorous sister being anyone's old-maid auntie. But as he drove to his parents' home, he wondered if all that wedding stuff hadn't pickled his own brain. Because try though he might, he couldn't get the image of Susan's pretty, vulnerable face out of his mind. Or shake the growing sense of disappointment that she hadn't shown more interest in going out with him.

"And they all lived together in the little house in the forest, happily ever after." Susan closed the fairy-tale book, then lovingly ruffled Timmy's sandy brown hair. "Time to brush your teeth, pal."

He wrinkled his nose at her. "Aw, Mom, just one more story."

"Not tonight. We've already read three, and it's been a long day. Go on now."

Obeying reluctantly, Timmy turned in the doorway. "Mom?"

"What is it, honey?"

He hesitated, scuffing the tips of his bare toes across the carpet. Then he planted his feet wide apart and crossed his arms over his chest. "Is Mr. Hunter gonna be your new boyfriend? Like Jason was?"

Susan's heart wrenched at his defensive stance, the wistful yet worried expression in his eyes, the suspicious tone of his voice. He'd been unusually quiet since the wedding, but she'd been too busy fighting her own emotions and cleaning the house to pay much attention to him. She patted the sofa cushion beside her. "Come here, Timmy. I think we'd better talk about this."

He walked slowly back to the sofa and sat a foot away from her. Susan raised an eyebrow at him, then patted the cushion beside her again. Timmy grinned sheepishly and scooted closer. She wrapped her arm around him in a quick hug, praying she could help with whatever was troubling him. Eric romped happily through life, as friendly and carefree as a puppy; Timmy was her sensitive one.

"What makes you think Mr. Hunter might become my boyfriend?" she asked quietly.

"He was hangin' around you at the wedding reception, an' he drove us home an' I heard him ask you for a date before he left."

"Then you heard me turn him down, too," Susan reminded her son. "How would you feel if I did go out with him sometime?"

The boy shrugged and looked down at his knees. "I dunno."

"Didn't you like him?"

Another shrug. "He was okay, I guess. He didn't get mad at Eric for barfin' all over him, and he seemed pretty nice."

"Yes, he was pretty nice. So, what's bothering you, honey?"

"I, uh, I guess I, uh, don't want you to be sad again, Mom."

Susan winced inwardly at her son's earnest little face. He was too young to know so much about getting hurt by people he loved. Though he adored his father, Ed Miller, and missed having him at home, he'd been ready and eager to accept Jason as a substitute. Perhaps it hadn't been intentional on either man's part, but Ed and Jason had both wounded Timmy as much, if not more than they'd wounded her.

"Timmy," she said slowly, "people don't always get hurt when they date someone. And you know Jason didn't mean to hurt us."

"But I thought he cared about us," he wailed, his chin trembling. "Why didn't he marry you instead of that dumb Melody lady? You're lots prettier than her."

Susan closed her eyes for a moment, groping for the words that would help him understand. "He *does* care about us, honey. But he never promised to marry me. He told me he loved Melody right from the start. We were just very good friends."

"You loved him, though, didn't you?"

"I was starting to love him," she admitted, "and it hurt when he left. But it won't hurt forever, Timmy. I can promise you that."

"But why didn't he love you back, Mom?" His voice broke, and he looked down at his hands. "Was it because of Eric and me? Did we do something bad?"

"Oh, no, sweetheart," Susan cried, reaching for him. He climbed willingly onto her lap, resting the side of his head against her breasts. She stroked his hair and rubbed his back automatically. "Jason enjoyed both of you. Didn't you notice how happy he was to see you today?"

Timmy sniffled and wrapped his arms around his mother's neck. "Yeah. But I wanted him to be my new dad."

"I know you did. You'll always have Eric and me, though. And we're doing okay, aren't we?"

"Yeah, we don't need anybody," Timmy answered, leaning back and looking Susan in the eye, his little chin thrust out at a defiant angle. "But I don't like big guys anymore. They always leave."

"I know it seems that way now, honey," Susan said quietly. "But it's not fair to say that about all men. Some of them stay with their families forever."

"What kind do you think Mr. Hunter is?"

"I don't know. But I doubt he'll be back, so you don't have to worry about him."

Timmy sighed and snuggled closer into his mother's arms, resting his head against her breasts again. "I love you, Mom."

"I love you, too, Timmy."

Susan hugged him tightly, dreading the day when he would no longer tolerate such emotional displays of affection from her. She held him until he let out a jaw-cracking yawn that made them both laugh, then walked him through his bedtime ritual and tucked him in. After checking on Eric, she made sure the doors were locked, went into her bedroom and sat down at the battered desk she'd bought at the Goodwill store.

She patted her aging electric typewriter out of habit and picked up the manuscript pages she'd finished the night before. Though no one else would ever read it, her latest novel was moving right along, and she was enjoying this set of characters immensely. Perhaps her writing hobby was a time-wasting escape from reality, as her ex-husband, Ed, had so scornfully and frequently reminded her. But tonight she needed to escape into the world of her imagination.

Her fingers danced over the keyboard, faster and faster as the words flowed from her mind onto the page. Three hours later, her eyes gritty with fatigue, Susan pushed back her chair and wandered into the living room. She opened the front door and looked up and down the street, marveling at how quiet the neighborhood always was at this time of night.

It would be wonderful if a nice family with playmates for Timmy and Eric would buy that empty house across the street, she thought idly, breathing in the cool evening air.

Then, unbidden, an image of David Hunter standing right here with one hand holding the screen door open popped into her mind. *"If you ever need a friend or someone to talk to, I'm available,"* he'd said.

Susan smiled bitterly and shook her head. The image vanished, but in its place lingered the treacherous yearning for someone to hold her and care about her. Resting her head against the doorjamb, she told herself it was stupid and dangerous for her to feel that way about any man, especially David Hunter.

In the first place she wasn't about to risk hurting herself or her boys again. Not in this lifetime. In the second place a playboy like David wouldn't want a woman with two kids, not really. And even if he did, he'd only be another man she couldn't depend on. Like her father. Like Ed. Like Jason.

Oh, she believed Jason Wakefield would be a wonderful husband to Melody. Though he'd been just as much of a playboy as David was, Susan couldn't doubt Jason's love for and devotion to his new wife. But Susan Miller was not Melody Hunter—she simply did not inspire the lifelong, till-death-do-us-part loyalty Melody had inspired in Jason.

Besides, she didn't need a man in her life. Jason had awakened pleasant fantasies and dreams, not unlike the silly dreams she used to have of becoming a famous author. But her hard-won independence since the divorce had taught Susan the proper place for fantasies and dreams—in the trash can. And not even a man as attractive as David Hunter would ever convince her to get them out and dust them off again.

Chapter Three

David Hunter stepped back for a better view of the neat little Cape Cod house, his chest feeling tight. It needed some work, but it practically shouted "home" to him. He'd paint it a light gray-blue, do the trim in white, maybe put in a hedge along the neighbor's fence....

"It's a great little house, Dave," Paul Stauffer, an old friend from high school who had become a real-estate agent, declared.

David smiled, silently saluting Paul's professionalism. The man had been patient beyond belief during the four straight days he'd been showing David houses. His enthusiasm rarely flagged, even though the homes in this neighborhood wouldn't yield him the kind of commission he'd probably hoped to earn from someone in David's income bracket.

Fully intending to tell Paul he'd take the house, David turned and caught sight of the little white rancher across the street. His smile faded and his heart sank. The hot-pink petunias Susan Miller had planted beside the steps bobbed, and the porch swing swayed in the breeze, as if beckoning him to come over and say hello. He hadn't seen Susan for nearly a week, but instantly a vision of her sweet, serious face when she refused a date with him popped into his mind.

"What else have you got to show me?" he asked brusquely.

Paul grimaced. "You've seen everything in this part of town. Unless you want to try Western Hills or Buffalo Ridge...."

David shook his head. "No, I told you I don't want to be that far from the station."

Paul's patience finally cracked. "Come on, Hunter. We've already looked at twenty-five houses, and we both know this is the one you want. For God's sake, this is the third time we've come back to it."

"It's not quite what I had in mind," David muttered, avoiding Paul's irritated gaze.

"It's got everything you told me you wanted in a house and more. It can't be the price that's hanging you up, so what's the real problem here?"

David stole another glance at the house across the street. Paul turned, following the direction of David's gaze with his own.

"You like that one better?" he asked. "I could always ask the owner if he'd like to sell it."

"No, I know the owner."

"Oh, yeah? Who is it?"

"Susan Miller," David answered with studied casualness. "Used to be Susan Wolcott. She was a couple of years behind us in high school."

Paul's eyes scrunched up at the corners, and he scratched thoughtfully at his receding hairline. Then he snapped his fingers. "Oh, yeah, I remember her. Skinny, bashful little sophomore who checked out books in the library? Always blushed and stammered when she had to wait on us?"

"That's the one."

"Is she married?"

"Divorced. Has two kids."

A knowing smile crept across Paul's face. "Does she still have those great legs?"

"What do *you* care?" David snapped. "Planning to step out on your wife?"

Paul threw back his head and laughed. "Never. Emily would do unspeakable things to my body if she ever caught me. But I think I've finally figured out why you're afraid to buy this house."

"I'm not afraid—"

"She's an old girlfriend," Paul went on, pointing a finger at David. "And you don't want to give her any encouragement, right? Huh? Am I right?"

"Wrong."

"Oh, *sure*, Hunter. You've got more ex-girlfriends in this town than anybody but Wakefield. I'll bet little Susan turned into quite a knockout if she ever grew any boobs. Did she?"

"Shut up, Stauffer."

"Oooh, touchy aren't we? You have the hots for this babe, or what?"

David laughed at Paul's waggling eyebrows in spite of his irritation. "Knock off the locker-room talk, will you? She's a nice gal. And I've never even dated her."

"Okay, she's nice," Paul said slowly. "If she's so nice, why aren't you grabbing up this house? You know you want it."

David shoved his hands into his jeans pockets. "She dated Jase before he married my sister. She's not over him yet, and I, uh, think I make her uncomfortable. She'd probably hate having me for a neighbor."

"David, David, David," Paul chortled, walking over to lay a beefy hand on David's shoulder. "Things have changed since you lived up on the avenues with your folks. Nobody's got time to socialize with the neighbors anymore. Oh, they might have a block party once a year during crime-prevention week, or get into a hassle over somebody's dog crapping in their yard, but for the most part they ignore each other."

David glanced from the Cape Cod to the rancher and back again. "You think so?"

"Hey, I *know* so," Paul assured him. "You think a single mom like Susan will have the time to bring cookies over to the new neighbor? No way. Hell, she'll hardly know you're here. And this is business, Dave. You can't let someone else influence your decision. Now, do you want the house or not?"

Feeling slightly foolish, David gazed at the little Cape Cod for another long moment. Damn, but he *did* want that house. And Paul was right; this was business. Turning to the other man, he grinned. "Let's go make the owners an offer they can't refuse."

Susan glanced at her watch, then scowled at the stacks of files and papers covering two-thirds of her desk. Cheyenne Security Bank faithfully paid her salary every two weeks. The least she could do in return was finish her work on time. Her assistant, Beth Campbell, was on a three-month maternity leave, but that was no excuse for Susan's being *this* far behind.

Beth loved to tease her about being able to block out distractions in the middle of a stampede. Unfortunately, during the week since Jason's wedding, Susan's powers of concentration had gone straight down the toilet. It had all started the first day back at work after the Labor Day weekend.

Cheyenne was still a small town at heart, and everyone had known she'd been dating Jason during the summer. Nearly every single woman in the building stopped by Susan's desk, eager to hear about the big wedding and offer sincere, and some not-so-sincere, sympathy for losing one of the most coveted bachelors in the state to another woman. Susan hadn't been particularly surprised or upset by the unwelcome attention she received. She'd simply gritted her teeth, smiled a lot and assumed the whole thing would blow over in a day or two.

But then, somehow the word spread that David Hunter had escorted her at the reception and driven her home. Now, every time she got a cup of coffee or went to the women's lounge, she encountered arched eyebrows, conspiratorial winks and sly advice about "hanging on to this one."

Susan muttered a curse and bounced her pen off the opposite wall. She looked down at the newsletter on her blotter, but the words all ran together and made no sense whatsoever. Darn that David Hunter.

Wasn't it bad enough that he popped into her thoughts all the time no matter how sternly she banished him? Did he have to invade her job, as well? Maybe she should have gone out with him once, just to get him out of her system.

The telephone beside her buzzed, and Susan gratefully snatched up the receiver. She'd rather deal with anyone, even an irate customer, than continue that line of thought. She spent the rest of the day frantically trying to catch up, without much success.

At five o'clock she cleared off her desk, then glanced around the office for a moment while she dug her car keys out of the depths of her purse. Her job provided variety and challenge but didn't pay enough, and she hated being away from the boys so much.

"Just one more year," she promised herself in a whisper, and headed out the door.

The thought of another twelve months of such frugal living depressed the daylights out of her as she drove to the sitter's house. If only Ed would pay his child support on a regular basis, she would be back in college right now, finishing up her degree in education. But since she couldn't count on him to do that, she would simply have to go on clipping coupons and scrimping every other way possible until she had enough money saved.

As always, however, Susan's spirits lifted when Timmy and Eric raced to meet her and filled the little car with their exuberant chatter on the way home. As long as they were happy and healthy, she could handle just about anything.

She parked in the driveway, nearly jumping out of her skin when Timmy suddenly shouted, "Wow, look at that!"

"What?" Eric asked.

"The sign across the street, dummy," Timmy answered, scrambling out of the car.

Susan automatically scolded her older son. "Don't call your brother names." Then she saw the reason for his excitement. A bright red Sold sticker had been pasted across the For Sale sign in front of the little Cape Cod house she'd admired ever since she'd moved into the neighborhood.

"What's he yelling about, Mom?" Eric demanded, tugging on her skirt.

"Somebody bought the house across the street, honey," she answered.

"Do they got any kids to play with?"

Susan smiled at his eager, hopeful expression and ruffled his sandy hair. "I don't know, Eric. I guess we'll find out when they move in."

"When will that be?"

"I don't know," Susan repeated, "but it usually takes about six weeks to finish all the paperwork. Come on. Let's go get dinner started."

"That's too long," Eric grumbled, following his mother and brother into the house. He brightened a moment later. "Hey Mom, does that mean we're gonna bake cookies? Like we did when Candy and Nancy moved in next door?"

"Yeah," Timmy agreed immediately, "the kind with the caramels and chocolate chips. Let's do it tonight."

Susan groaned inwardly. The boys loved "helping" her in the kitchen, but after all, it was Friday night, she had laundry stacked to the ceiling and bills to pay, not to mention a date with a long soak in a hot bath. "Not tonight, boys. You'll eat all the cookies before anyone moves in if we make them now."

"Oh, *please*, Mom," Eric begged, turning his most beguiling smile on her. "You said it was the neighborly thing to do."

"We can put 'em in the freezer. And we promise we won't touch 'em," Timmy added for good measure.

Knowing she had about as much resistance to her sons' pleading as a marshmallow to a camp fire, Susan struck the best bargain she could. "All right. We'll do it on one condition. You guys haul all your dirty clothes downstairs and sort them while I'm fixing dinner. Underwear and socks in one pile, shirts in another, jeans in another. Deal?"

"Deal, Mom."

Susan smiled as they thundered off to their bedroom. So she was an easy mark once in a while. Big deal. The laundry would eventually get done; the bills would get paid. She could give up that long hot bath to have some fun with her boys. And it would be nice to have some cookies in the freezer for the new neighbors.

Eight days later Susan lay in bed, smiling sleepily at the sound of Saturday-morning cartoons. The boys would still be in their pajamas, stretched out on the floor in front of the TV, each with a bowl of cereal on a cookie sheet to protect the carpet. When their favourite show was over, they'd come in and pounce, tickling her and demanding that she get up and make some real food, such as pancakes or waffles.

Hearing the familiar theme song, she braced herself for the invasion, but nothing happened. A moment later she heard the boys talking in excited whispers, the screech and thud of a tailgate being lowered out in the street, then the sound of her own front door banging open and shut and Timmy yelling, "Eric, come back!"

She raced into the living room. "What's going on?" Timmy pointed toward the house across the street. "Jason's over there, Mom, an' Eric went to see him in his pajamas!"

"Oh, Lord," Susan muttered, peeking out the diamond-shaped window in the door. Sure enough, there was Jason with Eric in his arms, a broad smile on his face as the boy talked a mile a minute. Melody stood next to him, and on the other side of the red pickup with the Lazy W brand stenciled on the door, were David Hunter, his parents and

Nicole and Becky, two of the women who had made such a point of approaching David at the wedding. The back end of the pickup was stacked high with furniture and cardboard boxes.

David pulled a key out of his pocket, walked up to the front door of the Cape Cod and opened it with a flourish. His parents, Becky and Nicole walked inside. Jason put Eric down and sent him home with a pat on his bottom. Then putting an arm around Melody's shoulders, Jason escorted her into the house. David followed them in, his bearing that of a proud master showing off his new domain.

"Oh, Lord," Susan muttered again, opening the door for Eric.

"Guess what, Mom?" he asked breathlessly. "Mr. Hunter's our new neighbor. He said I can come visit him anytime, and Jason said to tell you hello. Can we take the cookies over now? Huh? Can we?"

Susan shook her head sharply, hoping she would wake up and start this day over. This wasn't a swinging singles street. She didn't want David Hunter for a neighbor. Where was the nice family with little boys to play with Timmy and Eric she'd envisioned while that house was on the market? Unfortunately, when she looked out the window again David and Jason came outside, lifted a chocolate brown leather sofa out of the pickup's bed and carried it into the house.

Eric yanked on the hem of the oversized T-shirt she used for a nightgown. "Can we, Mom?"

"They're still frozen, Eric," she snapped. At his crestfallen expression, she sighed. It wasn't Eric's fault that David Hunter had bought the house across the street.

But darn it, if she took cookies over there, the man might think she was giving him some kind of a come-on. On the other hand, if Eric had blabbed about the cookies to Jason—knowing her son, he had undoubtedly done just that—the Wakefields would probably think she was avoiding them. Foolish pride or not, she couldn't stand that. Though she wasn't exactly wild to hear all about their recent honeymoon, she couldn't let them believe she was pining over Jason.

"Can I get the cookies out of the freezer, Mom?" Eric asked meekly.

Bowing to the inevitable, Susan gave him a weak smile. "Sure, honey. I, uh, I think I'll go take a shower. You guys get dressed, and we'll take the cookies over at lunchtime. Until then, you stay in our yard."

"Aw, Mom, can't we go over to Mr. Hunter's and watch?" Eric begged. "I wanna talk to Jason."

"No, Eric. They don't need kids underfoot."

Susan tried to disregard the activity across the street while she sped through her Saturday-morning chores, but it wasn't easy. Since it was the middle of September and there might not be that many warm, sunny days left before the weather turned cold, she refused to shut the windows. Masculine grunts of exertion, punctuated by frequent bursts of laughter, continually drew her attention away from the dusting and vacuuming, bed changing and mopping. Of course, it didn't help at all that the boys raced in and out to give her detailed reports of all the neat stuff the men were unloading, either.

She told herself it was only normal curiosity pulling her to the living-room windows from time to time. After all, who could ignore all that racket out there? She would even admit to a certain, healthy amount of feminine lust. Any woman with decent eyesight would enjoy watching those two strapping, handsome men in their tight jeans and body-hugging T-shirts flexing their muscles while they carted load after load into the house. She would *not* admit to a certain jealous satisfaction when Nicole and Becky roared off in a powder-blue convertible at ten o'clock.

But what really got to Susan, what really attracted her way down deep in her most private self, was the blatant bond of love and respect she witnessed among the five people left working together across the street. They argued. They touched each other with open affection. They teased each other without mercy, but they were first, last and always a family. Susan admired that, while at the same time it caused a funny little ache in her heart that was awfully close to yearning or envy or perhaps, loneliness.

Shaking her head in disgust at the direction her thoughts were taking, she turned away from the window and went into the bathroom. Might as well do her good deed and be done with it, she told herself as she put on some makeup and fixed her hair. She changed into clean clothes, piled a plate high with cookies and covered it with plastic wrap. Then she called the boys.

Susan groaned silently when they stepped out the front door and she saw that the only person outside the house across the street was Jason Wakefield. Willing someone, anyone else to join him and spare her the discomfort of being alone with him, she slowed her steps until she was barely moving. Eric proudly carried the plate across the street, his eager little legs propelling him ahead of Susan and Timmy.

"Jason!" he hollered. "Look what I got!"

Jason set the box he'd just lifted out of the pickup onto the ground and grinned when he saw the boy with his precious burden. He squatted down on the heel of one boot and tipped his Stetson farther back on his head. "Hey there, pard. Are those for me?"

"Naw, they're for Mr. Hunter," Eric replied. "I toldja we always take cookies to new neighbors. But maybe he'll share."

"Well, he'd better," Jason said, ruffling the boy's sandy hair affectionately. Then he looked up at Susan and Timmy, and his grin broadened into a full-fledged smile. "Hi."

Susan gazed into his gorgeous hazel eyes and waited for her heart to go crazy, as it always had before. But instead of racing at the sight of that handsome face, her pulse maintained a nice, steady rhythm. Surprised, but not at all unhappy with her reaction, Susan returned his greeting with a smile. "Hi, yourself."

Straightening to his full height, Jason studied Timmy for a moment, his eyes narrowing as he noted the way the boy hung back beside his mother. Rather than ruffling his hair the way he had Eric's, he offered Timmy his hand. "It's good to see you, pal."

Timmy hesitated, then shook Jason's hand and gave the big man a bashful grin. "It's good to see you, too, Jason."

"Where's Mr. Hunter?" Eric asked, dancing from one foot to the other.

Jason nodded toward the front door. "In the house. Why don't you guys take the cookies in and put them in the kitchen?"

The boys raced off at his suggestion. Jason watched them cross the threshold before turning back to Susan. "It's good to see you, too. How've you been?"

"Fine. Busy. How about you, Jason? Are you happy?"

He tipped his head to one side and rubbed his chin in a thoughtful pose. Then his eyes took on a wicked twinkle, and a broad grin stretched across his face. "Yeah."

That one word and the note of supreme contentment in his voice said it all. Susan held her breath for an instant, but the shaft of pain she'd expected didn't materialize. In its place a warm glow of friendship settled in her chest, and she exhaled a silent sigh of relief. If she'd ever really been in love with Jason, she was over it now.

Susan took his hand in hers and gave it an affectionate squeeze. "I'm glad to hear that," she said, smiling up at him.

David Hunter came out of the house at that moment, a cookie in each hand and one in his mouth. The sight of Susan and Jason standing so close together rocked him back on his heels. He swallowed the cookie in one hard gulp, then started walking again when he heard Melody, Susan's boys and his parents coming behind him.

"Hey, Jase," he called, "wait'll you taste what Susan brought."

Susan let go of Jason's hand and casually stepped away from him at the sound of David's voice. David felt his heart lurch when she turned toward him with a sunny smile. His throat suddenly clogged up, and he had to clear it before he could speak.

"These are really great, Susan," he said, holding up the cookie in his right hand. "Thanks."

"You're welcome." For the life of her, Susan couldn't think of another intelligent thing to say. David's dark brown eyes held a tantalizing intensity that stood the fine hairs at the back of her neck on end, dried up the saliva in her mouth and dampened her palms. It didn't make sense. Jason couldn't make her pulse race now, but David Hunter could? With one look? Was she getting fickle in her old age, or what?

The rest of the group converged on them, interrupting the silent exchange and greeting Susan as if she were an old friend. They all complimented her on the cookies and exchanged small talk.

"Do you still write those wonderful stories you used to have in the high school literary magazine, Susan?" David's mother, Karen Hunter, asked.

Susan nodded. "It's the only hobby I've ever had, Mrs. Hunter."

"Have you had anything published? You certainly had the talent," Karen replied.

Flattered that a professional writer had remembered her early attempts, Susan flushed with pleasure. "I tried for a while, but I'm so busy with the boys now, I don't really have the time. It's just something I do for fun."

"Oh, but Susan—"

"Mom," Melody interrupted with an indulgent smile. "Maybe you and Susan can talk writing next Saturday." When Susan looked at her in confusion, Melody added, "We're having a barbecue at the ranch. We'd love to have you and the boys come. There'll be lots of other kids."

"Oh, well, I don't know, uh—"

"Can we ride horses, Jason?" Eric asked while his mother groped for a polite refusal.

"Sure, pard," Jason answered. "And we'll play a little football, maybe a little baseball."

"Can we go, Mom?" Timmy asked eagerly.

Susan glared at Jason for a moment, thinking, *gee, thanks for giving me an out, pard*. What red-blooded American boy could resist horses, football and baseball, for heaven's sake? Jason simply grinned back at her, letting her know he'd done it deliberately.

"Please, Mom?" Eric chimed in, jumping up and down in excitement. "Please, please, *please*?"

A reluctant smile tugged at the corners of Susan's mouth. "All right," she said. "What can we bring?"

"Just an appetite and some riding boots," Melody answered. "We'll start about ten."

"It sounds like fun." Susan looked down at her sons. "What do you say, guys? Shall we let these people get back to work?"

"Melody was just about to go get us some lunch, Susan," David said quickly. "Would you like to join us?"

This time Susan firmly shook her head. "No, thanks, David. We've got errands to run this afternoon," she said, stepping out of the group. "But thanks for the invitation. Welcome to the neighborhood."

With that, she steered the boys toward home, feeling the heat of David Hunter's gaze following her every step of the way. She made Timmy and Eric peanut-butter-and-jelly sandwiches and sent them out to eat in the backyard. She was looking for some leftover salad in the refrigerator when she heard a familiar knock at her back door.

"Come on in, Candy," she called, going back to her search.

Candy Sorenson was an attractive, red-haired widow in her late forties who had moved in next door to Susan a year ago. The two women had become close friends, and Susan often hired Candy's sixteen-year-old daughter, Nancy, to baby-sit. Candy entered the kitchen, then walked over to the refrigerator.

"Who", she said, pausing for dramatic effect, leaning one hip against the counter, "is that gorgeous hunk of man moving in across the street?"

"Been spying on your neighbors again, Candy?" Susan asked, plunking the bowl of salad onto the counter.

"Of course. Why do you think God made windows?"

"God didn't make windows," Susan replied.

"Knock it off, Miller. Give. You obviously know him."

Susan shrugged. "I went to high school with him."

"Does he have a name?"

"David Hunter."

Candy raised an eyebrow at that. "One of the Hunter Communications Hunters?"

"That's right."

"So he's Jason's brother-in-law now? The one who helped you with the boys at the reception?"

Susan nodded. "He and Jason have been friends for years."

"Is he married? Engaged? Dating anyone seriously?"

"No to the first two questions. Not that I know of to the third," Susan answered with a laugh. "Anything else you want to know?"

"Sure," Candy replied, supremely unrepentant, "when are you going out with him?"

"I'm not interested in men right now," Susan said firmly, crossing her arms over her chest. "You know that."

"Baloney," the other woman snorted. "There are men and then there are *men*. And that one—" she pointed across the street "—looks too good to pass up."

"Read my lips. I'm not interested."

"That's why you trotted those cookies across the street?"

"I didn't know who was moving in when I baked them," Susan defended herself. "I did it for you, too, if you'll remember."

"Uh-huh." Candy studied her friend from head to toe, then picked up a paper plate from the stack Susan had used for the boys. Grinning wickedly, she waved it under Susan's nose. "Then why didn't you use one of these for your cookies so he wouldn't have to return the plate?"

Susan shook her head and chuckled. "Candy, did you happen to notice the two sweet young things helping out over there this morning?"

"The ones with the skintight jeans, big bazooms and tons of hair?"

Susan nodded. "That's the kind of woman David Hunter dates. There's no way I could ever compete with them. I wouldn't even want to try."

"Oh, I see," Candy replied with a smirk. "That's why you, queen of the Saturday slobs, put on your newest blouse, curled your hair and put on all your makeup before you went over there for five whole minutes."

"For Pete's sake," Susan huffed. "There were other people over there, too, you know. My ex-boyfriend and his new wife, included. Don't you think I have any pride at all?"

Her expression turning serious, Candy walked over and patted Susan's shoulder. "I'm sorry. I shouldn't tease you so much. It's just that you've been a good friend, and I care about you."

"I know you do," Susan replied, "and I appreciate that, but—"

"But nothing. I've always liked you a lot, Susan," Candy said earnestly, "but this last summer you really changed, and I don't want you to lose it."

"How did I change?"

"You were less intense, more ready to laugh…shoot, you were happy. You blossomed when you were with Jason. I hate to see you go back to being alone."

"I'm not alone. Remember those two little people I live with?"

Candy shook her head. "Eric and Timmy can't be your whole life, Susan. It's not fair to you, and it's certainly not fair to them. When you deny your own needs, you're not doing anyone a favor."

"I'm not trying to be a martyr," Susan defended herself. "But I don't need a man, and I don't really have time for one."

"Of course you don't, honey." Her eyes taking on a wicked twinkle, Candy added, "But for one that gorgeous, I'd *make* time."

"Go home, Candy."

"I'm going, Susan. See you later."

The back door opened and closed, and then Susan heard Candy laughing all the way over to her own back door.

Chapter Four

David set the last box of books on the floor in front of the living-room bookcase, then straightened up, wincing as his back and shoulder muscles protested. He'd been so busy with his job and buying the house the past few weeks, he'd neglected his workouts. Now he was paying the price. Stretching his arms over his head, he looked around the room and sighed.

The pink carpeting and flowered wallpaper would have to go, but he liked the light, airy feeling the bank of windows beside the bookcase provided. The fireplace on the north side of the room would give the place a warm, cozy atmosphere when the weather got cold enough to use it. He'd feel more at home once he had everything unpacked. He hoped.

Susan Miller's voice drifted through the open windows. "Okay, Timmy, go out for a long one this time."

David turned, looked through the sheers and chuckled when he saw her throw a child-sized football in a high, wobbly pass. Timmy charged the ball, and Eric charged

Timmy. Then Susan charged them both, and they all ended up in a giggling tangle of arms and legs.

"The woman must run on high-octane fuel," he murmured in admiration.

When he'd dragged himself out of bed this morning, she'd been ushering the boys off to church. They'd come back around noon, and the past four hours, she'd been working in the yard, playing with the boys and running in and out of the house doing only God knew what. He hadn't been spying on her, exactly, just sort of keeping track while he put away his stuff.

Speaking of which, he thought grimly, he'd better get back to work. He'd planned to finish yesterday, but there had been an emergency at the station and he hadn't wanted his mother and Melody imposing their system of organization on his house. He'd allowed that once before and hadn't been able to find anything for weeks.

"All right, Eric. One more turn for you, and then I have to go inside," Susan called across the street.

David swung back to the window and watched a repeat of the last play. Eric caught the ball, dodged to the left of the maple tree, then, shrieking at the top of his lungs, ran around the yard with his mother and brother in hot pursuit. Susan streaked by, giving David a tantalizing view of her cute little tush in well-worn jeans as she nailed Eric and bent over to tickle him.

"Damn, but I wouldn't mind tackling her," David muttered, feeling his groin tighten.

It was odd that he felt so attracted to Susan Miller. Not that she wasn't pretty in a subdued yet wholesome kind of way. Her sandy brown hair was soft and shiny, and he liked the way it curved under at her jawline. She had serious, intelligent hazel eyes, and a few freckles sprinkled across her cheeks and spunky little nose. There was nothing wrong with her figure, either, although he thought a few more pounds wouldn't hurt her a bit. But she wasn't nearly as striking or glamorous or outgoing as his other girlfriends had been.

Still, there was an elusive something about her that tugged at him. Was she nothing more than a challenge to his ego because she'd refused to go out with him? He didn't think so. He wasn't masochistic enough to go looking for rejection. Nevertheless, the one thing he wanted more than anything else at this moment was to be across the street, in the middle of that tangle of arms and legs, sharing in the fun.

Shaking his head, he turned away from the window and crammed the books onto the shelf. He carried the empty box through the kitchen to the garage, tossed it onto the growing pile and went back to the kitchen. He sighed in discouragement at the stacks still waiting for him there. The only bright spot in the room was the last, lonesome cookie sitting in the middle of the plate Susan had brought over.

David reached for it, bit into it, then closed his eyes in pleasure as the rich flavors of chocolate and caramel blended on his tongue. Lord, but it was good. Almost as good as sex. He wondered how Susan would react if he told her that.

Eyeing the empty plate, he told himself he wasn't looking for an excuse to see her again. He really *should* take the plate back in case Susan needed it. Besides, he needed to check in with the station and let his mother know he wouldn't be coming for dinner. Surely Susan wouldn't mind if he used her phone since his wasn't hooked up yet.

His decision made, David hurried into the bathroom, washed his face and combed his hair. When he returned to the kitchen, he brushed the crumbs off the plate and polished it with his shirtsleeve. If Susan was anything like his mother, she'd wash it again herself, whether he'd washed it or not. Holding it up for a closer inspection, he said, "Looks good enough to me," and headed off across the street.

Eric appeared on the other side of the screen door and opened it, greeting him with a cheery, "Howdy, Mr. Hunter."

"Hiya, sport." David stepped inside, his nose twitching appreciatively at a delicious, tangy smell coming from the kitchen. He glanced around the room, nodded at Timmy, who was flopped on his stomach in front of the TV, and noted with a grin that while the living room wasn't exactly ready for a layout in one of his mother's *Better Homes and Gardens* magazines, it looked a lot neater than the last time he'd seen it.

Eric studied David's battered Reeboks for a long moment, "Jason wears cowboy boots," he said as if anything Jason did was the *only* way to go.

"Yeah, he does," David agreed, squatting down closer to eye level with the boy. "But I've got bigger muscles."

"No, you don't," Eric answered, grinning while he shook his head vigorously.

"Wanna bet?" David flexed his arm for the boy. *Shoot, but this little guy is cute,* he thought as Eric reached out and squeezed his biceps. He had his mother's sandy hair and freckles, but he must have gotten those big blue eyes from his father. "Well? What do you think, sport?"

Eric giggled. "Yup. It's bigger, all right."

"Be sure to tell Jason that. Think I could talk to your mom for a minute?"

The boy nodded. "She's in the kitchen. C'mon, I'll show you."

The tempting aroma of dinner in the oven grew stronger as he followed the boy through a doorway on the north end of the room. Susan stood next to a rectangular formica table, the telephone receiver from a wall phone tucked between her ear and shoulder, one small, pink-stockinged foot braced on a chair seat, a coffee mug within reach. Her hands moved methodically while she talked, taking a little shirt out of the laundry basket on the table, giving it a quick snap, folding it across her raised knee and smoothing it, then adding it to one of the piles in front of her.

"Mom—"

"I'm on the phone, Eric. I'll be done in just a minute," she murmured without looking up or pausing in her work.

Eric looked up at David, shrugged and walked over to the cabinets beside the sink. He pulled out the bottom drawer, stepped onto it and hoisted himself up to sit on the counter.

Then he reached into a small paper bag and pulled out a handful of peanuts still in their shells.

Susan let out a low, husky giggle. "Candy, I swear, you're turning into a dirty old lady."

Leaning one shoulder against the door casing, David crossed one foot over the other, his gaze taking in the rest of Susan's small kitchen while it traveled back and forth between mother and son. The sink was piled high with pots and pans, some kind of casserole bubbled in the oven, and magnets and children's art projects covered the refrigerator. It reminded him of home.

Eric found a stubborn peanut shell. He squeezed it between his thumbs and fingers, flipped it over and squeezed again until his face turned red. Then he turned sideways and stuck the nut above the bottom hinge on a cabinet door. When he opened the door with a quick jerk, the shell cracked and the nuts dropped into his hand. He popped them into his mouth. David chuckled at the boy's ingenuity and his triumphant grin.

Susan glanced up and did a double take when she saw him lounging in the doorway. Her hands froze in midair, stretching a pair of silky panties between them. David couldn't help grinning at her shocked expression.

She must have realized what she was holding, because her eyes widened in horror, her cheeks turned a delightful shade of pink and she wadded up the garment and flung it at the laundry basket. It hit the rim and slithered slowly off the edge of the table and onto the floor. She lunged for it, almost lost the receiver, then said, "Candy, I've got to go. Talk to you later," and hung up the phone.

David leaned down and picked up the panties. "Blue is my favorite color," he said with a smile, handing them to Susan. She snatched her underwear out of his hand and crammed it down the side of the basket before turning back to face him.

"Hey, that's Mom's favorite color, too," Eric informed him.

Susan's fiery blush deepened and David almost wished he hadn't teased her. "You didn't need to interrupt your call for me," he said quietly.

"It wasn't important." She tugged her baggy purple sweatshirt down over her hips, then crossed her arms over her chest. "Just, uh, passing time."

David swallowed a sigh of disappointment at her nervous gestures. Susan's house was about the same size and age as his, and yet hers was a home and his was . . . just a house. He wouldn't mind sitting down, having a cup of coffee and talking with her while she folded her laundry. But it was obvious his presence made her about as comfortable as a mouse in a room full of starving cats.

"What can I do for you, David?" she asked, tucking a strand of hair behind her ear.

"I brought this back," he answered, holding up the plate.

"You already ate *all* those cookies?" Eric asked, wide-eyed with amazement. "Mom never lets us have more than two in one day."

Susan took the plate from David and set it on the table. "Eric, that's not very polite."

"It's all right," David replied with a grin. "My family put a pretty good dent in them yesterday, but they were too good to resist and I pigged out on the rest today. Thanks for bringing them over."

"You're welcome."

"I did have one other favor to ask. Could I use your phone? Mine should be connected tomorrow, but—"

"No problem." Susan turned and stacked the folded clothes back into the basket. "Just let me get this table cleared off, and we'll let you have some privacy."

"You don't have to leave. I'm just calling—"

She left anyway. Eric stayed where he was, still cracking nuts in the cupboard door and listening with obvious interest while David made his calls. David was finishing up with his mother when Susan returned with a basket full of jeans.

"Hey, Mom, guess what?" Eric said. "Mr. Hunter's not gonna have any dinner."

"What?" Susan asked, plunking the basket onto the table.

"He told his mom he wasn't gonna come home for dinner," Eric explained. "Can he eat with us? Please?"

She glanced at the glass pan in the oven, then over at her son. "Number one, Eric, you shouldn't listen to other people's conversations. And number two, maybe Mr. Hunter doesn't want to eat with us."

Eric scrambled off the counter and ran over to David. "My mom makes the bestest lasagna in the whole world," he said seriously, "so tell her ya wanna stay."

David scooped the boy up into his arms and turned to face Susan. "I'm sure she does, pal. But you know, she's had a busy day. I don't want to put her to any trouble, and I still have some unpacking to do."

Susan hesitated for a moment as she studied David and Eric. Then she gave David a wry smile. "It won't be any trouble, if you'd like to stay."

Wanting to accept her invitation and yet uncertain whether she really meant it or was simply being polite, David paused before answering. "Are you sure, Susan?"

She nodded toward the oven. "It won't be fancy, but there's plenty."

"All right. What can I do to help?" he asked, setting Eric on his feet. The boy immediately took off to tell his brother the news.

Smiling, she took a pair of jeans out of the basket. "Not a thing. The lasagna has to bake more, so you can go unpack for a while if you'd like. Why don't you come back about six?"

"Sounds good. I'll see you then."

David waved to the boys on his way out. Feeling absurdly pleased with himself, he went home and organized his kitchen. Okay, so his trip across the street *had* been an excuse to see Susan again. At the moment he didn't care. He wasn't sure why she hadn't flatly retracted Eric's artless invitation, but he wasn't in the mood to question a stroke of luck.

If Susan would only spend a little time with him, maybe she'd see he wasn't such a bad guy. And then what? Well, he didn't know that answer just yet. But he would.

By five-forty-five Susan wished she had wrung Eric's little neck and sent David Hunter off to a fast-food restaurant. It wasn't that having him over for dinner was any more work than feeding the boys. She would have made the salad, cooked the green beans and whipped up the instant pudding anyway.

Oh, she probably wouldn't have bothered with place mats and cloth napkins. She definitely wouldn't have changed into slacks and a nice sweater, put on makeup or combed her hair. But what really bothered her was that she wouldn't be feeling this tingling sense of anticipation, either. Those weren't butterflies zipping around in her stomach—they were full-grown eagles. It was ridiculous, if not downright dangerous, to feel so darn . . . pleased that David was coming for dinner.

Susan bit her lower lip and studied the table. Darn it, she should have nixed Eric's invitation. Taking cookies over to David had been bad enough. But he'd looked so tired and hopeful when Eric blurted out his plea, she hadn't had the heart to refuse. Maybe she should take off the place mats and change back into her jeans and sweatshirt.

On the other hand, maybe she was making too much of the whole situation. She hadn't invited David, Eric had. There was no reason to believe he would regard the dinner as anything more than a neighborly gesture. He'd come over, tired out and grubby from working all day, eat and go home. No big deal.

The doorbell rang at that moment. Eric and Timmy raced to answer it. Susan inhaled a calming breath and took the lasagna out of the oven. She heard David's deep voice mixing with the boys' higher tones, and then he walked into the kitchen carrying a bottle of wine.

Susan took one look at him over her shoulder, and the eagles in her stomach did swan dives. He'd changed into a

casual pair of dark blue slacks and a blue-and-white-striped
rugby shirt that emphasized the breadth of his chest and
shoulders. His dark hair gleamed with dampness, as if he'd
just stepped out of the shower, and his big, gorgeous brown
eyes didn't look the least bit tired.

His gaze roamed over her, his mouth curving in a smile of
frank, masculine approval. A rush of warmth that had
nothing to do with the hot oven spread through her nervous system, and Susan had to look away. She set the dish
on a trivet.

"Man, does that ever smell good," he said, walking over
to stand beside her. He held the wine out for her inspection. "Think this will go all right with dinner?"

Susan barely glanced at the bottle and caught a whiff of
an expensive after-shave. The lasagna wasn't the only thing
that smelled good. He looked at her, his eyebrows raised in
query, and she realized he was still waiting for her to answer his question. "Uh, that's fine. Thanks for bringing it."

"Have you got a corkscrew?"

It was a simple-enough question, but she was so caught up
in the compelling expression in his dark eyes, it took several seconds for it to sink in. When it finally did, she felt her
cheeks flush and turned away to rummage through the appropriate drawer. Feeling every bit as awkward and embarrassed as she had back in high school whenever she'd waited
on David or one of his pals in the library, she finally found
the corkscrew, dropped it into his outstretched hand and
hurried over to another cupboard for wineglasses.

David extracted the cork, then filled a glass for each of
them with deft, relaxed movements Susan envied. She
looked at the bottle again, recognizing a label that was far
beyond her budget.

"Aren't we supposed to let it breathe for a while?" she
asked when David held up his glass for a toast.

"I'm too nervous to wait."

She shot him a skeptical glance before touching her glass
to his. "Why should you be nervous?"

"I'm nervous because you're nervous, and I don't know how to help you relax.

Susan closed her eyes in mortification for a moment. Then the idiocy of the situation hit her, and she laughed. "I'm sorry, David. I don't have company for dinner very often."

"I'm not company," he answered with a broad grin. "Think of me as a pal Eric dragged home. You know, just one of the boys."

She eyed all six feet four inches of him and shook her head. "Eric's friends are usually shorter."

"Then why don't we just start all over again?"

"How do we do that?"

He set down his glass, grabbed the wine bottle and walked out of the room. He appeared in the doorway a second later, and without the least bit of self-consciousness, reenacted his entry. Susan found his performance both funny and endearing, and by the time they sat down to eat, her tension and awkwardness had drained away.

David ate her lasagna with flattering enthusiasm, and Susan couldn't remember enjoying a meal more. He was an accomplished storyteller, and he warmed her heart when he automatically included the boys in the conversation. Eric hung on his every word from the outset, but Timmy held back until David mentioned the magic words guaranteed to grab the boy's attention—football and the Denver Broncos.

"Didja ever see 'em play at Mile High Stadium?" Timmy asked eagerly.

"A few times," David admitted with a twinkle in his eyes. "My boss used to lend me his season tickets if he couldn't go to a game."

"Didja ever meet John Elway?"

"Sure did. In fact, I interviewed him when we were doing a Super Bowl Twenty-One promotion, and he autographed a ball for me."

"Wow."

"Would you like to come see it sometime?"

"You bet!"

"Do they still have show-and-tell in second grade?" David asked.

"Yeah."

"You want to take it to school?"

Timmy's eyes bugged out. "Do you mean it?"

"Sure. How about next week?"

"Oh, man! I'll be supercareful with it, Mr. Hunter. I promise."

"I know you will, Tim."

Susan took one glimpse of the sudden hero worship shining in her older son's eyes and lost her appetite. Timmy used to look at Jason the same way. She hadn't done a very good job of protecting him before, but she could and would protect him now, she thought fiercely.

"Is something wrong, Mom?" Eric asked.

She started at his question and gave him an embarrassed smile when she realized she must have been scowling. "Oh, uh, no. I was just thinking about something."

The boys drew David into a discussion about the Broncos' chances of returning to the Super Bowl. Susan excused herself to get the dessert and studied him surreptitiously while she worked. With every new burst of laughter from the table, her resentment grew.

Why did he have to be so damn handsome? Why did he have to be charming and make himself so at home during the space of one meal that he looked as if he belonged in her family even more than Jason had? Why did he have to come into her life now, of all times, make her enjoy his company and want him...no, want *things* she knew she couldn't have?

After dinner the boys went into the living room to clip the coupons from the Sunday paper, and David helped Susan clear the table and load the dishwasher. When they were finished, they settled in at the kitchen table with a second cup of coffee.

"That was a great dinner, Susan. Thank you." David said.

"You're welcome." She fiddled with her cup for a moment, then looked up at him, her forehead creased with concern. "That was a pretty generous offer you made Timmy. Did you mean it?"

"I wouldn't have said it if I didn't."

"What if something happens to your football? I know Timmy will be careful with it, but anything can happen around a bunch of kids."

David shrugged. "Don't worry about it. I never lend anything if I really need to have it back." He leaned forward, resting one forearm on the table. "But why do I get the feeling something else is going on here? What's really bothering you, Susan?"

She met his direct, questioning gaze and felt her resentment slip a notch. After all, what had the man done but befriend her son? "I guess I'm not sure why you made the offer in the first place."

"Timmy's a neat kid, and I like him. What's wrong with that?

"Nothing's wrong with it. You made him feel great, and I appreciate that. But he's awfully vulnerable right now, especially to men."

"Because of Jason?"

Susan nodded. "He was counting on having Jason as a father. When it didn't work out, he was crushed."

"So what are you saying?" he asked with a frown. "You don't want me to be friendly with your kids?"

"No, of course not. But I don't want you to raise their expectations, either."

"Well, how do I do that? I can't control what a kid thinks."

"I know." She sighed and twirled a lock of hair around her index finger. "But just don't get too close to him."

David leaned back in his chair and crossed his arms over his chest. "Is it the boys you don't want me to get close to? Or is it you?"

"Both." Susan felt a twinge of remorse at the quick flash of hurt that crossed his face.

"Man, you don't pull any punches, do you?" He rubbed his chin for a moment, studying her with a thoughtful expression. "Mind if I ask why? Do you dislike me, or have I done something to offend you?"

She shook her head. "It's nothing like that, David. But I'm not...maybe I should say *we're* not ready to get involved with anyone yet."

"Did I ask you to get involved with me?"

Though her face burned with embarrassment, Susan met his gaze squarely. "I didn't say you did. But I thought, with my bringing the cookies over and dinner tonight, maybe I was sending you mixed signals. I'd rather be honest with you than play games."

David reached across the table and captured her hand in his. "And I admire that. I don't like playing games, either. But I think we've got a problem."

His thumb brushed over the back of her hand in a soothing gesture, but the intense look in his eyes was anything but soothing. "What's that?" she asked, inhaling a shaky breath.

"I like you and your boys. A lot. All I want is a chance to get to know you better."

His dark eyes said more than his words. They coaxed her, promised her, tempted her. She tried to tug her hand away, but he held it fast. "Why?"

"Why not?"

"We don't have much in common, David."

"You don't know that. You don't even know me. But I'm attracted to you, and I think maybe you're attracted to me. Isn't that why you're trying to put me off?"

Her heart thumped against her rib cage at his long, searching look. She jerked her hand out of his grasp and moved out of his reach. Finally she said, "You don't pull any punches, either."

"I thought you wanted to be honest."

"I do. That's why I asked you not to get too close."

"I won't get any closer than you want me to. But can't we even be friends?"

Susan stuck her hands into her pockets. Could they be friends? Just friends? Maybe David could. If the rumors about his record with women were true, it might be a novelty for him to have a friendship with her. But there was something about him that was so darn appealing, she wasn't at all sure she could trust herself not to feel more for him.

"Let's just leave it at neighbors," she suggested.

His lips quirked into a wry smile. "Friendly neighbors."

"Maybe."

"Would one friendly neighbor let another friendly neighbor drive her and her boys to a barbecue next Saturday?" he asked with a teasing glint in his eyes.

She laughed and shook her head. "Your car isn't built for a family, Hunter."

"We can take your car."

"I'd rather go by myself. I want to be able to leave if one of the kids get crabby."

Chuckling, David climbed to his feet. "You're a stubborn wretch, Miller, but I like you anyway. Walk me to the door, and I'll get out of your hair."

Susan followed him into the living room. He told Timmy to come over and get the promised football the next evening before turning to Susan at the door. He thanked her again for dinner, then pulled her outside away from the boys' sight and hearing. "Are you sure you want me to back off?"

"No," she admitted honestly. "But I think it would be better if you did."

"All right. I will." His eyes gleaming with devilry, he lowered his head and dropped a quick, warm kiss on her lips that left her shaken and breathless. Then he strolled down her front steps and into the street. When he was halfway home, he turned and called softly to her, "But only for a while, Susan. Only for a while."

Chapter Five

Susan rubbed her forehead, read the page again, then gave up and slammed shut the file on the bank's new advertising campaign. Since she wasn't accomplishing anything, she might as well go to lunch. She'd like to blame David Hunter for her lack of concentration, but after loaning Timmy the precious football, David had backed off.

The man hadn't done anything except tell her he was attracted to her and kiss her. His kiss had been pleasant, even a bit... arousing, but it hadn't been what she would call spectacular. Unfortunately that hadn't stopped her from thinking about him at the darnedest times, keeping track of his comings and goings across the street like a besotted teenager, and worse yet, dreaming about him.

Of course, his last parting shot about only backing off for a while hadn't helped. Having the boys talking about him all the time didn't help much, either. But Susan had always considered her ability to focus on her goals her greatest strength. David Hunter did *not* figure into her present or future goals.

After four days of not seeing or talking to him, one would think she could at least stop wondering who owned the red Corvette that had been parked in his driveway on Sunday night and then again on Tuesday. It wasn't any of her business and it didn't matter. At least it *shouldn't* matter.

"Blast him anyway," she muttered, reaching into her drawer for her purse.

"I sure hope you didn't mean me," a male voice responded from the other side of the desk.

Susan straightened up and felt her face flush when she found herself looking into the amused gray eyes of her boss, Hal Baker, the bank's vice president of marketing and public affairs. She'd worked with Hal for four years now, and had come to view him as a fatherly friend as well as an employer.

"Not this time, Hal," she replied with a smile. "What can I do for you?"

He pulled up a chair and plunked himself down, then smoothed a hand over the few hairs left on top of his head. "How are you getting along without Beth? Do you need a temp?" he asked.

"I may need some help before her maternity leave ends, but I'm okay for now." Her eyes narrowed in suspicion. "Unless you've got a new project in mind for me?"

Hal folded his hands over his ample stomach, "Well, it just so happens I might. It all depends on Melissa Reed."

"And who is Melissa Reed?"

"A two-month-old baby. Her mother's a friend of my daughter Tracy. Real nice little gal as I remember her."

"What's this got to do with me?" Susan asked.

Hal's expression turned sour. "Melissa may need a liver transplant. They're still doing some tests to be sure, but it doesn't look good for the little tyke. Her dad's a mechanic, and Katie—that's her mother—works part-time, but their insurance won't cover a liver transplant."

"Aren't there government funds available for patients like this?" Susan asked.

"Nope. The Reeds don't qualify for Medicare. And Wyoming's Medicaid program won't pay for liver transplants anyway. They've been able to scrape up twenty-five thousand dollars between their savings and what Katie's folks can give them, but that won't even get Melissa on a donor list. They'll need at least eighty-five thousand more to do that. Then they'll need another ten to twenty thousand to pay for the rest of the surgery bill, and at least another twenty thousand to get Melissa through her first year of care."

Adding it all up in her head, Susan gulped at the staggering amount. "So, you want me to organize a fund-raising campaign?"

"Not just yet. There's no sense in getting people all stirred up until the final test results are in. But it wouldn't hurt to start thinking about it. If she does need the transplant, we'll have to move on this in a hurry."

"How long does she have without the surgery?"

"About two years, I guess. How do you feel about tackling this?" Hal said, pushing himself out of the chair. "You may have to work on it full-time for a while."

"I'll be glad to try. But that's a lot of money."

Hal reached over and patted her shoulder. "You'll do fine, Susan. Call if you need any help."

Susan sent up a silent prayer of thanks for her boys' good health as he walked away, then took out a yellow pad and started roughing out ideas for the campaign.

Saturday morning dawned cool and clear. Eric and Timmy were out of bed when the first pale streaks of sunlight appeared on the eastern horizon. They torpedoed into Susan's room, demanding to leave for Jason's ranch immediately. She moaned, rolled onto her stomach and pulled a pillow over her head.

"C'mon, Mom," Eric coaxed, lifting up one corner of the pillow. "We're starvin'. Ya gotta get up."

Slow to wake up at the best of times, Susan opened one eye and gave her younger son a baleful glare. "This is my one day to sleep in, Eric. Go get some cereal and watch cartoons if they're on yet.''

"Aw, Mom," Timmy protested, "we wanna get there before all the best horses are taken."

Susan struggled up on one elbow, looked at the clock and moaned again. "The barbecue starts at ten. It takes an hour to get to the ranch. That means we don't have to leave for four hours."

"But you'll find all kinds of jobs to do, and it takes you forever to get ready," Timmy argued.

"Let me sleep until seven. I promise we'll leave in plenty of time," Susan countered. "Now, will you please scram?"

"Oh, all right," Timmy grumbled. "Come on, Eric. Mr. Hunter told me he's going, too. If Mom's not ready on time, maybe we can ride with him."

The boys trudged out of the room, and a moment later Susan heard them rattling around in the kitchen. She turned onto her back, snuggled into her favorite sleeping position and closed her eyes. Then Timmy's last statement penetrated her foggy brain, and her eyelids popped right back open.

Damn the man! Did he have to haunt her every minute? The only times he'd been far from her thoughts all week were when she'd been writing or working on the campaign for Melissa Reed. She couldn't go on writing until mid night every night to get him out of her head when she had to rise and shine at six in order to get to work on time. Well, maybe seeing him again today would fix that.

She'd always had an overly active imagination. Surely David Hunter wouldn't be as handsome, as intriguing, as...sexy in reality as he was in her memory. He'd show up with some gorgeous young thing, no doubt the owner of the red Corvette that had been in his driveway again last night. He'd be friendly and polite, and Susan would know that he wasn't seriously interested in her after all.

With that comforting thought firmly entrenched in her mind, she settled back and tried to sleep one more time. Of course, it was no use. She finally gave up at six, dragged herself out of bed and went out to the kitchen to make coffee. By the time she'd fed and bathed the boys, straightened up the house and dressed in a comfortable pair of jeans and her Wyoming Cowboys sweatshirt, it was time to leave.

During the drive out to the ranch, her spirits lifted. The boys were too busy looking out the car windows for antelope to squabble. The sky was a deep, clear blue, and for once Wyoming's wind had settled down to a mere breeze. A carefree outing with the boys was a rare treat, and she intended to enjoy it.

They finished the last chorus of "Row, Row, Row Your Boat" as Susan parked behind the Wakefields' sprawling house next to David's black Porsche. Jason and Melody walked outside to welcome them, and when the social amenities had been concluded, Jason suggested they all go out to the barn to see a surprise.

Eric and Timmy walked alongside the big man, chattering all the way and skipping to keep up with his long strides. Susan and Melody followed at a slower pace. Not knowing quite what to say to her ex-boyfriend's new wife, Susan stuck her hands in her pockets and gazed at the barnyard and the pastures beyond. Her silence didn't appear to bother Melody, and Susan's discomfort gradually faded.

When they reached the barn door, however, Melody stopped walking and touched Susan's forearm. "I wasn't sure you'd come today."

"Jason didn't give me much choice," Susan answered with a wry smile. "But I suppose you would have been happier if I'd stayed home."

Melody shrugged, neither admitting nor denying the truth of Susan's statement. "He wanted you and the boys included, so I invited you. Does it upset you to see us together?"

Susan slowly shook her head, then looked Melody right in the eye. "No. What you really want to know, though, is if I still love him. Isn't it?"

Melody nodded. "He's really been concerned about losing your friendship."

"You know," Susan said, tracing the toe of one shoe around a rock, "it's hard raising kids alone, and it's lonely. I enjoyed having Jason around to talk to and do things with the boys. I'm not sure I ever really loved him as much as I loved the idea of having a man in my life again. But he was the best friend I've had in a long time, and it hurt to lose him."

"You don't have to lose him," Melody replied with a relieved smile. "At least not on my account. I hated your guts for a while last summer, Susan, but I wouldn't mind having you for a friend now, myself."

The sincere warmth in Melody's big brown eyes reminded Susan of the way David had looked at her on occasion. That warmth was every bit as hard to resist coming from Melody as it was from her brother. "I wouldn't mind it, either."

A delighted grin broke out across Melody's face, and she wiped the back of one hand across her forehead. "Whew! Am I ever glad we got that out of the way."

Susan laughed in response, then turned her head toward the sound of squeals and giggles coming from the barn. Melody linked her arm through Susan's and led her inside to an open stall. Susan's eyes widened at the sight of her sons rolling around in a pile of hay with six fat, wiggling puppies.

She dropped to her knees and scooped one of the little black-and-tan bundles of fur into her arms. The pup immediately licked her face until Susan got her hands around its middle and held it out at arm's length. "Oh, you little sweetums, aren't you just gorgeous?" she crooned.

"Mom, Mom, aren't they great?" Timmy asked.

Susan glanced over at him, then jerked her head back to the right when she realized the boys and puppies were not alone. David Hunter sat in a darkened corner of the stall, his long legs drawn up close to his chest and a seventh little animal cuddled against his neck. He grinned at her as if her reaction to the pups amused him to no end.

Her breath caught in her chest, and a warm, excited tingle hit her nervous system. The puppy slurped David's ear. He tipped back his head and laughed before lowering the pup farther down on his chest and stroking it gently with his big hand. Susan had to admit her imagination hadn't been working overtime at all.

His jeans had a rip in one knee, his blue work shirt was wrinkled and dusty and a piece of hay stuck out of the dark hair falling across his forehead. He looked boyish and disheveled, but at that moment he was the most appealing and, yes, the most sexy man she'd ever seen.

"Hi," he said softly.

"Hi," she replied, feeling ridiculously bashful and sheepish and yet awfully glad to see him all at the same time.

Timmy walked over to her on his knees, holding out a hand to coax one of the pups along with him. "Look at this one, Mom," he demanded.

Wrenching her gaze away from David's, Susan struggled to focus on her son. Timmy's eyes shone with devotion as he petted and talked to the puppy gamboling around him. "Isn't he neat?" he rattled on. "Jason said he's trying to find homes for them, and Mr. Hunter's gonna take that one he's holding. He's already named it Sheba. Can we have this one?

Susan looked into Timmy's eager little face for a moment, then studied the size of the animal's feet with a sinking sensation in the pit of her stomach. She turned and looked up at Jason, who stood outside the stall with Melody. "What kind of dogs are they?"

He shrugged. "I think their mother's got a lot of German shepherd in her, but since she was already pregnant when she wandered in here, who knows what their father was? From their looks and coloring, I'd guess he might have been a black Lab."

"Please, Mom?" Timmy begged.

Turning to her son, Susan bit back a sigh. "No, honey. Not this time."

"Aw, Mom," the boy protested, gathering the pup into his arms. "I'll take good care of him. I'll feed him and walk him and clean up after him. I promise."

Her heart aching, Susan reached out and smoothed his hair off his forehead. "I know you would. And I hate to disappoint you, but we can't afford a dog," she said gently but firmly. "Especially not one that'll be as big as this one will."

Timmy glared at her over the top of the puppy's head, but his lower lip quivered as if tears might be close. "You always say that. What if I buy his food out of my allowance?"

"I doubt your allowance would pay for it," Susan replied. "But there's more to taking care of a dog than food. There are vet bills and license fees and boarding fees, too, sometimes. I'm sorry, honey, but I just can't swing it right now."

David stretched his legs out in front of him and laid his puppy down beside him. "You know, Tim, I'll probably need some help taking care of Sheba when I take her home next week. Would you be interested in a job once in a while?"

Timmy gave him a stiff shrug and answered in a monotone, "I guess so."

Jason cleared his throat, then announced, "Well, guys, looks like mama dog's comin' back. Whaddaya say we go pick out your horses?"

Eric clambered to his feet and ran over to Jason with a rambunctious, "Yeah!" After giving his puppy one last longing glance, Timmy followed them out of the barn. Unable to face David for a moment, Susan stood and made a production out of dusting off her knees. David got up and walked close to her.

"That was pretty rough on you," he said.

Susan straightened and managed a crooked smile. "Yeah, well, that's motherhood."

David petted the puppies' mother as she rejoined her offspring. Then he slung one around Susan's shoulders and gave her a reassuring hug. "He'll get over it."

"I suppose he will. But he'll never know how much I wanted to say yes to that puppy and a lot of other things, too."

"I could see that. But I thought you handled it pretty well, Susan. At least you didn't say he could never have a dog."

Struggling for a more cheerful expression, Susan stepped away from him. "If my plans work out, we should be able to get one in a couple of years. But to a seven-year-old, that seems like forever."

"Ready to go outside now?" David asked.

She inhaled a deep breath, then nodded and ambled out of the barn beside him. Two pickups and three more cars, one of them the flashy red Corvette that had piqued Susan's interest all week, were lined up behind the house now, and a happy mixture of male and female voices came from the corral. Susan scanned the crowd for a gorgeous, unattached young woman, but every female present had a man standing beside her.

"Look at me, Mom!" Eric shouted.

"Yeah, Mom, look," Timmy called.

Susan followed David over to the corral, then smiled and waved to the boys, who were already mounted on a couple of sleepy-eyed old horses. David rested an elbow on the top rung of the fence and hooked the heel of one boot over the bottom rung. He gestured toward Timmy with his thumb before turning a grin on Susan.

"He doesn't look like he's suffering much."

"No, he doesn't," Susan replied, joining him at the fence with a relieved sigh.

"Which one are you going to ride? How about that Appaloosa over there?"

Susan gazed at the horse in question and winced inwardly at its size and the way it pranced around in the herd. It was a beautiful animal, but the thought of climbing onto its back held about as much appeal as walking barefoot into a den of rattlers. She might be able to fake it on an old plug from a riding stable, but her courage wouldn't stretch to a horse that looked as if it couldn't wait for a hard gallop across the prairie. She suddenly found the toes of her boots extremely fascinating.

"I thought I'd stay here and help Melody with the food," she said.

David studied her, one side of his mouth twitching. "You wouldn't happen to be scared of horses."

"Who, me?" she asked, feeling her cheeks heat up at the knowing look in his eyes. "No, of course not." Hoping to distract him, she asked, "Which one are you going to ride?"

He chuckled. "The damn things always run away with me. Even the old crippled ones. You couldn't get me up on one of those mangy critters for anything."

She gaped at him in disbelief for an instant, then burst out laughing. "You're afraid of them, too?"

"Not everyone from Wyoming is a cowboy, Susan," he answered with a shrug.

"And here I thought that since Jason's your friend, you'd be another Clint Eastwood. Don't you come out and help him with branding or anything?"

"No, ma'am," he drawled, shaking his head. "Steak and prime rib are the only things I like about cattle." He paused and shuddered. "And I especially hate what they do to the little boy cows. It's downright cruel, if you ask me."

She let her eyes roam over his Western clothes, then sniffed as if in disgust. "You're nothing but a drugstore cowboy, Hunter."

He reached over and gently punched her arm. "Well, you don't have to broadcast it, Miller. It's bad enough having Jason call me Slick whenever he wants to feel superior."

Smiling at his disgruntled expression, Susan patted his forearm. "Your secret is safe with me." She looked down at her own jeans and boots. "Besides, who am I to talk?"

"I'm glad you realize that."

They watched the commotion of getting the rest of the horses caught and saddled in a companionable silence. Susan recognized David's parents and the usher David had introduced her to at the wedding. What was his name? Alan Jordan? Yeah, that was it. She didn't know anyone else, but it looked like a congenial group.

When everyone else had been matched with a mount, Jason tried to wave David and Susan over. "Hey, Slick. Susan. Come on and pick out your horses."

"We'll pass this time, Jase. Go on ahead," David replied.

Jason tipped his hat back, propped his hands on his hips and gave them a long, searching look. "Sure you don't want to come, Susan?"

"No, thanks, Jason. You'll keep an eye on the boys for me?"

A slow, thoughtful smile spread across his mouth. "Be glad to. See you guys later."

With that, he whispered something to Melody and gave her a quick kiss before swinging himself into his big black gelding's saddle. David opened the corral gate and held it while the horses walked through in single file. Melody followed the last one out on foot, grinning at her brother as she approached him.

"Don't say it, Squirt," he warned, scowling down at her.

"Say what, Slick?" she asked with wide-eyed innocence, then giggled and jumped away, avoiding the swat he took at her rear end.

Walking over to Susan, Melody gestured toward the house. "Come on in and have a cup of coffee. You can talk to me while I put the salads and relish trays together."

"Sounds good to me," Susan agreed. "I'll be glad to help."

"I never refuse an offer like that," Melody told her.

David joined them, and in a few moments they were all seated at the kitchen table, coffee mugs in front of them. Enjoying the lighthearted banter between David and his sister, Susan sat back and relaxed. When they'd finished their coffee, Melody hauled a giant bowl of raw hamburger out of the refrigerator and put Susan and David to work making patties.

"Stand back and watch a master at work," David told Susan, rolling up his sleeves with a flourish.

He plunged his right hand into the bowl and pulled out at least a half-pound glob of meat. He shaped it into a tight sphere the size of a softball, plopped it onto the table and smashed it with the side of his fist. Then he mashed down the lumps and smoothed the ragged edges with his fingers before looking up at Susan.

"Is that a perfect hamburger, or what?" he asked, shooting her a triumphant grin.

"Your method reminds me of Timmy and Eric with their Playdough."

His eyebrows drew together in a fierce scowl, and Susan and Melody laughed at his indignant snort. "Just for that, Miller, you don't get to help me. Go make salad with the squirt over there."

She stuck her nose in the air. "All right. I will."

The teasing and infectious humor continued throughout the morning, but somehow the work got done. When the tables were set and the charcoal had been lit, they all went out to rest on the lawn chairs while they waited for the riders to return. Melody leaned back and closed her eyes with a weary sigh. David pulled a twelve-string guitar out of a battered case and started picking out the tune to "On Top of Old Smokey."

Susan tipped her face up toward the noonday sun and felt a sense of contentment wash into her soul along with David's soft music. Despite all the aggravation he'd caused her during the past week, it was good to be with him now. He started humming along with his playing, and his deep, rich voice sent a pleasant tingle of awareness through her body.

She turned her head to look at him and found him looking right back at her with a bemused, somewhat moody expression in his dark eyes. The tingle flashed into a sizzle, and her gaze moved down to rest on his mouth. Her heart stopped beating for a moment, and gooseflesh sprouted on the backs of her arms. Lord help her, she wanted to feel his lips on hers again.

His fingers hit the wrong strings, and he glanced down at his instrument, breaking the sudden tension between them. Susan looked away from him, inhaled a deep breath, then let it out on a quiet sigh. She didn't want an involvement with him or anyone else, but her earlier conversation with Candy echoed in her brain.

Maybe her friend was right. She was a big girl, after all. She could go out with David, enjoy his company and have a good time without falling in love with him. She had gained a great deal from Jason's friendship, and she'd gotten over him well enough, hadn't she?

Why not give David a try?

Because he's more dangerous to your peace of mind than Jason ever was, a voice piped up inside her head. Susan ordered the little voice to hush, but it went on relentlessly. *There's more chemistry with David. He's more sensitive to your feelings. He's more open with his own feelings than Jason is. You understand him better, and that makes him more attractive, more exciting.*

To Susan's intense relief, Melody straightened up at that moment and pointed toward the western pastures. "Here they come," she said, shielding her eyes with her other hand. "Guess we'd better bring the food out now."

When the riders arrived, Melody introduced Susan to the people she didn't know, while David and Michael Hunter manned the grills. Getting the meal on the table and helping the boys with their plates gave Susan the distraction she needed to get her emotions back in perspective. She ended up at a table with David, his parents and the Wakefields, and soon found herself drawn into a conversation as naturally as if she were an old friend.

She talked writing with Karen Hunter and was delighted when the older woman offered to loan her some books about fiction techniques. She learned about the master's degree program in counselling Melody had enrolled in at the University of Wyoming. She told David's father about Melissa Reed and received an immediate commitment of help from Hunter Communications for the fund-raising campaign if one became necessary.

"Why don't you let me take that on, Dad?" David suggested. "You'll be leaving for Europe soon, so I might as well get in at the beginning."

"Sounds like a good idea to me," Michael answered. "You've done plenty of promotion work before." He turned to Susan. "Just give Dave a call. He'll give you all the help you need."

Susan's misgivings about getting close to David surged up inside her, but she hid her feelings behind a polite smile. "Thanks. I'm sure he will."

"Well, Slick," Jason said with a challenging smile. "Ready for that football game?"

"Whenever you are, cowboy," David retorted.

"Better you guys than me," Michael put in with a laugh. He climbed off the picnic bench, walked around the table and gave Melody a hug. "Great party, honey. We'll see you next week."

"You're not leaving yet, are you?" Melody protested.

"We've got to get back to town," Karen said, kissing her daughter's cheek. "I need to finish a column and get ready for a hot date with your old man."

Michael and Karen walked across the lawn toward the cars hand in hand, laughing and talking all the way. Susan watched them go, touched by their obvious closeness to each other. Her mouth nearly dropped open in surprise when they climbed into the red Corvette and roared off down the drive with a cheery honk and a wave.

"Honestly," Melody said, starting to clear the table, "those two have been acting like a couple of kids since they bought that car."

"They've earned, it, sis," David said.

"Yes, they have. Has Dad eased up any at work?" Melody asked.

"Some." David's grin widened. "But I have high hopes this vacation will convince him it's time to turn more of the decisions over to me."

Susan gathered up a load of paper plates. "Is it hard working for your father?"

David shrugged and reached for a bowl of potato chips. "Most of the time it's not hard at all. Then something happens and he remembers what a rotten kid I was, and, well, I guess it's hard for him, too, sometimes."

"Are we gonna stand here and talk all day?" Jason grumbled. "Or are we gonna play football?"

"We'll play just as soon as we get this mess picked up, honey," Melody replied, giving him an impish smile and handing him a tray loaded with condiments.

The football game was a chaotic, hilarious affair. Everyone played, even the youngest toddler, who was only two years old. David and Jason made up rules as they went along, adding confusion and fun to the process. When the contest ended in a tie two hours later, Susan wasn't sure if she was more exhausted from running or from laughing.

Everyone gravitated toward the picnic tables afterward for homemade ice cream. Susan helped the boys get some dessert, then flopped down on the grass between them. Someone convinced David to play his guitar, and before long he had a rousing songfest going. He played everything from the University of Wyoming's fight song, "Ragtime Cowboy Joe," to rock and roll, to sweet country ballads like "Down in the Valley."

Eric crawled into Susan's lap. She put her arms around him, rested her chin on top of his head and watched David's performance with ambivalent emotions. She couldn't help liking, even admiring him. She couldn't deny she felt drawn to him both physically and emotionally, in ways she'd never been to anyone else. And yet he still scared her spitless.

The reason she felt that way, Susan mused, was that he seemed too damn good to be true. He was funny and talented, kind and considerate, affectionate and sexy as hell. He had a powerful but loving family behind him, money and a sound future most people only dreamed about. The man literally had everything going for him; he'd *always* had everything going for him.

She didn't think he was shallow, exactly; he'd shown too much empathy for her to think that of him. But what did someone like David Hunter know about abandonment, insecurity and low self-esteem? About struggling to keep a roof over your head, clothes on your children's backs and put food in front of them on the table? About sitting up all night with a baby screaming from the pain of an ear infection and wondering how in the world you were going to pay the doctor and the pharmacist?

Eric sighed and stuck his thumb in his mouth. Susan looked down at him for a moment, then over at Timmy, then back up at David. She felt immensely flattered that David had shown so much interest in her and in her sons. She had to smile at the memory of his antics during the football game.

Eric had been on Jason's team and was running with the ball toward the goal line. David had scooped the boy up, ball and all, charged in the opposite direction and scored a touchdown for his own team. It was hard to resist a man who obviously liked kids as much as he did.

But it was easy to love Eric and Timmy when they were in a sunny, cooperative mood. It was not so easy to love them when they had temper tantrums or trashed the house or tormented each other into a screaming fit. Their father hadn't been able to tolerate the daily grind of family life. Her own father hadn't, either. Why should she expect more from David?

As if the kids weren't enough, there was the matter of fidelity to consider. Some women might be able to have an affair with a man without some kind of a commitment, but Susan Miller wasn't one of them. Some women could look the other way when their husbands strayed, but Susan wasn't one of them, either.

Okay, so she'd been wrong about some gorgeous young thing owning the red Corvette, and David hadn't been entertaining a woman at his house last week. That didn't mean he hadn't done so in the past or wouldn't do so in the future. The man attracted women to him like picnics attracted ants.

David looked up from his playing, caught her eye, then gave her one of those deliciously wicked smiles of his—the kind that made her toes curl inside her boots and invited her to wonder if he'd really look as good without his clothes as she thought he might. Damn, but the man was tempting despite all her misgivings about having a relationship with him.

Timmy yawned and leaned against her arm. Susan glanced down at his dusty, tangled hair and tired little face and decided it was time to go home. As if he'd come to the same conclusion, David put away his guitar and walked over to her. He studied her intently for a long moment before reaching down to take Eric from her arms. Susan and Timmy scrambled to their feet.

"That was really great, Mr. Hunter," Timmy said. "I wish I could play like that."

"Maybe you will some day, Tim," David told him. "All it takes is practice."

The other guests started gathering up their possessions in preparation for leaving. Susan found her purse next to one of the picnic tables, thanked the Wakefields for their hospitality and went back to collect her sons from David. He insisted on carrying Eric to the car for her. When the boys were settled inside, he opened Susan's door.

"Great party, wasn't it?" he said quietly.

Susan nodded. "It was a nice day for everyone."

He reached out and gently stroked the backs of his fingers across her cheek. "I'd still like to spend more time with you and the boys."

She looked into his dark eyes, and the sincerity she found there nearly convinced her to agree. She hesitated, forcing herself to remember all the reasons she'd decided a relationship between them would never work. Then she slowly shook her head. "I'd rather not, David."

Impatience glinted in his eyes. His lips clamped shut, forming a thin, grim line across his face. Finally he said, "All right, Susan. If that's the way you want it."

She slid into the car, shut the door and started the engine. David stepped out of the way and put his hands on his hips while he watched her drive away. He started when a hand fell on his right shoulder. Turning around, he found Jason beside him, a frown creasing his forehead.

"What was that all about?" Jason asked.

David shrugged as if his gut wasn't clenched in a knot of disappointment. "Damned if I know."

"You weren't hitting on her, were you?"

"Well, I asked her out, not that it's any of your business. But she turned me down, and I don't know why."

Letting his hand fall to his side, Jason backed off a step. "Why'd you ask her out?"

"Why shouldn't I?" David shot back. "You don't have a claim on her anymore."

"She's not your usual type, Dave."

David smiled wryly at that remark, remembering Jason's preference for tall, buxom redheads before he'd fallen in love with Melody, a short, skinny brunette. "And I suppose my sister was your type?"

Jason chuckled in response. "Your sister's in a class by herself." Then his eyes took on a worried expression. "But what about Susan?"

"What about her?"

"Just how interested in her are you?"

"How can I answer that if she won't even let me get to know her?" Running one hand through his hair, David turned a suspicious glare on his friend. "Did you do something rotten to her I don't know about?"

"Hell, no." Jason shoved his hands into his pockets and looked down at the toes of his boots. "I mean, I know she was hurt when we broke up and all, but I was honest with her from day one."

"C'mon, Jase, *something* must have happened. Did you sleep with her?"

Jason shot him a warning look. "Do you really think that's any of your business?"

When David stared right back at him without even blinking, Jason sighed and answered the question.

"All right. I thought about it. Plenty. I mean, Susan's a damned sexy little gal in a quiet sorta way. But it just didn't feel right when I was still so far gone over Mel."

David relaxed slightly at his friend's admission. "Well, then, what is she so afraid of?" he asked, shaking his head in confusion. "Is it men in general or just me personally? She's warm and open for a while, but when I try to get a little closer, she clams up and gets this damn wary look in her eyes. When I try to be nice to her kids, she warns me off. What does she think I am, for God's sake? A child molester or a rapist?"

"I doubt she thinks that, Dave," Jason chided him. "From the way you two were lookin' at each other all day, I reckon she's just as interested in you as you are in her. That's probably what's got her so spooked."

"I still don't understand—"

"She's just not ready yet, that's all. I don't know much about why her marriage broke up, but I do know she was damn near crushed when it did. And then I came along. Shoot, you're talkin' about a woman who's been burned at least twice. It's only natural for her to feel skittish as hell."

"Yeah, I guess you're right," David muttered. "Maybe I should just forget about her."

"Is that really what you wanna do?"

David shook his head again. "I'm not sure I could if I wanted to, especially with her living right across the street. When I look at her, I see...hell, I don't know. Picket fences and romantic evenings in front of a big fire in the fireplace and Christmas mornings with the kids ripping into their presents—"

"Don't forget great meals," Jason put in. "She's one helluva good cook."

David flushed at his friend's dry tone, realizing he must have had a sappy expression on his face. "Yeah. She sure is."

"Geez, you've really got it bad, pal."

"Well, then, help me, you big ox. You know her better than I do."

"First I want your word that you won't hurt her or those kids. Susan's not the kind of woman you can have your jollies with and then dump."

"I figured that out all by myself," David said indignantly. "Cripes, why does everybody think I'm some kind of a heartbreaker? First Liz, then Barbara, now you. I'm still friends with every woman I've ever dated but Liz. Doesn't that say something good about the way I treat women?"

"Sure, it does," Jason agreed. "Hey, I'm the last one to throw any rocks at you, Dave. I'd just like to know if you're really ready to settle down."

"I am. So how do I get through to Susan?"

Jason rubbed his chin thoughtfully for a moment. "I'm not sure. She can be stubborn as hell, but if she's got a weak spot, it's those boys of hers. Get close to them, and Susan won't be far away. But ya gotta be subtle. Give her a little time, and don't crowd her too much or she'll bolt for sure."

"All right. I'll give it a try. But tell me something, will ya?"

"What's that?"

"Has being married to my sister been worth all the hell she put you through last summer?"

Jason threw back his head and let out a deep, booming laugh. Then he clapped David on the back with one hand and held up a Scout's honor sign with the other. "I swear, she's been worth every bit of that hell and more."

Chapter Six

"Only four more days," David muttered under his breath as his father closed the office door behind him. "Just four more days and he'll be on his way to England."

He picked up the new nameplate Michael had delivered and read it out loud. "David Hunter, General Manager." Then he slammed it back down on the desk and snorted in disgust. He might be the general manager of KBOY TV, but his dad was still the CEO and he didn't hesitate to let everyone know it.

David had spent the past two years pulling double and sometimes triple duty, managing the company's radio stations and putting in time at the television station, as well, doing every grunt job imaginable in order to learn the business from the ground up. His promotion to general manager had finally been announced a month ago, but the staff still went over his head to Michael if they didn't like one of David's decisions. And damn his hide, Michael let them.

Unable to sit another second, David stalked over to the window and looked out at the empty field behind the station. There wasn't much out there but dried grass, litter and a lot of blue sky. The view agitated him even more. Michael should have bought that field when he'd had the chance a year ago. There wasn't enough parking at KBOY for the staff, much less visitors.

Why in the hell had his father had to get so damn cautious and conservative on him? Why couldn't he give David's ideas a fair chance once in a while? Why couldn't he understand that change wasn't inherently bad? Cheyenne was a pretty small market, but that didn't mean they had to run this station like a bunch of hicks.

"Maybe I should go back to Denver," David grumbled.

Being a disc jockey had been fun for him. His show had been popular enough that nobody had given him much flak about anything. But here he faced continual demands, daily challenges to his authority, and his own father cut him off at the knees all the damn time. He could do this job, if only Michael would get the hell out of his way.

David's phone buzzed. He muttered a curse at yet another interruption, stomped over to his desk and snarled, "What?" into the receiver. He heard a gasp on the other end of the line, then a moment of dead silence. *Oh, hell,* he thought, *now I'll have to apologize to Rita or she'll sulk for the rest of the day.* The woman was inefficient and snotty half the time, but he couldn't fire her because she'd worked for Michael for twenty years. "What is it, Rita?" he asked, moderating his tone.

"There's a Susan Miller on line one," the secretary responded icily. "Do you want to take the call?"

"Yes, thank you. And I'm sorry I snapped at you," David replied, wincing when she disconnected without another word. He let out a sigh, then punched the button for line one, hoping Susan would be less hostile than his darn secretary. "Good morning, Susan. What can I do for you?"

"Good morning. I'm calling about the fund-raising campaign we discussed last Saturday. My boss just told me Melissa Reed needs the liver transplant. I'd like to get started as soon as possible. Are you still interested in helping?"

She sounded crisp and professional, but there was a hint of hesitancy in her soft voice. He pictured her sitting at a desk, wearing the rust-colored suit she'd had on when she left her house this morning—the one that showed off her slim legs so well. He smiled at the thought of what a nosy neighbor he'd become, and some of his tension eased. "You bet. What have you got in mind?"

"I, uh, thought it would be best if we started with a meeting of business and civic leaders here at the bank on Thursday night. That doesn't give us much time, but the more people we can get involved, the better, don't you think?"

"That sounds fine." David reached for a legal pad and a pen, visualizing the sweet, earnest expression that must be in her pretty hazel eyes. "What can I do to help?"

"Could you start planning some public-service announcements?"

"No problem. What's the disease called? We may have some file tapes we can use to educate the public about it."

"Biliary atresia." She spelled it for him. "As I understand it, the bile ducts from the liver to the intestine have been destroyed. Nobody knows what causes it, but it's almost always fatal without a transplant."

"I'll get our health reporter right on it. How soon do you want to start running the announcements?"

"Yesterday," she answered. "The average life expectancy for these kids without the surgery is only two years, and it can take a long time to find a compatible donor. The sooner we get Melissa on that waiting list, the better her chances will be."

"All right. What else can I do? Want me to call the civic organizations for you?"

"Would you? I've been wondering how I'd ever get everyone contacted in time, but I don't want to wait until next week."

"Sure. My dad's belonged to just about every one of those groups at one time or another. I'll cover the other media, too. We can probably get an ad or a short article in the paper about the meeting in case we miss anyone.''

"That's a great idea.''

"What time are you planning to start?''

"Seven o'clock. And you can tell everyone we'll be serving refreshments.''

"That'll help bring people in,'' David replied with a chuckle. "Anything else I can do?''

"That's plenty for now. And thanks. I really appreciate this, David.''

Hating to have this conversation end, David racked his brain for another question he could ask her. Unfortunately he couldn't come up with one. "You're welcome. I'll see you Thursday night, Susan.''

He leaned back in his chair, propped his feet on the corner of his desk and linked his hands behind his neck. Susan would have to spend more time with him now, he thought with a satisfied smile. What a golden opportunity. While he was proving he could handle the station and a major civic project to his dad, he could also show Susan he was a guy worth knowing.

He swung his feet to the floor, grabbed the phone book and went to work. Susan hadn't been easily impressed so far. But by the time this fund-raising campaign was over, she wouldn't be able to resist him.

On Thursday night Susan checked the refreshment table one last time, then glanced at her watch and sighed. The bank's meeting room was ready, and her notes were organized, but her stomach felt ready to reject what little dinner she'd managed to choke down. No matter how many times she forced herself to do it, she despised public speaking. Especially before a group as large as she hoped this one would be.

The thought of David watching her fumble her way through this presentation didn't help much, either. After the way they had parted on Saturday, it had been darn hard to call him Tuesday morning. He'd been gracious and helpful, of course, but it hadn't been a personal conversation. She couldn't help wondering if he was still angry with her.

The door swung open, and she turned toward it. As if she had conjured him up with her thoughts, David walked into the room carrying a bulky case in each hand. His eyes lighted up with pleasure when he saw her, and Susan's breath caught in her chest. Lord, but he looked handsome in that dark blue suit.

"Hi," he said, walking right up to her. He lifted the cases a little higher. "Where can I set these up?"

"What are they?" she asked.

"A television and a VCR. One of the Denver stations had a tape about biliary atresia, and they shipped us a copy. It's pretty good." He tipped his head to one side and studied her for a moment. Then a teasing grin appeared on his face, and he raised an eyebrow at her. "Unless you wanted to explain it yourself?"

Though her palms suddenly felt damp and her lips tingled from the way he was gazing at her mouth, Susan returned his grin. "No, that's wonderful." She led him to the front of the room and indicated a spot to the left of the podium. "Will this do? There's an outlet right back there."

"It's perfect."

He set up the equipment so quickly, Susan shook her head in admiration. "How'd you do that so fast?" she asked.

David turned to her with a shrug. "I've worked with electronics for years. It's no big deal."

"Maybe not to you," she said, "but I have to read the directions at least five times to hook one of those monsters up. And even then, I'm holding my breath to see if the darn thing will work."

"Call me any time you have a problem. I'll be glad to help."

Susan couldn't doubt his sincerity in making the offer. "Are you always so generous?" she asked softly.

Resting back against the table, David crossed one foot over the other. "I try to be," he replied in a serious tone. "Mom used to tell me that if you want to have a friend,

you've got to be a friend. It's always made sense to me."
Then his eyes twinkled, and he leaned toward her until their
noses almost touched. "You should give me a chance, Miller. I can be a real handy guy to have around."

"Yeah, I'll just bet you can, Hunter," she said with a wry
smile.

Other people started filtering into the room then, and before long a need for more chairs became evident. Susan
flagged down a janitor, but even with the extra thirty chairs
he brought in, there still weren't enough seats. By seven
o'clock the room was packed beyond the fire marshal's legal limit, but Susan wasn't about to turn anyone away.

She started the meeting, her case of nerves banished by
the concerned, receptive audience. After David had played
the tape, she opened the floor for suggestions. Ideas poured
out of the group. Without waiting to be asked, David came
forward and started writing them down on the pad of
newsprint Susan had set up on an easel before the meeting
started.

The Lions Club proposed a community garage sale. The
Kiwanians offered to raffle a month's worth of groceries.
The Boy Scouts volunteered to pick up aluminum cans from
all the city parks and donate the profits from recycling them.
The cattlemen's association donated a side of beef for another raffle. The Central High School cheerleaders promised a car wash.

It went on and on, faster and faster, until David capped
his marker, threw it up in the air and hollered, "Uncle!"

Everyone laughed, then looked at him expectantly when
he walked over to stand next to Susan. "May I make a suggestion?" he asked her.

"Please do." She stepped aside so that David could use
the microphone.

"Actually I have two suggestions," he told the crowd.
"First, I think we need a steering committee to act as a
clearinghouse to make sure we're not duplicating our efforts or scheduling too many events for one day."

"Are you gonna be on it, Hunter?" a man in the back called out.

"I'd be glad to. And I think Susan should be on it, as well, since the bank started this project." he looked to her for consent. When she nodded, he continued. "How about three other volunteers?"

It only took a minute to add the requested names to the list. Then David rested an elbow on the podium. "I've got an idea for a project, but it would take a lot of community support. I'd like to try it out on you folks before we break up."

"Let's hear it," several people answered at once.

"What would you say to a dance at the Frontier Park Exhibition Building? Hunter Communications will provide a disc jockey and records from the forties right up to today. Different groups could serve food and soft drinks. Maybe some of the junior-high and high-school kids could donate baby-sitting services. What do you think?"

From the front row, a voluptuous young woman who owned a popular dress shop batted her eyelashes at him. "I'd come if you were the disc jockey, David."

"Thanks, I'll do that," he replied with an oh-so-charming smile.

The audience tittered. Susan smiled, but felt a flicker of irrational dislike toward the woman. Before she could think much about it, one of the ranchers broke in.

"Why don't you get Wendy Wyoming to play the records, Hunter? Then you'd *really* draw a crowd."

"Hey, yeah!" three-fourths of the men in the room agreed instantly.

David rubbed his chin in a thoughtful gesture. Susan held her breath along with everyone else while she waited for his answer. The previous January, Hunter Communications' FM Country-and-Western station, KBOY, had introduced Wendy Wyoming to the city of Cheyenne. Her playful, sexy patter and down-to-earth sense of humor enthralled her listeners to the point that the local newspaper had run a Who is Wendy Wyoming? contest. Nobody had been able to prove a correct guess, but Wendy had been sorely missed since she'd announced she was leaving Cheyenne in August. If David could produce Wendy Wyoming, the dance would be a guaranteed sellout.

"You know," he drawled when the tension in the room reached a crisis point, "I can't promise anything, but Wendy's a real sucker when it comes to kids. I think she just might do it."

The volunteers hooted and applauded until Susan thought she'd go deaf. When the noise finally abated, she announced another gathering in two weeks for progress reports and adjourned the meeting. An hour later the last straggler walked out the door. Susan collapsed into the closest chair and kicked off her high heels. David packed up his equipment before sitting down beside her.

"Well, Ms. Miller, I haven't seen this much excitement since Frontier Days," he said. "Your first meeting was a smashing success."

"That's an understatement, Mr. Hunter," she answered. "Do you really think you can deliver Wendy Wyoming? You'd better, or some of those guys might lynch you."

His eyes sparkled with mirth. "That's a distinct possibility. But I don't think she'll turn me down." He looked around the room. "I'll help you clean this place up if you'll have a drink with me on the way home."

Giving him a weary smile, Susan shook her head. "All I have to do is unplug the coffeepot and turn out the lights. I promised the Reeds I'd stop by and tell them about the meeting."

"Why don't I come with you?" David suggested. "I'd like to use them in some of the public-service announcements. I can meet them and set up a time for a film crew to visit."

It was a blatant excuse to spend more time with her, but Susan was too tired and too grateful to David for all his help to argue. Besides, what he'd said made sense. "All right." She poked her feet back into her shoes. "Let's get going, then."

He walked Susan to her car and followed her north on Carey and then west on First Street to a small house on Snyder Avenue. Tom Reed answered the door only seconds after Susan rang the bell. He was shorter than David by three or four inches, but with a huskier build. His wife, Katie, was a bit taller than Susan and painfully thin. They both looked strained, exhausted and heartbreakingly young, but they eagerly invited Susan and David into their home.

When everyone had been introduced, they all sat down in the living room. Tom's eyes grew misty, and tears of gratitude slid down Katie's cheeks while Susan and David related the evening's events. A faint cry came from another room. Katie excused herself and came back a few moments later with the baby wrapped in a soft pink blanket.

"Here's the star of the show," she said, bringing Melissa to the sofa where David and Susan sat.

Susan instinctively held out her arms. "May I hold her?"

"Of course. Just be careful of her tummy. It's pretty tender."

Katie handed over the baby, and David scooted closer for a better view. Melissa squalled and thrashed her tiny arms and legs. Her skin had a yellowish cast, and her abdomen looked painfully distended. Though her face was all scrunched up from crying, Susan could see she had delicate, even features.

"Hello, sweetheart," Susan crooned, gently stroking the wispy blond fuzz on the child's head.

Melissa quieted for a moment and gazed up at Susan with big blue eyes.

"She's a pretty little doll," David said quietly, smiling down at Melissa with a tenderness that made Susan's throat tighten. Ed had never looked at Timmy or Eric that way. David touched the baby's tiny hand. Melissa latched on to his finger, then pulled her knees up against her belly and started squalling again.

"There's nothing wrong with her grip or her lungs," David said, giving the Reeds a lopsided grin.

"No," Katie said sadly, taking the baby from Susan, "just her liver." She raised watery eyes to David and Susan. "Do you really think you'll be able to raise all that money in time to help her?"

David unfolded himself from the sofa and gave Katie a one-armed hug. "We'll give it one hell of a good shot. You and Tom concentrate on taking care of yourselves and Melissa and let us worry about the money. Do you have anyone who can handle Melissa sometimes so you can get some sleep?"

Katie gulped and wiped her eyes with the back of her free hand. "My mom comes over whenever she can, but she and my dad are both still working full-time. Dad's scared to touch her. But Tom and I are doing fine."

"All right," David said, giving her another squeeze. "But don't be afraid to ask for help. It won't help anyone if you two wear yourselves out."

Susan stood beside David and added her agreement. "That's right. Most new parents need a hand once in a while. I'd be glad to take her for an evening, so call if you need a break."

"We'll do that," Tom promised.

They set a time for KBOY's film crew to come over the next day, and then Susan and David left. Her heart aching for the Reeds, Susan drove home with David following close behind her. They parked in their respective driveways ten minutes later.

Susan waved good-night and headed for her front door. When David jogged across the street calling her name, she made a detour and met him at the sidewalk. He studied her face under the light of the street lamp.

"Are you okay?" he asked softly.

"Of course," she answered, looking down at her feet.

He tipped her chin up with his index finger and forced her to look at him. "What is it? I thought everything went pretty well tonight."

"It did. But seeing Melissa . . ." Susan's throat closed up and she couldn't go on.

David pulled her into his arms and gently pushed her head down against his chest. "Yeah, that really brought it all home, didn't it?"

There was nothing threatening about his embrace. She nodded and wrapped her arms around his waist. His heart beat a comforting rhythm beneath her cheek. The warmth of his arms around her soothed her ragged emotions. She sighed with pleasure and wondered how he had known she needed to be held so badly. Then Susan pulled away slightly and looked up at him.

"You know, parents are so weird," she told him. "Your kids yell and scream and act like obnoxious brats, and you wish they'd disappear. But just let them get sick, and all you can think about is how much you wish they'd get up and yell and scream and act obnoxious. If something like that had happened to one of my babies, I'd have lost my mind."

David smiled and shook his head. "No, you wouldn't. You're a survivor if I've ever met one. And you're doing a great job for Melissa."

"But what if we don't get the money in time?"

"Cheyenne won't let that little girl down. We have to believe that. Just look at how many people showed up tonight with only two days' notice."

"Thanks to you." she answered. "You must have called groups I've never even heard of."

"Hey, what can I say? I've got connections."

Grinning, she poked him in the ribs. "Don't get smart with me, Hunter. I've got your number."

"Oh, yeah?"

"Yeah. You've got this hotshot, playboy image, but you're really just a nice guy at heart."

His cocky smile faded, and his tone turned serious. "I've been trying to tell you that since Labor Day."

Susan suddenly became aware that their bodies were intimately aligned, that his hands rested possessively on her hips, that if she stood on her tiptoes, she could kiss him. Did she want to? She sighed inwardly. Did birds have feathers? Did bees buzz? Did kids make messes?

"I never thought you were anything else, David," she said. "Not really."

"Then why don't you want to have anything to do with me? Why don't you like me?"

The pain in his voice finished off what little was left of Susan's defenses. Perhaps it was risky to be so honest with him, but after this evening, she didn't care. "I like you too much," she admitted. "And it scares me. I don't want to get hurt again."

He raised his right hand and caressed the side of her face with the backs of his knuckles. "I wouldn't hurt you or your kids for anything.

"I know you wouldn't mean to. Jason didn't mean to. But he did. I haven't had much luck with men, David. I can't help feeling scared."

"All right. I can understand that. But we're neighbors and we're going to be working together for a while. Can't we at least be good friends? You know, have a cup of coffee together once in a while, pal around together sometimes, tell each other to get lost when we feel like it. Does that sound so bad?"

"You oughta sell life insurance," she grumbled, trying and failing miserably to suppress a smile.

"Is that a yes or a no?"

"I think it's a yes."

David heaved out a horrendous sigh that made Susan laugh, then put an arm around her waist and escorted her up to her door. "Good night, friend," he said, dropping a quick, tender kiss on her lips. "I'll talk to you tomorrow."

Susan watched him walk across the street with his smooth, athletic stride. She told herself she hadn't wanted more of a kiss than he'd given her, but she didn't believe it for a minute. She was too attracted to David Hunter in too many ways to maintain a platonic friendship with him for long. She also suspected he knew that.

When he reached his own sidewalk, he started whistling as if he hadn't a single worry. Susan wrapped her arms around her stomach in an attempt to quell the uneasy feeling she'd just gone off a high-diving board head first. Would she make a clean entry into the water this time? she wondered. Or would she belly flop again?

Chapter Seven

On Saturday morning David drove his parents to the airport in their sedan, continually reassuring his father that he could run Hunter Communications for six weeks. He waved them off on their trip to Europe, then went back to their house, switched cars again and whistled all the way home. After parking in his driveway, he climbed out of the Porsche, gathered up the books his mother had given him for Susan and froze when he glanced across the street.

The crazy woman was perched on top of a rickety-looking stepladder, clinging to the rain gutter with one hand while she scooped leaves and other debris out with the other. "My God," he muttered, his heart pounding with fear. "She'll kill herself!"

He hurried across the street, clearing his throat as he aproached so he wouldn't startle her. She glanced down and gave him a sunny smile. "Hi. What are you up to today?"

Dropping his mother's books, he grabbed the ladder with both hands and scowled at her. "What the hell do you think you're doing?"

Her smile vanished. She stared at him for a long moment before going back to work. "What does it look like?"

David eyed the proud tilt to her chin and, mentally cursing his lack of tact, he sucked in a deep breath and blew it out. "I didn't mean to yell at you, Susan, but you darn near scared me to death. Why didn't you hire somebody or ask me to help you with such a dangerous job?"

"I can't afford to hire anybody, and I don't need any help," she informed him, dropping a handful of leaves in front of his nose. "I've done it lots of times before. Don't you have anything better to do than stand around here and bother me?"

"I'm not leaving. You're liable to break your fool neck up there."

She paused and looked down at him as if she were considering pelting him with the handful of twigs she'd just picked up. "One of the few benefits of being a single parent, David, is that I don't have to answer to anyone. So why don't you go home?"

He tightened his grip when she shifted her weight and the ladder wobbled in response. "I thought we agreed to be friends," he argued. "Our friendship isn't worth much if we can't give each other a hand once in a while."

Susan snorted at that remark, but avoided hitting him with the twigs. "Right. And just how often are you going to need help from me?"

"As a matter of fact, I could use a little help this afternoon."

"Oh, yeah?"

"Yeah. Maybe we could work out a trade."

"That depends on what you have in mind," she told him. "I don't do windows or ironing."

"It's nothing like that. Would you mind coming down here for a minute? I'm getting a crick in my neck."

She went up on her tiptoes and looked into the gutter. "All right. It's time to move over, anyway."

He watched her slowly back down the ladder, resisting the temptation to pat her cute little tush when it reached his eye level. The wary, almost hostile expression in Susan's hazel eyes when she lowered herself two more steps told him that had been a wise move on his part. She straightened away from the ladder and rotated one shoulder at a time as if her muscles ached.

His irritation with her evaporated. A black smudge decorated the tip of her nose. Bits of leaves and twigs clung to the front of her ratty sweatshirt. Despite the chilly October wind, perspiration plastered the hair at her temples to her skin, and she looked as if she needed a hug. He would have happily given her one, but he knew she wouldn't accept it. Not yet, anyway.

She pulled off the cotton gloves she'd worn to protect her hands, tucked them into the back pocket of her jeans, then crossed her arms over her chest. "Okay, Hunter. What's the trade?"

David thought she was cuter than hell with that feisty glint in her eyes. He bit back a grin and copied her stance to prevent himself from reaching out and wiping away the smudge on her nose.

"I need to pick up Sheba, but her portable kennel won't fit in my car." He nodded toward the Subaru wagon parked in her driveway. "I'll help you finish up here, if you and the boys will drive me out to Jason's ranch."

After considering the idea for a moment, she agreed. "Sounds fair enough."

Without another word, she tugged her gloves back on and showed David where she wanted the ladder. It was heavier than it looked, and he wondered how such a small woman had managed to carry it to the house. He glanced at the garage, saw two strips of grass mashed flat and felt sympathy and admiration well up inside him as he guessed that she'd dragged it.

The next few minutes passed in silence. David held his breath every time Susan leaned out farther to the side than he thought was safe, but kept his mouth shut. He rewarded himself for his restraint by watching the play of muscles in her trim legs and backside under her tight jeans until his thoughts turned in a carnal direction.

In an effort to keep his attention where it belonged, he started talking about the fund-raising campaign. Susan responded enthusiastically to the news that Wendy Wyoming had agreed to appear at the dance, and before long they were chatting away like the good friends they had agreed to become on Thursday night. Finally David dropped the question he'd wanted to ask for a long time.

"What happened to your marriage, Susan?"

She shook her head and let out a sad little laugh. "It's such a cliché—"

"C'mon. Tell me about it."

"All right, but don't say I didn't warn you." She wiped her forehead with the back of one arm. "I met Ed during my sophomore year at UW. He was just starting law school and hurting for money. We fell in love, got married at the end of the year, and I dropped out of school to support us until he finished up his degree."

"Go on," David coaxed, giving her an encouraging smile.

"He got a job with a law firm here in Cheyenne, and I got pregnant before I could go back to school. Ed was furious because he wanted to concentrate on his career and sock away lots of money before we started a family. I worked right up until the day Timmy was born and went back to work two months later, until he started having ear infections one right after another."

She sighed and stared off into the cloudless blue sky for a moment, then climbed down the ladder so David could move it again. When she was perched back on top, she tossed down a handful of leaves and continued with her story.

"Ed started working longer and longer hours and telling me I needed to spruce up my image so I wouldn't embarrass him. We fought a lot, and I went back to work for a year, hoping the extra money would smooth things over. But then I got pregnant with Eric. By the time he was born, I suspected Ed was seeing someone else, and three months later, he moved in with another woman. That was right after Eric had his first ear infection."

"He left you with a tiny baby?" David asked, outraged at the idea. "How old was Timmy then?"

"Three."

"The bastard," David muttered.

"I thought so at the time," she admitted with a shrug. "But he wasn't really a bastard, David. He loved the boys in his own way, but he just wasn't mature enough to be a father."

"Then he damn well should have been more careful."

"That wasn't entirely his fault. The first time I got pregnant, we were using birth control and it didn't work. The second time"—she paused, and her cheeks turned a bright pink—"uh, neither of us was thinking about contraception."

"That still doesn't justify his leaving you like that."

"Well, he did. Last year he moved up to a bigger firm in Denver."

David started to say something, hesitated, then closed his mouth.

"What is it?" Susan asked.

"Nothing. It's none of my business."

"None of this was your business, Hunter," she answered with a smile "so you might as well go ahead and ask."

It was David's turn to shrug. "It's just that I've heard you say you can't afford something twice now, neither of which was very expensive. Didn't you get anything out of the divorce settlement?"

"Ed always liked the finer things in life, so there wasn't much money to divide. I got the car and put my share of the money into a down payment on this house."

"But doesn't he have to pay child support?"

"He does sometimes, but not regularly enough for me to count on it. I bank what he sends for the boys' education."

"If you put him through law school, though, can't you sue for a part of his practice? At least force him to pay on time?"

"That takes a lot of time and money for lawyers I don't have. It's especially complicated since he's moved out of state. And I'm afraid it would make him so mad, he'd never see the boys again."

"Does he see them often?"

She shook her head. "Three or four times a year. But it's important for the boys to have some contact with him and think well of him, David. I've left things alone for their sake, not Ed's."

"It's still not right, Susan."

"Hey, I get by better than most single mothers do. At least my job provides health insurance. And I'll finish my degree in the next couple of years, so I'll be earning more before long."

"What about your family? Do they help you at all?"

"My folks are divorced and have both remarried. They didn't want me to marry Ed in the first place, so we haven't had much contact. We were never very close, anyway."

"Do you still love Ed?" David asked.

Susan tipped her head to one side and stared at the roof, considering his question for what seemed like forever to David. Finally she looked down at him, her expression honest and direct.

"I don't love him romantically. I mean, I wouldn't reconcile with him for anything. He shattered my trust too completely for that. But I don't hate him, either. I try to remember the good times we had together, and I'll always be glad I have Timmy and Eric. And who knows? Maybe he did me a favor by forcing me to be independent. It's been good for my self-esteem to find out I can make it on my own."

"That sounds like an amazingly healthy attitude."

"Well..." She gave him a rueful smile. "I don't always manage to keep it that healthy. When the bills stack up on me, I've been known to get petty and resentful. And when he disappoints the boys, I get downright hostile."

"How does he do that?"

"He promises them things he can't or won't deliver. Or he makes plans to spend time with them and then cancels at the last minute because of work or one of his girlfriends. That really upsets Timmy."

Susan climbed down the ladder and shook out the muscles in her arms while David moved it again. When she saw that he'd moved it too far, she protested. "Hey, my arms aren't that long."

"They don't have to be," he answered, testing each rung cautiously to make sure it would bear his weight. "It's my turn to do some of the hard stuff."

"But you don't have any gloves." She laughed at the disdainful look he shot her. "All right, tough guy. Have it your way. It's your turn to bare your soul, too, by the way."

"What do you want to know?"

"What do you think? Tell me about your engagement."

"Oh, that."

"Yeah, that. Come on, Hunter, you heard all the gory details of my marriage. If you don't want me to feel too exposed to be your friend, you have to open up a little, too."

"I guess it was a combination of things," he said slowly, dropping a fistful of leaves over the side of the ladder. "Liz was really a neat person in a lot of ways, but she was always afraid I'd cheat on her, even after I gave her a ring."

"Did you give her any reason to feel that way?"

"I didn't think so at the time. I mean, I didn't cheat on her. I didn't even want to. But I was working pretty long hours then, and I could never get her to understand that there were a lot of women I'd dated who were just friends. If we were out someplace and one those women stopped to talk with me, Liz would get furious and accuse me of making dates with them."

"How did you feel about that?"

"At first it made me mad, because I felt she was accusing me unjustly. Later it really hurt that she wouldn't trust me. Melody told me one time that Liz was just too young to have the self-confidence she needed to deal with me. But I don't know if that's true or not."

"How old was she?"

"Twenty-one." David glanced down and defended himself when he saw Susan's raised eyebrow. "Hey, you know as well as I do what dating is like in Cheyenne. Most of the gals my age are either married or bitter over a divorce. Who am I supposed to date?"

"It's not my business to judge, David," Susan answered quietly.

"Yeah, but I can see that you do, and so does everyone else apparently."

"What do you mean by that?"

He looked away for a moment and ran one hand through his hair in frustration. Then he went back to work. "Lately I've been hearing a lot about my wild past. It's like everyone has an image of me as this superstud playboy. Even my sister Barbara and my dad."

"Don't you see yourself that way?"

"Hell, no." He shrugged, feeling more uncomfortable than he'd ever felt before, but it was important somehow to make one other person understand how he felt. "I'm no monk, but I'm not a Don Juan, either. I never have been. I'll admit I sowed my share of wild oats in this town. So did Jason, and he had a hard time with Melody because of it. But I've grown up since then, and nobody seems willing to believe that."

"How do you see yourself, then?" Susan asked.

At the curious tone in her voice, David looked down and felt a moment's relief that she wasn't laughing her head off at him. In fact, she looked as if she wanted to understand him, to believe him, and his heart swelled with gratitude. "I'm a responsible adult. I work hard and I play hard. I want a wife and kids and a home, but I'm beginning to wonder if I'll ever have them."

"Then why do you flirt so much?"

"I don't flirt that much."

"Oh, yes, you do, Hunter."

"How?" he demanded. "What do I do that makes you and everybody else I know say that?"

Susan crossed her arms over her chest and frowned up at him as if trying to decide whether he was serious in asking the question. "You do a lot of little things. Your body language is open and inviting. You say flattering things. You use a lot of eye contact . . . you just make a woman feel special."

"What's wrong with that?" he shot back, throwing his arms toward the sky. The ladder wobbled, and he had to grab the rain gutter until Susan steadied it again. They exchanged sheepish grins, and then David said more quietly, "I really don't understand, Susan. I honestly like women, and I don't want to change that about myself. I guess I don't know the difference between being friendly and flirting."

"I don't think you should stop liking women. And maybe it's not you," she said thoughtfully. "Maybe it's the way women react to you."

"What's that supposed to mean?"

Susan grinned up at him. "It's just that you're so handsome, Hunter." She chuckled at his snort of disgust before going on in a more sober tone. "No, I mean it, David. You really are an exceptionally attractive man, and you've got those big dark bedroom eyes and that wonderfully deep, sexy voice. Maybe women think you're flirting with them because they want you to be flirting with them. Maybe they think you've got lusty thoughts because they have lusty thoughts about you."

David finished the last section, then came down the ladder and stuck his face close to Susan's. "You think I have bedroom eyes, Miller?" he asked, waggling his eyebrows at her.

She eyed his wicked grin and moved back a step. "Spare me the false modesty. You know you do."

He dropped his voice to its deepest register and moved closer. "You think my voice is sexy?"

"Knock it off, Hunter," she demanded with a laugh, taking another step back. "I wasn't talking about me. I was talking about women in general."

"Well, I'm talking about you." He advanced on her again, enjoying her furious blush immensely. "I have lusty thoughts about you, sometimes, Susan. Do you have lusty thoughts about me?"

"For heaven's sake, David," she hissed, her backside hitting the house. "The boys are right inside watching cartoons."

He planted a hand on either side of her head and leaned down as if he would kiss her. "Aw, c'mon, tell me," he coaxed. "Don't you have a few lusty thoughts about me?"

Susan's right hand brushed against the spigot and garden hose she used to water the front lawn. She laid her right hand against David's chest and gave him a coy smile, then cranked on the water full blast, grabbed the hose and drenched him from waist to sneakers. He squawked and jumped back.

"Did that cool you off a little?" she taunted, letting him have it again, aiming higher this time.

David wiped his face off with both hands before putting his head down and charging her like the linebacker he had been in high school and college. He fought her for the hose, soaking them both in the process. When he figured she was as wet as he was, he turned off the water and leaned against the house, laughing at Susan's outraged expression. A moment later she looked down at herself, and her shoulders started to shake with laughter, as well.

Timmy and Eric ran out the front door. "What's the matter, Mom? Why were you screaming?" They halted in front of the dripping grown-ups. Eyes wide, Eric said, "You guys are all wet!"

Susan exchanged a guilty, silly grin with David. "We, uh, had a little water fight," she admitted.

"Oh, boy!" Timmy shouted, reaching for the hose.

"No, honey." Susan laughed and grabbed his arm. "I don't want you two to get all wet."

"Why can't we play, too?" Eric demanded.

"It's really too cold for this, and it's almost lunchtime. Have you finished your jobs?"

"Aw, Mom," Timmy grumbled.

David went down on one knee and told the boys about the plans to pick up his puppy. "If you guys stay dry while your mom and I get cleaned up, I'll take you to McDonald's first." He held out a hand to Timmy. "Deal?"

"Can we have a Happy Meal?" Timmy asked.

"You can have anything you want."

"All right!"

Both boys slapped David's palm enthusiastically, then raced back into the house to finish their chores. When David climbed back to his feet, he found Susan scowling at him. "What's wrong?"

She clamped her hands on her hips. "I wish you wouldn't do that, David."

"Do what?" he asked, completely mystified by her change of mood. "I owe you guys a meal after that dinner you fed me. What's wrong with lunch at McDonald's?"

"Nothing's wrong with it," she told him. "But I don't like anyone making plans for the boys unless they check with me first. Then if I want to say no, I don't have to be a bad guy to them."

"I hadn't thought of that," David admitted. "I won't do it again."

"See that you don't." She laid a hand on his arm, her mouth twitching at the corners before slowly curving up into a smile. "But this time I think you had a great idea. Whaddaya say we finish up here and get on with it before we freeze to death in these wet clothes?"

"Sounds good to me."

David hauled the ladder back to the garage while Susan swept the piles of debris into one big heap. He helped her bag it up, gave her the books his mother had sent and promised to meet her in half an hour. Then he hurried home and stepped gratefully under a hot shower, his thoughts on Susan.

She was stubborn and pricklier than a porcupine about her independence, which could be a royal pain in the butt. But after hearing about her ex-husband and her family, he couldn't fault her for that. In fact, he admired her for it. She wouldn't wait around for him like Liz had and fuss over every minute he couldn't be with her.

He admired other things about her, too. Such as the way she stood up for herself and told him she didn't want him inviting the boys to do something unless he checked it out with her first. He didn't want to spend his life with someone who would only tell him what she thought he wanted to hear. Hell, he loved a good argument, and she sure wouldn't hesitate to give him one.

As for her remarks about his eyes and hair and lusty thoughts, it tickled him no end that she'd had to turn the hose on him to avoid answering his question. He probably shouldn't have teased her the way he had, but he knew darn well she was attracted to him. Well, he hoped she was, anyway.

The problem for Susan was that she didn't have it in her to lie about it. Shoot, she couldn't even lie about having a water fight to her kids. He suspected a lot of parents might have concocted a story about an accident with the hose.

Scrunching up his eyes to keep the shampoo out while he rinsed his hair, he wished she could just relax with him a little more, the way she had for a while this morning. He wasn't going to hurt her or the boys. He wasn't going to push her into going to bed with him, either, though the prospect of that was enticing enough to keep him awake at night.

He doubted it would take much for him to fall headlong in love with Susan Miller, but this time it was going to be different. This time he would stomp on his impulsiveness and take it slow and easy. He would earn her trust and show her he meant what he'd said this morning. It wouldn't be easy, but he didn't want easy.

He wanted the kind of rock-solid relationship his parents had built over their thirty-five years of marriage. He couldn't settle for less. His gut instincts told him he wouldn't have to settle for less with Susan. But for now, he'd just have to wait and see.

* * *

Susan turned off the shower and stepped onto the bath mat, her face pink from more than the steamy heat in the bathroom. Lord, every time she remembered all the things she'd told David about her marriage, she cringed with embarrassment. She hadn't told Jason half that much in two months of dating.

"And then you just had to babble on and on about his eyes and his voice and lusty thoughts," she muttered, toweling herself off with rough, angry swipes. "The big ape's not conceited enough about his looks?"

She stomped into her bedroom, yanked on underwear, clean jeans and a fuzzy violet sweater, then ran back to the bathroom and dried her hair. She leaned closer to the mirror to put on her makeup and blew out a disgruntled sigh when she caught sight of her troubled eyes in the mirror. It was time to be honest with herself.

David Hunter was not an ape, nor was he conceited. So what if she had lusty thoughts about him? Any woman with her hormones intact would find him physically attractive, so why should she beat herself over the head for wondering what it would be like to make love with him?

The truth was, her emotional reaction to David worried her much more than her physical reaction to him did. Talking with him was so easy, she forgot to be cautious. She'd told him all those things about her marriage because he listened as if he was really interested in what she had to say. That was more seductive to Susan than an impressive set of pecs, tight buns and a handsome face would ever be.

If she could believe what he'd said about himself this morning, and she supposed she did, he was even more dangerous to her peace of mind than she'd thought before.

"So what are you gonna do about it, Miller?" she whispered to her reflection. "Push him out of your life the way you did Jason?"

A surprisingly sharp ache pierced her heart at the thought. She didn't see how she could do that now, anyway, not with him living across the street and working with her on the fund-raising campaign. But she might as well be *really* honest with herself and admit she didn't want to push him out of her life.

Okay, she'd been hurt in her dealings with men more than once. But she was tired of trying to keep her distance from David when she liked him so much, tired of dredging up all of the old reasons she shouldn't get involved with him or anyone else, tired of letting fear control her. No matter what her common sense might be shouting at her, she wanted to get closer to him.

The doorbell rang, and her heart jumped into her throat. She shoved her makeup back into the cosmetics bag and took one last look at herself in the mirror.

"Maybe he *is* too good to be true, but you'll never know if you don't give him a chance," she told herself firmly. "You don't have to fall in love with him. You don't have to sleep with him. All you have to do for now is be his friend."

Susan turned off the bathroom light and walked out to the living room. She found David on his hands and knees on the floor with Eric and Timmy, racing toy trucks and making the appropriate noises. He looked up at her and grinned. She gazed into those big dark eyes of his, and her knees started feeling mushy. Her pulse beat loudly in her ears, and her heart twinged with a familiar anxiety. "Anybody hungry?" she asked before her newly found courage deserted her completely.

All three males scrambled to their feet. The boys trooped out to the car with Susan and David close behind them. When they arrived at McDonald's, Susan and her sons staked out a table while David ordered the food. He returned a few minutes later, carrying a loaded tray.

Eric and Timmy tore into their Happy Meals and spent more time playing with the enclosed toys than eating, but Susan hated to nag when they were having such a good time. David solved the problem for her by letting them catch him snitching their French Fries and initiating a bet-I-can-finish-my-Big-Mac-before-you-can-finish-your-hamburger game. The results were gross but effective.

During the trip out to the ranch, he entertained them all with corny jokes and riddles. When Susan parked behind the Wakefields' house, Jason came out the back door with a suitcase in his left hand. He looked surprised to see Susan's car, but sent them a wave. Then he stowed the case in the back seat of his Blazer and walked over to greet them.

"What's with the luggage?" David asked. "Running away from home?"

"Nope," Jason replied. "We're goin' to a dinner theatre down in Greeley. Thought we'd spend the night in a motel just for fun."

"Can we go see the puppies?" Timmy asked eagerly.

"Sure thing, pard. Sheba's been waiting for her new daddy all day. Just don't go in the stall with mama dog until I get there."

The boys raced for the barn, and the adults strolled along after them.

"I'm not going to be Sheba's daddy," David informed his friend indignantly.

Jason exchanged an amused glance with Susan. "Uh-huh. And I suppose you're not gonna coo and fuss and cuddle her like you did the last time you were out here, either."

"She's a dog, Wakefield."

"But she's a baby dog, Slick," Jason retorted. He looked at Susan and said in a mock whisper, "The guy loses all his macho points whenever he sees a baby critter of any kind. He'd go nuts over a baby rhino."

David's neck and ears turned red. "Knock it off, Wakefield. What're you giving me such a hard time for?"

Jason stopped walking and gave David a hard stare. "You're a bright enough guy, Hunter. Can't you guess?"

David returned his stare for a moment, then ducked his head as if he felt guilty. "Yeah. I guess I can."

"Would you guys mind telling me what's going on?" Susan asked.

Jason looked at her and smiled in apology. "It's personal, Susan. Would you mind going in with the boys? We'll be along soon."

Mystified but unwilling to intrude, Susan stepped into the barn and found Eric and Timmy hanging over the gate to the puppies' stall, arguing over which one of the little mutts was Sheba. She heard a deep rumble of angry voices a time or two, but couldn't understand what they said. Ten minutes later Melody came in with two bright spots of temper coloring her cheeks and two grim but subdued men trailing in her wake.

She greeted Susan and the boys with a determinedly cheerful smile. Jason entered the stall and coaxed the mother out. David and the boys went in and played with the puppies for a short while, then carried Sheba out to her crate in the back end of the Subaru.

After a brief goodbye, Susan put the car in gear and drove away from the ranch. David and the boys were unusually quiet until they reached Interstate 80 and Sheba started crying piteously.

"She misses her mom," Eric said.

"She does not, dummy," Timmy chided him. "She just wants to come up here with us. Can I let her out, Mr. Hunter?"

"I don't think that's a good idea right now, Tim," David answered. "She'll settle down pretty soon."

Sheba, however, had other ideas. She whined and yipped and finally broke out into full-fledged barking. David twisted around in his seat and talked to her in soothing tones. Sheba ignored him. In desperation he finally sang to her.

The pup sat back on her haunches, tipped her head to one side and listened. Of course, the minute he tried to quit, she started yapping again. Timmy suggested they try the radio, but Sheba wanted David and nobody else. Susan thought the dog had impeccable taste. At the Cheyenne city limits, the puppy finally curled up for a nap.

"Are you going to sing her to sleep every night?" Susan asked David, struggling to keep a grin off her face.

He scowled at her, his eyebrows forming a dark V across his forehead. "Just drive, Miller. Will ya?"

Susan drove.

The puppy woke up when Susan parked in David's driveway. He set the crate on the lawn and let her out. The boys joined him on the grass, laughing while she ran from one to the other, nipping and licking and celebrating her freedom Ten minutes later Sheba flopped onto the ground, panting.

David asked the boys to keep an eye on her while he got some water and hauled the crate into the house. Curious to see if he'd done any decorating, Susan followed him inside. He hadn't done much. She grinned at the sight of his dark leather sofa and easy chair set against the pink carpet and flowered wallpaper.

If this were her living room, she'd install a beige carpet— no, with Sheba's arrival, a soft chocolate color would be more practical. Of course, then the walls would need to be light to keep the room from looking gloomy. David walked out of the adjoining room. Since he carried a plastic bowl of water, she assumed it must be the kitchen.

He smiled and walked over to her. "I like what you've done with your place. Got any decorating ideas for me?"

She feigned surprise. "Don't you like all these pretty flowers, David?"

His grimace said volumes. She laughed and then turned toward the sound of a car's brakes squealing somewhere to the south. "Maybe we'd better check on the boys," she said, heading for the front door.

Susan stepped outside in time to see Sheba run for the curb with Eric in hot pursuit. The car she'd heard a moment ago took the corner on two wheels, swerved, then straightened out and roared down the middle of the street toward David's house.

Time lost all meaning. The disaster unfolded before her as if in slow motion. Sheba jumped off the curb and raced across the street. Eric followed. The car closed in on them. She couldn't breathe, couldn't scream, couldn't move.

Timmy's voice filtered faintly into her brain, screaming, "No, Eric! Come back!"

A violent shove from behind knocked Susan to her knees. David hurdled over her and charged the street, his long legs whipping so fast they blurred her vision. The car kept coming and coming, faster and faster. David launched his body at Eric in a flying tackle. The car whooshed past, and they disappeared from view.

Susan covered her eyes with both hands, her gorge rising into her throat. Then the car's noisy engine faded into the distance, and she heard Timmy sobbing. She scrambled to her feet and stared in horror at the still figures piled up against the opposite curb.

"They're dead, they're dead," Timmy cried.

Candy's front door banged open. The sight of her plump friend hurrying toward Eric and David finally jarred Susan into motion. She ran across the street and knelt down beside David. His body curved protectively around her son like a big C, his right arm draped over the boy.

Sheba wiggled out from beneath Eric. As if sensing something was wrong with her playmate, she whined and licked his face. Eric moaned and feebly pushed her away.

"Timmy, come get Sheba," Susan called, frantically searching for a pulse on David's neck. It was there, thank God, steady and strong.

"Did you see the bastard?" Candy muttered. "He didn't even slow down." She handed the pup to Timmy, then turned her attention to Eric. She checked his arms and legs for broken bones, murmuring, "It's okay, sweetie. You're gonna be fine," to him when he started to cry.

Susan leaned across David and stroked Eric's hair off his forehead, gasping when her fingers encountered sticky red blood. She turned his head slightly and found a large patch of skin on the left side of his face had been scraped away by the pavement. A whimper escaped her lips, and Candy moved beside her.

"Are you ever lucky, Eric," she told the boy with a reassuring wink for Susan. "You've peeled off some hide, but that'll heal up in no time." She asked him if he hurt anywhere else, and when he shook his head, she put an arm around his shoulders and helped him sit up. He swayed a little at first, but soon righted himself.

"Where's Sheba?" he asked.

David groaned and rolled onto his back. His face was scraped, too, and he had a bump on the side of his forehead. Then his eyelids fluttered and opened a moment later. He looked up at Susan, confusion clouding his eyes. He tried to get up, but she gently pushed him back down. "Take it easy. Everything's all right."

He sucked in a deep breath, blew it out and shook his head. "Eric?"

"He's banged up," Candy said, "but thanks to you, he's alive."

"How about you, David?" Susan asked. "Do you hurt anywhere?"

David blinked, then muttered, "My head. Left leg."

"I'll go call the ambulance," Candy said, struggling to her feet. "And the cops. I got the license number on that car."

"No," David protested. He sat up slowly. "At least not for me. I'm okay."

"Eric needs to see a doctor and so do you," Susan said firmly.

"I don't need a damn ambulance," he insisted. "An ice pack will be enough."

Despite vehement protests from both women, he put his hands on the pavement, bent his right knee and pushed himself to his feet. Susan rose with him, her hands ready to catch him if necessary.

"See? Good as new," he said with a shaky grin.

He stepped off on his left foot, and his leg gave way. Susan barely managed to keep him from hitting his head again when they fell down together. She caught her breath, then nodded at Candy. "Go ahead and call. He's not going anywhere."

Susan sat behind David, supporting his head and shoulders against her chest. She rested her cheek against his hair and heard him inhale a breath with a sharp hiss. She leaned sideways for a look at his face. His forehead glistened with sweat, and his jaw was clenched.

"David, what is it?"

"My damn knee," he muttered, then sucked in another hissing breath. "I think it's busted."

She looked around for Timmy and found him standing three feet away, his eyes round with fear, Sheba clutched tightly in his arms. Motioning him closer, she said, "Are you all right, honey?"

He nodded. "Is Mr. Hunter gonna be okay? And Eric?"

"They'll be fine," she assured him. "But I need you to do something for me."

"What?"

"First, go put Sheba in her crate in Mr. Hunter's kitchen. Then get the keys out of my purse—I think it's still in the car—and get a couple of blankets out of our house. Can you do all that?"

"Sure, Mom."

He took off and Eric started to sob. Susan beckoned him over and wrapped an arm around him when he sat down beside her.

"It's all my fault, isn't it?" he asked, his eyes puddling up with tears.

"No, it's not all your fault," she told him. "Whoever was driving that car was going way too fast. But you shouldn't have run into the street without looking first. We've talked about that before."

He wiped his nose with the back of his hand. "I know. I won't ever do it again, Mommy."

"Eric," David called, "come here a minute."

Eric leaned around his mother and looked into David's eyes. "I'm s-s-sorry, Mr. Hunter."

"Hey, pal, I'm not mad at you." David reached out and wiped away the boy's tears with his thumb. "It was an accident. Looks like you're gonna have a shiner. Does your face hurt?"

"A little. Does yours?"

"A little."

"Does your knee hurt real bad?"

David gave him a lopsided grin. "Yeah. If I get a cast, will you sign it for me?"

"I'll practice my letters real hard," Eric promised solemnly.

Candy and Timmy came back and wrapped Eric and David in the blankets. When they were finished, the paramedics and a policeman arrived. The next fifteen minutes passed in a flurry of activity. Finally Susan rode in the ambulance with Eric and David to the hospital, and Candy promised to follow in her car with Timmy.

A nurse and an orderly whisked David off for an X ray. Susan stayed with Eric while a nurse cleaned and bandaged his cuts. A doctor came in and checked him over and pronounced him fit to go home. They found Candy and Timmy in a small waiting room next to the emergency entrance.

"What did the doctor say?" Candy asked immediately.

"He's fine, but he should take it easy for a day or so," Susan told her with a relieved smile.

"Any word on David yet?"

Susan shook her head. "I don't want to leave him here alone. Could Nancy babysit for a while?"

"If she can't, I will," Candy answered. She picked up her purse and stood. "What about the puppy?"

They went over all the necessary arrangements before Candy left with the boys. "We'll bring your car over and leave the keys at the desk. Stay as long as you want, Susan," she called over her shoulder as she ushered them to the door. "They can spend the night with us."

Susan watched them go, then leaned her head back against the wall and shut her eyes. Lord, what a day. A moment later she got to her feet and went in search of David. The nurse at the emergency room desk smiled when Susan asked if she could see him.

The nurse gestured toward the hallway on Susan's right. "He's in room three. See if you can get him to take something for pain."

Clutching her purse under one arm, Susan thanked the woman and hurried to David's room. She paused in the doorway when she saw him. He lay on an examining table in a hospital gown that barely covered him. His arms were crossed over his chest, and his left leg rested on a stack of pillows, an ice pack draped over his knee. Lines of pain bracketed his closed eyes and his mouth.

Though her heart ached with compassion for him, Susan mustered up a smile and entered the room. "Eric's just fine," she said cheerfully, walking over to stand beside the table. "How are you doing?"

He opened his eyes and gave her a grim smile. "You want the truth?"

"Of course."

"Lousy."

She picked up one corner of the ice pack and peeked under it. His knee had swollen to the size of a grapefruit. She winced at the sight and carefully laid the ice pack down. "I can see that. How bad is it?"

"Kneecap's broken into five pieces. They've called in an orthopedic surgeon."

"Oh, David," Susan murmured. She took his hand and looked deeply into his eyes. "I'm so sorry this happened to you. Have I even thanked you for saving Eric's life? God, I've never been so scared—"

"No thanks necessary," he interrupted gruffly. "Anybody would've done the same thing."

"Well, I didn't. I just stood there like a damn rock, and he's my kid." She leaned over and kissed his unbattered cheek. "So thank you. Is there anything I can get for you?"

"How about my pants?" he grumbled, tugging the skimpy gown down over his right buttock.

Susan grinned. "I don't think the nurses would approve. Would a blanket help?"

"Sure."

She found one in a storage cupboard and covered him with it, then pulled a chair alongside the table. "Want me to call someone for you? Maybe I can track down Melody and Jason in Greeley.''

"The hospital's already trying," he said. "Look, you must be exhausted. Why don't you take the boys and go on home? I'll be fine."

After telling him about the arrangements she'd made with Candy, Susan settled back in her chair. "I'm not leaving you, Hunter, so you might as well get used to the idea. Is there anything I can do for you? Like call the nurse for some pain medication?"

David shook his head, a smile hovering at the corners of his mouth. "I don't want any pills, but there's something you can do."

"What?"

He shifted, turning his torso toward her, and held out his right hand. "Will you hold my hand again?"

"You bet." She laced her fingers through his and rested their clasped hands on the edge of the table.

They chatted quietly until Dr. Ambrose, the surgeon, arrived. David insisted he wanted Susan with him while they discussed his treatment and a nurse prepped him for surgery. His eyelids drooped from the shot, but he held fast to Susan's hand until they wheeled him to the operating room.

The next five hours dragged by. Susan phoned Candy's house to check on the boys, bought a sandwich in the cafeteria she couldn't eat, then went back to the waiting room, where she alternately paced and flipped through the outdated magazines. At last Dr. Ambrose stopped by and told her David would be out of the recovery room within the hour. Before he left, he promised to send a nurse to get her once David was settled.

She sent up a silent prayer of thanks for David's safety, found a ladies' room and freshened up. Half an hour later a nurse escorted her to a private room on the fourth floor. David lay silently in a regular hospital bed with an IV stand next to it. A bulky bandage covered his left leg, which was raised by some kind of traction apparatus.

When she approached the bed, he opened one eye, gave her a groggy smile and held out his hand. "What're you still doing here?" he asked, his speech slurred from the anesthesia.

Susan's heart filled with tenderness at his gesture. She clasped his hand in a firm grip and smiled back at him. "I told you I wasn't leaving, Hunter. How do you feel?"

"Fuzzy. Kinda floaty." He shook his head as if to clear it, then closed his eyes and sighed. "Glad you're here."

"I am, too," she assured him, smoothing his hair back off his forehead with her free hand.

"Feels good," he murmured. "Stay with me a little while?" he asked, his voice trailing off at the end.

"As long as you want me to."

Though he still clung to her hand, his respiration deepened and his mouth dropped open, emitting gentle, rumbly snores with every exhaled breath. Susan continued stroking his forehead and enjoyed the opportunity to study his features without those disturbing eyes of his watching her.

Nobody would call his face pretty or handsome now. The bump on his forehead had darkened with a purple bruise. The left side of his face was scraped and swollen. The lines around his eyes and mouth had relaxed somewhat, but were still visible. Bristly black stubble covered his lower cheeks and chin.

He looked like a battered warrior, but when she thought of what he'd done for her that afternoon, he was the most beautiful human being she'd ever seen. Tears leaked down her cheeks, and she let them come. It seemed silly to cry now that all the danger had passed, but it was a blessed relief, all the same.

A nurse came in to check David's pulse and apparatus. "He'll probably sleep through the night now," she told Susan quietly. "Why don't you go home and get some rest?"

Susan nodded and tried to extract her hand from David's, but he muttered in protest and tightened his grip. The nurse smiled at Susan in understanding and brought her a chair.

An hour passed, and he still held on to her as if touching her made him feel safe in his dream world.

Her back and shoulder ached from holding her arm up; she would have stood on her head all night if it would make him happy. She shifted the chair to a more comfortable position and rested her head against the bed rail. Her eyelids felt as if they weighed a ton. She yawned and looked over at David's peaceful face and thought, *Oh, God, it would be so easy to fall in love with you.*

Chapter Eight

David awoke to a grayish blur and a clattering sound somewhere in the distance. His lips were chapped, but his tongue felt so dry, he doubted he could lick them. Wondering what had put such a foul taste in his mouth and where in the hell he was, he blinked rapidly. Gradually the grayish blur swam into focus and became a leg suspended by a weird contraption hanging over the end of the bed.

He inhaled a breath and caught a sharp, antiseptic smell. Raising both hands to rub his eyes, he discovered his left one was taped to a board and had a needle and a thin plastic tube sticking out of it. He tried to shift his butt, and was rewarded for his efforts by a deep grinding pain in his knee. David decided he must be in a hospital, but what in God's name had happened to him?

Rolling his head to the left, he saw a call button clipped to the sheet, a portable bedside table with a plastic glass and pitcher and an open door that revealed bathroom tiles on the wall inside. On his right he found a window with half-opened venetian blinds letting in pale stripes of light and a woman curled up in a blue vinyl chair, sound asleep. As if sensing his confused stare, she turned toward him slightly and exhaled a gentle sigh.

Susan! What was she doing here? Then his brain cleared, and he remembered the accident. He looked at her again and felt his heart contract. He hadn't expected her to stay with him all night, but it touched him deeply that she had. She looked so soft and cuddly and damn uncomfortable, despite the little smile on her lips.

He hoped that smile meant she was dreaming about him. He'd love to wake her up with a kiss. He'd love to do a helluva lot more than that if he weren't trussed up like a stupid chicken.

Susan squirmed in the chair as if the wooden armrest were digging into her back. David tried to call her name softly, but his voice came out in a raspy croak. He poured himself some water from the pitcher, sipped it and tried again.

"Susan."

"Huh? What time is it?" she muttered, opening one bleary eye for an instant.

"Time to wake up, honey. It's morning."

"What?" She opened both eyes, saw him and shook her head as if to clear it, then jerked upright and hobbled stiffly over to the bed. "What's wrong?"

"Take it easy," he answered, smiling inside at the anxiety in her eyes and in her voice. "I'm okay."

She swayed and grabbed the bed rail for support. "Are you in pain? Do you want me to call the nurse?"

David reached out and smoothed her tousled hair away from her face. "Hey, calm down. I'm fine. Give yourself a minute to wake up."

"It takes two cups of coffee to do that." She rubbed a hand over her face, yawned, then gave him a crooked grin. "I'm sorry. I didn't mean to conk out on you."

"You should have gone home and slept in a real bed," he answered, laying his hand over both of hers on the railing.

Susan pulled her hands away and ran them through her hair. "Lord, I must look like a train wreck."

"You look beautiful," he informed her quietly. "I was pretty darn glad to see you when I came to this morning. Why didn't the nurses throw you out of here when visiting hours ended?"

She shrugged and glanced away as if she felt embarrassed by his compliment. "They tried, but you, got so, uh, restless every time I let go of your hand, they finally gave in."

David wondered what she meant by the term, "restless," but wasn't at all sure he really wanted to know. He vaguely remembered dreaming that he was holding something infinitely precious and somebody trying to take it away from him. Had that been Susan's hand?

"Can I get you anything, David?" she asked.

"No, but I think you need to get some rest."

"I guess you're right," she answered, stifling another yawn. "Want me to bring you some stuff from home?"

He thought about that for a moment. "Yeah, if you don't mind. There's a shaving kit in my closet, and my robe's hanging behind the bathroom door." He looked at his leg and grimaced. "I guess I'll need a pair of sweatpants to wear when I leave. They're in my dresser somewhere."

"I'll find them. We'll take care of your house and Sheba, so don't worry about anything." She patted his hand, then picked up her purse and walked to the door. "See you later."

"Susan?" he called.

"What?"

"Thanks."

"What for?"

"For being here with me."

She smiled and shook her head. "I'm so grateful to you for saving Eric, it was the least I could do. Call if you need anything."

David frowned as the door closed behind her. Dammit, he didn't want her gratitude. He wanted . . . her love.

The realization hit him like a fist in the diaphragm. But it didn't surprise him. Not really. Remembering the pep talk he'd given himself in the shower the day before about stomping on his impulsiveness and taking it slow and easy with Susan, he shook his head. What a pile of bull that had been.

"It's too late for that now, you fool," he whispered with a resigned smile.

Of course, if he told Susan he loved her, she'd run from him faster than he'd run after Eric yesterday. He sighed and rested his head back against the pillow. He'd just have to stick to his original plan. Somehow he would earn Susan's trust. With luck and patience on his part, surely the rest would follow. If only patience were one of his virtues . . .

Susan rushed home and went next door to check on Eric and Timmy. Candy greeted her with a cup of coffee and a plate of pancakes still warm from the boys' breakfast. Her daughter Nancy had taken them to David's house to visit Sheba ten minutes earlier.

Gratefully accepting the coffee and pancakes, Susan seated herself at the kitchen table and told Candy about David's surgery. They both had a second cup of coffee, and after Candy insisted on keeping the boys for the rest of the day, Susan went home for a nap.

She woke up at noon, showered and dressed in a pair of navy blue corduroy slacks and a white blouse. She picked up David's keys at Candy's house and spent a few minutes with the boys, then went across the street. Sheba barked and whined until Susan let her out of the crate and took her into the backyard.

Ten minutes later, they were back inside. Sheba followed Susan to David's bedroom and happily investigated this new part of her territory.

The king-size water bed with a mirrored headboard and built-in bookcases drew Susan's attention first. An image of David lying there in masculine splendor popped into her mind. Her pulse quickened. Her palms grew damp. She hastily averted her eyes and went into his bathroom.

A soft black velour robe that would probably reach his knees hung right where he'd said it would be. Susan grabbed it and caught a whiff of the after-shave she'd noticed him wearing before. She imagined him putting the robe on after a shower. She imagined him taking a shower. She imagined taking a shower with him. She rushed back into the bedroom, tossed the garment on the bed and marched over to the closet.

"The man is flat on his back. In the hospital. With a broken knee," she muttered. "Even you're not that kinky, Miller."

The shaving kit sat on the shelf above the clothing rod. A small suitcase lay on its side next to the kit. Susan put them both beside the robe. Feeling more like an intruder with every second, she approached his dresser.

The top drawer contained an assortment of masculine junk—a manicure set, a shoehorn and extra laces, a box of condoms. She slammed the drawer shut and yanked open the next one. Neat stacks of underwear and socks greeted her. David hadn't asked for any, but she added four pairs of shorts and socks to the growing pile on the bed, grinning when she noticed the shorts were royal blue.

The third drawer held sweatshirts and T-shirts, and the sweatpants turned up in the fourth drawer. Susan selected a matched set in Wyoming's brown and gold, then packed everything into the suitcase. Taking one last glance around the room, she found a suspense novel opened facedown on the nightstand, marked his place with a tissue and stuck it in on top.

After fighting a tug of war over a sneaker with Sheba, Susan put the pup back into her crate, locked the house and drove back to the hospital. Anxious to see how David was feeling, she hurried inside. She entered his room with a cheery smile, stopping short when she realized he wasn't alone. He didn't look very happy, either.

Jason sprawled in the chair Susan had slept in. Melody stood beside the bed. David lay back against the raised head of his bed, his eyes flashing with anger and his jaw set at an obstinate angle. Jason looked up and smiled at Susan, but David and Melody were too involved in an argument to notice her.

"Mel, so help me, if you call Mom and Dad, and tell them anything about this, I'll never speak to you again," David threatened his sister.

"Be reasonable, you big dope. You can't run the company when you're laid up like this."

"Yes, I can. I'll be out of here by Tuesday. I can do most of my work over the phone for a while, and Rita can bring whatever needs to be signed to my house."

Melody shook her head. "Who's going to take care of you there? Sheba? You've got to come out to the ranch with us."

David pointed a finger at his sister. "No way. I can't be that far from the station. I'll figure out something else."

"How are you going to eat?"

"I'll order pizzas."

"You can't even get yourself to the doctor."

"I'll rent a car with an automatic transmission."

"You can't drive when you're taking pain pills. And you shouldn't be alone, either. What if you fall and can't get back up? You could hurt your leg even worse."

"Hell, lots of people get around on crutches everyday."

"Not three days after surgery. You either come home with us for a week, or I'm calling Mom, David. I mean it."

"Dammit, Melody! I've waited too long for this chance to show Dad what I can do to let you screw it up for me."

They glared at each other like two gunfighters facing off in a dusty street at high noon. Then David leaned back and closed his eyes with a disgruntled sigh. His skin looked pale, and the deep lines of strain around his nose and mouth worried Susan. She raised an eyebrow at Jason, silently asking, *What can we do to stop this?*

He shrugged as if to say, *Who knows? They're both nuts.* Then he climbed to his feet and walked over to stand beside Melody. "You have a visitor, Dave."

David opened his eyes. His mouth curved into a welcoming, if somewhat tired, grin when he saw Susan. "Come on in. Feeling better?"

"Much," Susan answered, approaching the other side of the bed. She set his suitcase on the floor and rested an elbow on the bed railing. After greeting Melody, she asked David with a teasing smile, "What's going on here? Are you causing trouble already?"

"He certainly is," Melody said.

"Go home, Squirt," David grumbled in response.

Jason took off his Stetson and played with the brim. "Why don't you hire a nurse?" he suggested.

"And have some old prune-face telling me what to do all the time?" David shuddered at the idea. He held out his hands in a plea for understanding. "Look, I'm not a little kid. I can handle this."

"No, you can't, " Melody argued. "But if you're going to be so damn stubborn, I guess I'll have to drop out of school and take care of you myself. Jason can get along without me for a while—"

"Whoa," Jason interrupted. "Just hold it right there, Melody."

"Yeah, nobody's asking you to be a martyr, sis," David agreed.

"Well, *somebody's* got to take care of you," Melody insisted.

The three of them all looked as if they were ready to go another fifteen rounds, but Susan couldn't stand it any more. "May I say something?" she asked. They all looked at her expectantly. "David can come to my house when he gets out of the hospital. I have some vacation time coming, and I'll be glad to help him until he's steady on his crutches."

A flicker of hope entered David's eyes for an instant. Then it died, and he shook his head. "No, I can't let you do that, Susan."

"I thought you said our friendship isn't worth much if we can't help each other out once in a while," she said.

"That's asking too much of a friend," he answered with a rueful smile.

"Boy, I'll say," Melody agreed fervently. "He's the world's worst patient, Susan. He moans and whines and—"

"Mel," Jason cut her off. "Be quiet, will ya? Susan's on to something here."

Susan shot him a grateful smile. "Now, look, Hunter," she said firmly, "my kid got you into this mess. Let me help get you out of it."

"But I hate for you to give up your vacation," he protested.

"My boss is pretty flexible. Maybe he'll let me work at home for a week. Think how much we can get done for Melissa Reed. Come on, whaddaya say?"

"We'll help her all we can, Dave," Jason promised.

David sighed and shook his head. "Well, all right, but on one condition. You let me buy all the groceries while I'm at your house.

"Better take him up on that offer, Susan," Melody warned. "You won't believe how much food he can put away."

"It's a deal," Susan replied, extending her hand to David.

He shook it with his right hand, holding it far longer than necessary. Looking steadily into her eyes, he said quietly, "Thanks, friend. I'll try not to be a pain in the rear."

"You won't be," she assured him. "Now, don't you think it's about time you get some rest?"

"Yeah," he admitted. "Fighting with the squirt is hard work."

By the time Susan and Melody unpacked the suitcase for him and followed Jason out of the room, David was already asleep. When they reached the lobby, Melody turned to Susan, a concerned frown creasing her forehead.

"It's awfully generous of you to help David out like this, but I don't think you know what you're getting yourself into. I wasn't kidding when I said he was a terrible patient."

Susan replied with more confidence than she felt. "You're his family. He won't act as rotten with me as he would with you."

"Call us if you need anything or if he gets to be too much for you," Jason said. "Promise?"

"I promise."

Melody's words echoed in Susan's ears on the way home. In all honesty, she *wasn't* sure what she'd gotten herself into. Whether he was a rotten patient or not, however, was hardly the issue that concerned her. No, what worried her was that in the space of a few weeks, David Hunter had insinuated himself into her life more than any other man besides Ed.

The accident had forged a strong bond between them, but her feelings for David went way beyond gratitude. Sure, she'd decided she wanted to get closer to him, but *this* close? If she had erotic fantasies about him now while he was still in traction, how on earth was she going to deal with him living in her house?

"Ah, well," she said to her reflection in the rearview mirror, "It's only for a week. What can happen in seven days?"

Susan rushed home from work at noon on Tuesday and scurried around the house, getting it ready for David's arrival. Watching from her front window, she ran outside when Jason's Blazer roared into the driveway and parked. David sat sideways in the back seat. He looked pale and exhausted, but he sent her a chipper wave. Jason stepped out of the vehicle with a big grin for her.

"Your patient has arrived, Nurse Miller," he said, opening the passenger door at David's feet.

Jason picked up the crutches lying on the floor and gave them to Susan while David scooted himself across the seat, then propped himself up on his good leg. Susan handed over the crutches, he then propped himself up on his good leg. Susan handed over the crutches, her heart contracting with sympathy when David took three wobbly steps and had to rest before he could continue.

By the time they got him inside, he was sweating profusely and swearing like a cowboy whose horse has run away and stranded him ten miles from home. Susan led the way into her bedroom. David and Jason followed. When he realized she intended to give up her bed for him, David balked.

"No. I can't let you do this." He looked over his shoulder at Jason. "Better take me out to the ranch, after all."

"Don't be silly." Susan turned back the bedspread and blankets. "This is the only bed in the house that's big enough for you. I'll be fine on the sofa sleeper. Now sit down before you fall down."

He gazed longingly toward the bed for a moment, then grudgingly acquiesed. She helped him take off his coat and shoes while Jason went out to the car to get his suitcase and the five bouquets of flowers he'd received from his old girl-friends. David's fiberglass cast poked out of the elastic cuff at the bottom of his sweatpants and covered his left leg right up to his bottom.

Though he assured her it wasn't all that heavy, it was awkward, demanding a major effort just to get him over to the center of the bed. His face blanched with every movement. Once he was settled, he leaned back and closed his eyes, his breathing heavy and ragged. Susan gathered extra pillows to elevate his leg and covered him with a blanket.

Jason brought in the suitcase a moment later and motioned for Susan to follow him out of the room.

"When can he have something for pain?" she asked when they entered the kitchen.

"He was supposed to take a pill before we left the hospital, but he wouldn't do it." Jason gave her a rueful grin and took a prescription bottle out of his coat pocket. "But I think he'll take it now."

"Oh, for heaven's sake, Ed was the same way," Susan fumed, getting a glass of water. "Why do men do stupid things like that? Is being macho that important?"

Jason shrugged. "I don't think it has anything to do with being macho, Susan. Dave's always been pretty sensitive to any kind of medication, and that stuff makes him groggy. He doesn't like feeling out of control."

"Well, I can't stand to watch him hurt so much." She took the bottle of pills from Jason and marched into the bedroom. "Time for your medicine," she said, softening her tone with a smile.

David accepted the pill without a murmur of protest. Susan perched on the side of the bed while she waited for him to finish the water. "Do you want anything else?" she asked when he handed her the glass.

He shook his head. "Not now. I think I'll take a nap."

"All right. Call if you need me."

She left the door halfway open and went back to Jason in the kitchen. He handed her a list of instructions the hospital had given him for David's care and offered to run errands for her. She asked him to bring over more clothes for David and added that he might as well bring Sheba, too, since it would be easier to care for the pup there than at David's house. When he'd done that, Jason promised to stop by again the next day and left.

The rest of the afternoon passed quietly. Susan worked on Melissa Reed's campaign at her kitchen table with the radio turned low and Sheba curled up at her feet. She checked on David every half hour, but found him sleeping peacefully every time. At three-thirty she propped a note against the bedside lamp and went to pick up Timmy from school and Eric from the sitter's house.

She shushed the boys when they roared into the house in their normal, boisterous manner, but David called out to her from the bedroom that he was awake. The boys ran in to see him, and by the time Susan joined them, David looked and sounded more like himself.

He admired what remained of Eric's shiner and listened to their stories of what had happened that day. After the boys had signed his cast, they took Sheba out to their fenced backyard to play. David patted the bed beside him, and Susan sat down to talk for a minute.

"We could have Jason take Sheba back out to the ranch if she's too much trouble," he suggested.

Chuckling, Susan shook her head. "That'll confuse her, and the boys would hate me. Are you hungry? Thirsty? Need a pain pill?"

"No, but—" he hesitated "—I'd kill for a real shower. I think I'm getting cooties in my hair.

Remembering her thoughts when she'd picked up his robe, Susan felt her cheeks grow warm and looked away. "What about your cast?" she asked. "You can't get it wet, can you?"

"There's a rubber guard for it in my suitcase." He studied her face for a moment, and a teasing grin spread across his mouth. "I can wait for Jason to come back if it'll embarrass you too much."

Susan sniffed as if the idea were ridiculous, got up and put his suitcase on a chair. "I've been married, and I have two sons, Hunter. I doubt you've got anything I haven't seen before."

She rummaged through his things until she found a box with the appropriate label. Shooting David an unconcerned smile, she opened it, pulled out the bright yellow guard and held up one end. It slowly unrolled, gradually taking on the shape of a giant condom. Susan took one look and choked on a startled giggle. David threw back his head and howled with laughter.

Struggling to keep a straight face, she sat back down on the bed. "Are you sure it will fit?"

David inhaled a deep breath, his eyes dancing with merriment. "The nurse told me one size fits all."

Clutching her stomach, Susan sagged against the headboard and lost it. "Oh, oh, dear," she sputtered, certain her face was flaming, but too tickled to care. She picked up an extra pillow and tossed it at David's head. "You knew what that thing looked like," she accused him.

He threw it right back at her. "I did not. The box hadn't been opened, and you know it."

She held up one forearm to ward off the pillow. David reached out, grabbed her wrist and dragged her close beside him. "Lord, it feels good to laugh again," he said.

Susan nodded in agreement, feeling more giggles rising in her chest like champagne bubbles. She looked into his gorgeous eyes, and suddenly the laughter caught in her throat and she felt an almost irresistible urge to reach up and kiss him.

He leaned a fraction of an inch closer, his eyes darkening as if he'd read her mind. She shook her head slightly, laid one hand against his chest and sat up. He let go of her wrist and scooted back against the headboard.

"Well, Miller," he said casually, "are you going to help me or just let me sit here and stink?"

She retrieved the cast guard from the foot of the bed. "All right. Let's get this show on the road. What do we do first?"

"I don't know about you, but I usually take off my clothes for a shower.

Susan eyed his devilish grin and decided she'd better not let him provoke any more blushes. She peeled off his socks with brisk efficiency, then crossed her arms over her chest. "Okay, Hunter. Drop your pants."

His grin faltered for a second, but he untied the drawstring at his waist and worked the sweatpants down to his knees. Susan slid them off over his feet and draped them over the chair at her desk. When she turned back to face him, he'd pulled off his sweatshirt, as well.

Struggling for an impassive expression, Susan stifled a sigh of admiration. He was beautiful. Downright beautiful. His shoulders were broad and well-muscled. His chest was lightly covered with springy black hair that arrowed down his lean torso and flat stomach toward the waistband of his briefs.

Her heart banged against her rib cage so hard, she was afraid he might hear it. She couldn't meet his eyes for fear of what her own might reveal. Instead, she picked up the cast guard, opened the top and bunched it up in her hands like a nylon stocking.

She pushed it onto the end of his foot and tugged it up over the fiberglass. The material stretched, but David's leg was so long, it was slow, hard work. Her hand grazed the inside of his right thigh as she neared the top. He sucked in a quick, audible breath, but didn't move. Susan's hands trembled for a moment. She gritted her teeth and concentrated on her task. The higher she got, the more the guard resisted, and she feared she would tear it.

The edge of his royal blue briefs came into view when she edged the rubber guard over the rim of the cast. Finally she let it close tightly around his upper thigh, her knuckles pressed unavoidably against his crotch. A hard ridge under his briefs twitched at the contact.

She yanked her hand away and raised her eyes to meet David's. His neck and ears were crimson, and she guessed his cheeks must be, too, though she couldn't see them well with four days' worth of black stubble covering them. He gave her a lopsided smile.

"Well," he said, his voice husky, "that certainly was, uh, up close and personal."

Since she wasn't at all sure she could speak coherently, Susan nodded and went to get his crutches. *Lord,* she wondered, *how do nurses do this every day and maintain an emotional distance?* Tension hung over the room, thicker than the smog over Denver during a temperature inversion.

Behind her, David let out a sigh that reeked with discouragement. "Look," he said, "maybe I'd better wait for Jason."

Holding the crutches in front of her like a shield, Susan turned and faced him. He was gazing at the ceiling as if something fascinating were going on up there. Guilt niggled at her conscience when she realized this sudden intimacy was just as hard for David as it was for her. Was she going to deny the poor man a shower because she couldn't act like an adult instead of a nervous twit? Not likely.

Gathering up her composure, she marched back to the bed. "Don't be silly," she said, achieving a brisk tone.

"We're both feeling awkward because this is new to us, but we'll get over it. You'll feel much better when you're clean."

He sent her a long, searching look, then nodded, lifted his leg off the pillows and scooted to the edge of the bed. With a little ingenuity, they managed to preserve David's modesty and return to the lighthearted atmosphere they'd shared earlier. By the time he was back in bed wearing clean shorts and a pajama top Jason had brought over, he looked completely refreshed.

Admitting to herself that whatever embarrassment they'd suffered had been worth it, Susan brought David a light supper of soup and sandwiches and persuaded him to take another pain pill after he'd finished eating. She spent the next three hours with the boys and put them to bed, then tiptoed into her bedroom to check on David.

His eyes were closed; his book lay open on his chest. He stirred when she picked it up and set it on the nightstand. Susan tried to soothe him back to sleep, but his lashes fluttered and finally opened.

"What time is it?" he asked with a sleepy smile.

"About eight-thirty. I'm sorry I woke you."

"It's all right. I'm not really tired, just dopey." He rubbed his eyes with his fingertips. "Where're the boys?"

"I just tucked them in. Do you need anything?"

"Maybe a glass of water."

Susan went to get it for him, then gathered up her manuscript and typewriter from her desk. "I'm going to write for a while in the kitchen. Yell if you need me."

"Don't leave because of me," David protested.

"The typewriter will drive you crazy."

"Hey, I grew up with that sound, remember? It won't bother me a bit. I'll appreciate the company."

"You're sure?"

"You bet." He picked up his book and opened it. "I'll even be quiet so I don't bug you."

With a shrug Susan put her things back down and settled in to work. It felt strange at first, knowing there was another person in the room. But David was true to his word, and before long, she was immersed in her story and hammering out pages at a satisfying clip.

At eleven she finished the chapter and decided to quit for the night. She stacked up the manuscript and covered the typewriter, then stood and stretched out her back and shoulder muscles. David had dozed off, and his book was back on his chest.

Smiling, Susan walked over to the bed and put the book on the nightstand again. Tenderness blossomed inside her at the sight of his tousled dark hair and his long eyelashes spread like little fans across his cheeks. He'd been through so much in the last few days....

Without stopping to think about it, she bent over, brushed the hair off his forehead and gently kissed the vivid bruise over his left eyebrow. His eyelids flew open. His arm shot up, grabbed her around the waist and tumbled her onto the bed with him.

His other hand grasped her chin, aligning her lips with his. "Don't waste kisses on my forehead," he murmured.

Susan had no time to think, no time to protest before he captured her mouth in a kiss that stole her breath and her resistance. His whiskers were prickly against her chin, but his lips were warm and soft yet firm as they moved over hers with just the right amount of pressure to coax them apart. He sighed with pleasure, and the tip of his tongue darted in, gliding over her bottom lip, skimming the edges of her teeth.

She breathed in the aromas of her shampoo in his hair, her soap on his skin, mingled with a muskier scent all his own. His arms tightened around her, pulling her side against his chest, and she felt the heat of his body sinking down deep inside her, his heart pounding against his rib cage. Her hands slid over the crisp cotton of his pajama top and buried themselves in the silky hair at the back of his head.

He deepened the kiss, and she ached with a delicious need too long denied. It was heaven; it was hell. She wanted to stay in his arms all night; she had to stop him before this went one step further.

"God, you're so sweet," he whispered, planting hot nibbling kisses across her cheeks and eyelids.

She whimpered, then finally found her voice. "Stop. Please, let me up."

David released her slowly and leaned back against the pillows. Susan sat up and combed her hair out of her eyes with shaking hands. When she finally found the courage to meet his troubled gaze, she said, "This can't happen again, David."

"It was just a kiss, Susan." He reached for her hand, but she pulled away. His expression hardened. "You enjoyed it as much as I did."

"It doesn't matter whether I enjoyed it or not. We're supposed to be friends. Platonic friends."

"We can't kid ourselves about that anymore." He glanced down at his lap and sighed. "After what happened here this afternoon, you have to know I don't feel one damn bit platonic about you. And I don't think you feel that way about me, either."

Knowing he was right didn't make it any easier to admit. Susan climbed off the bed and looked down at him for an agonizing moment. "You're not in any condition to know what you feel," she said quietly. "You're hurt and vulnerable and right now, you need me."

"That's a crock of bull."

"No, it's not. At least I don't think it is. And even if I'm wrong, I can't get involved with you, David. I'm just not ready for a relationship."

He returned her implacable gaze, but didn't say anything. Then he swung his casted leg over the side of the bed and reached for his crutches.

"Where do you think you are going?" Susan asked.

"To the bathroom," he answered, pulling himself up on his good leg. "And I don't need any damn help."

She stepped out of the way and spent the time he was gone finding her nightgown, robe and clothes for the next day and listened intently for any sound indicating he'd gotten himself in a fix. When David returned, his face was drawn in pain and his muscles quivered with the exertion it took to get himself back into bed.

"I can't believe how weak I've gotten in four lousy days,' he grumbled as Susan pulled the sheet and blanket up over him.

"That's because you've been in bed. Once you're up and around more, you'll feel stronger," she assured him. "Do you need another pill?"

He gave her a pathetically hopeful grin. "No, but I could use a good-night kiss."

Smiling, Susan shook her head at him. "Forget it." Then, holding her clothes against her breasts, she said seriously, "I meant what I said. If you can't accept being here on my terms, you'll have to go out to the ranch."

Chapter Nine

David gritted his teeth and bit back a moan. Hot needles of agony shot up and down his leg, but he'd be damned if he would call Susan for help. She'd brought him breakfast and lunch, and stood sentry while he used the bathroom, but it was obvious she was doing her best to avoid him—and her best was pretty darn good. If it hadn't been for his foresight in having call forwarding installed on his phone line before leaving the hospital, he wouldn't have heard another human voice all day.

Of course, it was his own damn fault. Maybe his dad was right about him, after all. Maybe he *was* still too impulsive for his own good. He'd sure as hell acted on impulse last night when he yanked Susan down on the bed and kissed her like that.

He sighed and tried to shift his leg to a more comfortable position. Unfortunately, if there was a more comfortable position, he couldn't find it. His knee felt as if someone were deliberately trying to crush it with a pair of pliers. Biting into his lower lip, he wondered if a cast could shrink.

In an attempt to distract himself from the pain, he turned his thoughts back to Susan. Darn the woman, what did she expect from him, anyway? That he would ignore the sexual attraction between them forever? Did she honestly believe he was so wacked out on the painkiller his surgeon had prescribed, he couldn't tell if he wanted her? Tell that to his libido.

And why was she so flipped out over a little kiss? For Pete's sake, he hadn't even touched her breasts or anything else he'd wanted to. Didn't she know how appealing she was to him? How her shy blushes intrigued and delighted him? How her compassion and gentleness turned his guts to mush? How her flashes of humor when she forgot to be nervous around him made him feel as if he'd just won a million bucks? How the hell could he *not* want her?

She wasn't afraid of sex or a prude. She couldn't be, after the way she'd laughed with him over the cast guard. He didn't think she was put off by the idea of having sex with him personally, either. She'd kissed him back last night with enthusiasm, if not downright hunger. And when he'd stripped down to his shorts yesterday, she hadn't exactly acted repulsed.

Oh, she hadn't been obvious about checking out his assets. Not at all. But she'd done it, all right—when she thought he wasn't looking. And dammit, he just *knew* she'd wanted to touch him as much as he'd wanted her to. So what was holding her back? Why was she so doggedly determined to keep their relationship platonic?

"Damned if I know," he muttered, unconsciously tensing his leg in irritation.

The resulting pain made bright spots dance in front of his eyes. A groan escaped his clenched teeth, and he knew he'd have to give in and take another pill or be reduced to a whimpering baby. The bottle sat right over there on the desk. He still had water in the glass on the nightstand. Surely he could handle this without involving Susan.

Bracing his cast with his left hand, he swung his leg to the side of the bed. Sweat popped out on his forehead and upper lip, and he couldn't suppress a quiet moan. Cripes. This was worse than anything he'd felt yesterday. Marshaling his strength, he took three deep breaths before grabbing his crutches and pulling himself upright.

He rested a moment, then took a step, rested, and took another. Damn, but he was weak and wobblier than the newborn colt he'd seen out at Jason's ranch last spring. Panting with exertion, he told himself one more big step and he could reach the pills. David stood on his good leg, planted the crutches firmly in front of him and heaved his body forward. His right crutch snagged in the carpet pile, but he had too much momentum going to stop himself.

The crutch jerked out of his hand and fell to the floor with a muffled thud. He fought for balance, swaying and windmilling his free arm until he grasped the edge of the desk. His brain reeled with the irate messages blasting from his wounded knee, and his stomach did a nauseating somersault. When the room finally righted itself, he cut loose with a stream of epithets that would have sent his mother running for the nearest bar of soap.

"Could you hold on for just a moment?" Susan said into the phone's receiver. She covered the mouthpiece with one hand, turned her head toward the bedroom and listened. Yes, that was David, yelling about something in there. She promised to call her office back, hung up and ran to see what was wrong.

David leaned on one crutch beside her desk, his face ashen and a creative combination of cuss words spilling from his mouth. She gasped at the sight of him, then ran to his side, retrieved his other crutch and helped him back to bed.

"Good lord, what were you doing up?" she asked when he was settled.

"Needed a pain pill," he answered between gasps of pain.

"Are you all right?" Studying his contorted features, she chided herself, *Now that was a stupid question if you've ever asked one, Miller. Of course he's not.*

"Don't know, but it . . . hurts like hell."

She waited while he caught his breath before handing him a pill and the glass of water. When he'd swallowed it, she sat gingerly on the edge of the bed. "Should I call the doctor for you?"

He shook his head, grimaced, then finally nodded. "Maybe you'd better. Something's wrong. Tell him it feels like my cast is too tight."

Susan made the call from the bedside phone. "The nurse said to bring you right in," she reported. "Your knee is probably swelling and they can cut a window in the cast for you."

Though Susan could see he dreaded the pain it would cause him to move again so soon, David took the news stoically. She helped him get dressed and out to the Subaru, and could have wept when they realized his legs were too long for the back seat. He struggled out of the car and propped himself against the passenger door while she rushed to lay the rear seat down.

David half crawled, half dragged himself through the open hatchback. Susan shut it carefully and scurried around to get behind the wheel. "How are you doing back there?" she called over her shoulder as she backed out of the driveway.

"Okay. I think the pills are starting to kick in."

Feeling guilty as a teenage girl caught making out on the front porch by her father, Susan headed for the doctor's office. Good Lord, the man had saved Eric's life. She shouldn't have been so snotty to him just because she felt uncomfortable about her response to that kiss last night. She should have spent more time with him at noon. At the very least, she should have checked on him more often and asked if he needed anything.

They arrived at the clinic in record time. Susan left David in the car and marched inside to get him a wheelchair, certain an orthopedic surgeon's office must have one. A behemoth nurse named Zelda McCracken helped her haul him into the building, ordered her to stay in the waiting room and whisked him through a doorway at the side of the receptionist's desk.

Susan alternately paced and flipped through a stack of *Time* and *Newsweek* magazines, and wondered why clocks move slower in a doctor's office than anywhere else on earth. Forty-five endless minutes later, Zelda rolled a wan but happier-looking David into the waiting room. She gave him some additional instructions for his care and zipped him back out to the car so fast, Susan had to trot to keep up.

She drove home, helped David inside and into bed, picked up some ice for his leg, collected the boys from school and the sitter and cooked dinner. Sheba piddled on the floor twice. The phone rang constantly, with all of David's old girlfriends calling to see how he was feeling. Vans from every florist in town pulled in and out of the driveway every ten minutes, delivering bouquets and plants for him for which she had no space.

When the doorbell rang at seven o'clock, Susan felt more strung out than a brand-new clothesline. She let the boys answer it and dumped the pots and pans that wouldn't fit in the dishwasher into a sink full of soapy water. Jason's booming laugh filtered into the kitchen, then trailed down the hall toward the bedroom.

A moment later Melody Wakefield entered the room carrying a tray loaded with aluminum-foil dishes. "Hope you don't mind us barging in like this, but we couldn't get through on the phone." She set the tray on the table and unloaded it.

Susan pulled her hands out of the dishwater and wiped them on a towel. "No, that's fine. What's all this?"

"We thought we'd save you some cooking." Melody started with the loaf pan and worked her way down the line. "That's a meat loaf, that's a chicken casserole and that one's chili. There's a box of cookies out in the car, too, but Jason will bring it in once he's set up the television we bought for David."

"Television?" Susan echoed weakly.

"It's got earphones and a remote control so he won't have to bother you with it," Melody hastened to assure her.

"That's very—" Susan paused and took a deep breath "—kind of you."

Tipping her head to one side, Melody studied Susan's face intently for a moment. "Is David being a pain in the butt?" she asked darkly. "If he is, so help me, I'll—"

"No, he's b-been fine." To Susan's horror, a tear rolled down her cheek, then another, then another. She swiped at her eyes with the backs of her hands, but nothing could stop the cloudburst that had been brewing inside her all day.

Melody pulled out a chair, gently pushed Susan into it and set the tea kettle on the stove. She found two mugs in a cupboard and tea bags in a canister. Susan grabbed a tissue from the box on the counter and composed herself enough to give David's sister a shaky smile when she brought the tea over and sat in a chair at the end of the table.

"Okay, tell Aunt Melody what's going on," Melody ordered with an encouraging smile.

Susan chuckled, then blew her nose and briefly detailed the day's events. "He was in such pain," she said toward the end, "and if I'd just thought to put an ice pack on his cast, it wouldn't have happened."

Melody raised an eyebrow at her. "Did anyone tell you to put ice on it?"

"Well, no. But any idiot knows ice will reduce swelling."

"Did anyone warn you his knee might swell like that?"

"Not in so many words, but—"

"But you've been to medical school, so you should have realized that," Melody said dryly. "Of course, I wouldn't have thought of it, either, but I definitely think you should feel guilty as sin, Susan."

Susan eyed the younger woman with admiration. "You're very good at this," she said with a wry grin.

"At what?"

"Tea and sympathy and a gentle whack alongside the head when it's needed."

Melody shrugged and laughed. "Jason says I've been counseling everyone I know for years, so I might as well get my degree and make some money at it."

"How much do I owe you for this session?"

"Since you're putting up with my obnoxious brother, it's on the house."

"He hasn't been obnoxious," Susan replied. "I'm just tired tonight."

"I don't doubt that," Melody said, "but I think there's more bothering you than the problem with David's cast."

"Like what?"

"Oh, like maybe he's attracted to you." Melody paused and fiddled with her cup. "And that could be a problem for you. How'm I doing so far?"

"Not bad," Susan admitted. "Are you psychic or what?"

"No. I just know my brother. I could tell he was interested in you at our barbecue, but what really tipped me off was his agreement to come here when he got out of the hospital."

"You didn't give him much choice about that."

"David *always* has a choice." Melody shook her head and smiled. "Just before you came into his room on Sunday, I suggested some of his old girlfriends might be willing to take care of him, but he wouldn't even consider it. Believe me, Susan, he wouldn't be here if he didn't want to be."

"And that convinced you he's attracted to me."

"Well, isn't he?"

Susan nodded. "He says he is."

"And you're not attracted to him?"

"I didn't say that." Susan shrugged, then laughed at Melody's impish, knowing grin. "All right, I'm attracted to him. But that doesn't mean I want to get involved with him. I mean, in a way I do, but I don't think we're right for each other."

"I think you're perfect for him."

"You do? Even though I'm divorced and have two kids?"

"Your kids would never be a problem for David," Melody assured her. "He's been dating too many women who are so much younger than he is, they treat him like God. He gets bored with that before long and goes on to the next one.''

"It didn't sound like he got bored with Liz," Susan pointed out. "In fact, I'm not sure he's really over her yet."

"Oh, I think he is by now. You're right that he didn't get bored with her, but she didn't have enough of her own identity to handle him. She just got mad and jealous when she thought he wasn't paying enough attention to her."

"You think I wouldn't get jealous?" Susan asked, raising an eyebrow in disbelief. "With all his little friends calling and sending him flowers?''

Melody dismissed that concern with a wave of her hand. "You've got both feet on the ground, Susan. You've built a life for yourself and your kids. You know what you want and need from a relationship. He can't overpower you with his charm and experience, and that's exactly what he needs in a woman."

"But what happens to me if he gets bored and leaves?"

"How do you know he'll do that?" Melody asked. "Granted, his track record's not great. Neither was Jason's. I had a hard time dealing with that, but I've learned to trust him."

"And you think I could trust David?"

"I just think it wouldn't hurt to give him a chance. David's as capable of fidelity as Jason is. He certainly had a better role model with my dad than Jason did with his."

"I don't know, Melody," Susan answered with a sigh. "I'm scared, and I'm not sure, and I don't know what to do."

"Why don't you take things one day at a time?" Melody suggested. "Don't let him railroad you into anything you're not ready for, but try to keep an open mind."

"I'll think about it."

"That's all I can ask."

The two women chatted while they stored the food. Then Melody went in to visit her brother, and Susan sat down to read with Timmy and Eric, breathing a silent sigh of relief when she heard Jason helping David into the shower. By the time she tucked the boys in bed, the Wakefields were ready to leave.

Susan waved them off before going into her bedroom to see David. He sat propped up against a mountain of pillows with his leg elevated and an ice bag covering the center section of his cast. He wore the earphones to his new television and was happily zapping through channels with the remote control.

"How do you like your new toy?" she asked, walking over to the bed.

David took off the earphones and gave her a welcoming smile. "It's great." He gestured toward a spot beside him. "Have a seat. We need to talk."

"All right. That sounds like a good idea." She sat at an angle for a better view of his face. "How does your knee feel?"

"Better. That window they cut really did the trick." He turned off the television, then faced her with a serious expression in his dark eyes. "Are you still mad at me for last night?"

"I wasn't mad at you, exactly." She paused, searching for the right words. "I was more confused and uncomfortable than angry."

He reached over and sandwiched her hand between his palms. Susan left it there because . . . well, because it felt good.

"The last thing I want is for you to feel uncomfortable with me," he said. "Why don't we call a truce?"

"What kind of truce?"

"This is a pretty weird situation we're in right now. We can't avoid a certain amount of physical intimacy, but you shouldn't have to worry that I'll grab you every time you come anywhere near me."

"That would be nice," Susan agreed in a dry tone.

"On the other hand, I can't promise I won't ever touch you or try to kiss you again."

Susan snorted with laughter. "This is some truce, Hunter."

"Hey, I'm just trying to be honest. I'm a physical kind of guy, you know? I need hugs and stuff."

"Maybe we should let Sheba sleep with you."

"Will you please get serious and let me finish?"

She plastered a suitably dignified expression on her face, though it tickled her no end that he would come up with this outrageous line of malarkey for her benefit. "Certainly."

"Thank you. Now, what I propose is, I'll give you fair warning if I feel an insatiable urge to grab you."

"You mean like a code phrase?"

"Sure. How about something like, uh . . . hug attack?"

"Hug attack?"

"Yeah. If you don't want to hug me, all you've got to do is get out of my reach. Isn't that simple?"

"How much time do I have to get out of your reach after you use the code phrase?"

He scratched the side of his head thoughtfully for a moment. "About two seconds."

"What if I want to hug you, but I don't want anything else?"

"No problem," he said, sounding like a used-car salesman. "If I get too frisky, all you gotta do is say the other code phrase."

"Which is?"

"Stop, David. Down, boy. It's your turn to think one up, Miller."

"Oh, I definitely like 'down, boy'." Susan returned his teasing grin for a moment, then asked quietly, "Do you really think it'll work, David?"

"We'll make it work," he promised. "If you want me to leave, just say so. After what happened today, I wouldn't blame you. I can still hire a nurse or go out to the ranch."

Susan considered what Melody had said to her in the kitchen and slowly shook her head. "I don't want you to do that. You'll probably be able to manage by yourself in a

week or so, anyway. And in the meantime, we have a benefit to plan. It'll be easier if you're right here.''

"We'll start on it tomorrow morning, and I'll call in to my
office the next day. I need to get up more and practice with
my crutches, too.''

"But not by yourself just yet."

"Agreed." He hesitated for a moment. "Are you planning to write tonight?''

"I don't think I'd get very far."

"Then how about scooting up here and watching television with me for a while?'' he asked. "I'll even let you hold
the remote control.''

She eyed him skeptically until he held up both hands in a
classic show of innocence.

"I'll behave,'' he told her. "I just want some company.''

The idea was immensely appealing, and she didn't doubt
his sincerity. With a muttered, "Why not?'' Susan turned
around and accepted the pillows David offered to share. She
stretched her legs out beside his and felt her muscles relax
for the first time all day.

She rarely watched TV after the boys went to bed, but
David made it interesting by pointing out some of the tech-
nical aspects of programming. His favorite show began at
nine o'clock, and he didn't talk as much. Gradually Susan's
eyes started feeling heavy. She told herself she'd get up and
go to bed on the sofa sleeper at the next commercial.

David started when Susan slumped against him. He
whispered, "Susan, hug attack,'' silently counted off two
seconds, then put his arm around her shoulders and gently
pressed her head into a comfortable position on his chest.
She murmured something in her sleep and turned toward
him, snuggling closer in the process.

Gazing down at her serene face, he noted the circles of
weariness under her eyes, the lingering puffiness and red-
ness around her eyelids, and his gut ached at the thought
that he'd made her cry. He knew she could be tougher than
rawhide when she needed to, but at the moment she looked
infinitely fragile and in need of protection. Shoot, she

looked as if she needed a lifetime supply of hugs in one big dose.

Was he being fair to her? he wondered. There was no doubt in his mind that Susan was the kind of woman he'd always wanted and needed. But was he the kind of man she wanted and needed? He'd barged his way into her life and now her home with about as much subtlety as a tank, whether she'd wanted him to or not. Maybe what she really needed was protection from him.

His heart wrenched at the idea, but the thought of hurting her, even unwittingly, was more unbearable than his knee had been this afternoon. It wasn't too late to back off from this relationship. He could sell his house and move away, leave her alone. Was that the best thing he could do for her?

He didn't know. If it was, he was too selfish and too much of a coward to admit it. He couldn't, wouldn't let her go. Not just yet.

Chapter Ten

The next Sunday morning, Susan fed the boys and sent them to church school with some friends from her congregation. After checking to make sure David was all right, she put on the coffeepot and glanced through the front section of the newspaper, enjoying the rare moments of peace and quiet. A familiar knock sounded on her back door five minutes later. Susan grinned when she opened it and found Candy Sorenson waiting impatiently on the step, holding a box of doughnuts.

"Come on in." Susan moved back to allow her neighbor entrance. "Your timing is perfect. The coffee just finished dripping."

Candy set the box on the table and took a seat. "I was hoping you'd say that. I haven't talked to you in ages."

Remembering her neighbor's frequent phone calls all week, Susan snickered. "Not since yesterday, anyway."

"You know what I mean," Candy retorted, wrinkling her nose. "We haven't sat down together over a cup of coffee since David's accident. By the way, where is he?"

"Still asleep."

"Good." Candy reached for a chocolate doughnut. "That means we can really talk. How are things going with him?"

"Not bad. We've settled into a routine now, and he's getting around better on his crutches." Susan delivered coffee cups and paper napkins to the table and took a cherry-filled doughnut.

"I saw an older woman coming out of your house Thursday and Friday when I came home from work. Who was she?"

"David's secretary. She brought him some papers from the station."

"How much longer is he planning to stay?"

"Just until tomorrow morning. I'm going back to work at the bank, and Jason's planning to help him move home."

"Is he managing that well already?" Candy asked.

"I'm not sure," Susan admitted. "I'd feel better about it if he was completely off the pain medication, but he only takes it at night, so I guess that's not such a problem. Anyway he's determined to go, and I can't stop him."

"Well, I suppose you'll be glad to have your bed back, unless—" Candy paused and arched a wicked eyebrow at Susan "—you finally got smart and crawled in with him."

Laughing, Susan wadded up a napkin and pelted her friend with it. "You're getting so nosey in your old age, I don't know what to do with you."

"Well, did you?" Candy asked, completely unrepentant.

"Of course not. The man is injured."

"He's not injured where it counts. I don't see how you can keep your hands off him."

Susan shook her head and thought, *Candy, if you only knew how hard it's been....* Not that she could fault David's behavior since Wednesday night. He'd been a model patient and a model guest, and had only used their code phrase twice to tease her. But that hadn't stopped her attraction to him from growing stronger every day.

When she helped him with his cast guard, her palms actually itched to stroke his broad chest or his shoulders or his muscular right leg. If she happened to be in the room when he woke up from a nap, his sleepy, oh-so-sexy smile of greeting curled her toes inside her shoes and sent her blood pressure into the danger zone. And God help her, getting him settled at night and going out to her lonely bed in the living room was sheer, unadulterated torture.

"Yo, Miller. Where are you?" Candy asked, waving a hand in front of Susan's nose.

"Huh? Oh, I'm, uh, right here," Susan answered, feeling a guilty flush wash over her cheeks.

Candy hooted with laughter and shook her index finger. "You can't fool me. You've got the hots for that guy, all right."

Susan made a production out of checking her watch. "Time to go pick up the boys. Sorry you have to leave so soon."

"Aw, come on, Susan." Candy reached across the table and patted her friend's hand. "Don't shut me out. If I couldn't tease you, I'd go completely nuts. And since my love life has been zilch for the last year, let me have a few vicarious thrills, okay?"

"I'm trying my best to avoid all possible thrills," Susan told Candy with a rueful grin.

"Boy, would I ever love to get my hands on that ex-husband of yours. He did such a number on you, you're too scared to recognize Mr. Right when he's sleeping in your bed."

"Oh, I can recognize him," Susan said dryly. "I'm just not sure what I want to do with him."

"So you admit David is Mr. Right?"

"He could be. But neither of us is going anywhere, Candy. What's the rush?"

Candy snorted and rolled her eyes at the ceiling. "I keep forgetting you're still on the right side of thirty. Just wait'll you're staring fifty in the eye, and you won't have to ask that question."

"No, really. David's a special man, and I like him a lot. But this time I have to be absolutely sure I'm doing the right thing for me and the boys."

"How will you know that? Men don't come with money-back guarantees. At some point you're going to have to make a leap of faith and trust him."

"I'm thinking about it, all right?"

"That's better than your old no-way-in-hell attitude, I guess."

"I'm glad you approve. It's the best I can do for now."

Candy pushed back her chair and stood. "Okay. I get the message. But you'd better remember one thing, Susan."

"What's that?"

"David Hunter's a go-getter if I've ever met one. Guys like him tend to be short on patience. Think about what your life would be like without him."

Without waiting for a reply, Candy walked out the back door. Susan stared after her for a long moment and shook her head. If she got one more piece of advice about handling David, she'd...she'd...well, whatever it was she'd do, it wouldn't be pretty. Still, she had to admit, Candy might have a point. It was awfully nice having David around the house, sharing meals and jokes. She would miss him when he went home tomorrow. A lot.

David awoke to the happy voices of the Millers outside the bedroom window. "Go get it, Sheba," Timmy yelled. "Atta girl. Now, bring it here."

"Here, Sheba. Here, girl," Eric chanted.

"Give her a minute to catch her breath, Eric," Susan said with a laugh.

Wondering whether she was laughing at the pup or at Eric, David glanced at the clock radio beside the bed. Good Lord, it couldn't be eleven-fifteen. Susan must think he was a real slug. Of course, she didn't know he'd stayed up until almost four, watching old movies on his TV with the earphones because he was suffering massive hug attacks.

Having her so close and yet so untouchable, was... Well, it was just a damn good thing he'd be back in his own house by tomorrow or he'd blow any chance he might have with her for sure. The thought of going home depressed the hell out of him, but the thought of driving Susan completely away with his impatience gave him cold sweats.

David sat up in bed, scratched his chest and decided to get up. Since he was going home tomorrow, he might as well get dressed by himself today. That should convince Susan he was ready for independence.

He swung his left leg to the side of the bed, grabbed his crutches and hobbled into the bathroom. His knee still hurt some when he moved around, but either it was getting better or he was getting used to pain. There was no way he could get his cast guard on by himself—he'd tried that last night about two—but a spit bath would do until Jason could help him tomorrow.

Studying his face in the mirror, David wondered how Susan felt about men with beards. If he left his whiskers alone, he'd have a pretty decent growth in another week. But the hairs were so darn wiry, even when they were grown out.... Nah, if he ever got as close to Susan as he wanted to, he wouldn't risk tearing up her soft skin.

He lathered his face and, balancing on his good leg, managed to shave without slicing open his jugular vein or hacking up his chin. Spurred on by that small success, he brushed his teeth and went back to the bedroom for some clothes. He sat on the edge of the bed and hooked the waistband of his sweatpants over the toes of his left foot on the third try.

With a few contortions, he got his right foot inside, as well, and yanked them up around his waist, cursing mildly when he realized they were on backward. Oh, what the hell. He'd wear them that way for today. His sweatshirt would cover the drawstring. He put a sock and sneaker on his right foot and left his other foot bare.

Susan and the boys were still outside playing with Sheba when David hobbled into the kitchen. His stomach growled, and he decided it was time to show Susan he could feed himself, too. Moving carefully on the tile floor, he collected bacon and eggs from the refrigerator, a skillet from the cabinet next to the stove and bread from the bread box.

Women were such worrywarts, he thought smugly as he drained the bacon on a paper towel and broke the eggs into the pan. Ignoring the inevitable fatigue from standing up for so long, he buttered his toast and carried it to the table. By the time he made it back to the stove, his eggs were ready to turn.

David flipped them over, ferried some silverware and a napkin to the table and returned to the stove. He found a stoneware plate in the cupboard, scooped the eggs onto it, sprinkled on some salt and pepper, slapped the bacon beside them and finally rested for a moment. Then he picked up the plate between his right thumb and forefinger.

Straining to keep the plate level, he wrapped the other three fingers around the handgrip on his crutch and swung himself forward. His breakfast tilted dangerously to one side, and the food slid to the rim, but he managed to steady it. Damn. This was harder than he'd thought it would be.

He took a deep breath and tried a second step. So far, so good. On the third step, however, the plate's weight made his thumb and forefinger tremble. Knowing he needed to get to the table fast, he hurried the fourth step. The muscles in his hand cramped and went into a spasm.

The plate slipped from his grasp, landing with a crash when the stoneware shattered on impact. David glared at the disgusting pile of glass shards and exploded egg yolks, counted to ten, then sighed and hobbled back to the counter for the roll of paper towels. Why in the hell hadn't he left well enough alone and eaten standing up by the stove?

"Because you just had to show off for Susan, you dumb ass," he muttered, carefully lowering himself to the floor beside the mess. "If she catches you before you get this out of sight, she'll have *loads* of confidence in you."

The back door swung open at that precise moment, and Sheba galloped into the kitchen. While David tried to bat her away from the glass, Timmy, Eric and Susan entered the room. Timmy grabbed the pup. Eric halted dead in his tracks and stared in astonishment. Susan rushed over to David and knelt down beside him.

"Did you fall?" She asked anxiously. "Are you hurt anywhere?"

Frustrated to his toenails, David felt his neck and ears heat up. "Nah, just my pride. I, uh, had a little accident with my breakfast. Would you mind bringing the garbage can over here so I can clean it up?"

Susan turned to the boys. "Why don't you guys take Sheba to your room for a while so she doesn't get glass in her paws?"

"Okay, Mom," they answered in unison and trotted out of the room.

After getting the garbage can from under the sink, Susan sat down next to David. "Why didn't you call me?"

He shrugged and swiped at the mess with a handful of paper towels. "You were busy. I thought I could do it myself."

"You know, you don't have to go home tomorrow," she said. "Has it been that bad staying here?"

"Of course not. You and the boys have been great. But I've imposed enough."

Susan shook her head at him and stroked his hair back off his forehead, the same way she did when she soothed Eric and Timmy's ruffled feelings. David smiled to himself. Damned if it didn't soothe him, too.

"You're not imposing. Without you, I'd probably have an only child," she said in a firm, no-nonsense tone that made him smile even more. "If Rita will bring you lunch, there's no reason you can't stay here until your cast comes off. It's only three more weeks."

David took her hand and pressed its palm against his cheek. "There's one problem with that, Susan."

Her eyes widened at his action, but she didn't pull away. "Oh? What's that?"

"Whenever I'm around you, I keep having hug attacks. Really bad ones."

"Are you having one now?" she asked, moving closer with a smile that sizzled clear down to his groin.

"Yeah." His voice sounded so husky, he cleared his throat. "A kiss attack, too. It's pretty fierce."

Susan pursed her lips slightly, but the smile remained. She looped her arms around his neck and rested her forehead against his. "Well, maybe we should do something about it."

His pulse rate kicked into overdrive, and he laced his fingers together behind her waist. "What did you have in mind?"

Instead of answering, she tipped her head to one side and brushed her mouth across his. David closed his eyes and gave himself up to her gentle teasing, fighting an immediate, insistent urge to crush her against him and deepen the kiss. She rewarded him for his patience by leaning closer until the tips of her breasts touched his chest. Her hands framed his face, and her tongue darted out and skittered across his lower lip.

Moving his hands over her back, he let out a soft moan of delight and opened his mouth in invitation. She accepted it eagerly, even hungrily, her tongue tasting of coffee and something sweet as it stroked his. His arms closed convulsively around her, and he felt her heart pounding against his.

Much, much too soon, Susan pulled back, her breathing every bit as ragged as his own. Though it was the last thing he wanted to do, David slackened his hold on her and opened his eyes to find her gazing back at him with a dazed expression. He braced himself for her emotional withdrawal, that look of regret and self-recrimination she always had whenever he overstepped her invisible boundaries and got too close.

This time, thank God, it didn't happen. Her pretty hazel eyes gradually focused and then lighted up with a smile to match the one curving her delectable lips.

"Still want me to stay?" he whispered.

"Yeah. As long as we don't do this too often."

"I kinda liked it," he said, making the understatement of his life.

"So did I," she admitted, grinning at him, "but let's not get carried away."

David didn't even try to argue. He felt too exultant over her change in attitude to do anything that might spoil the moment. She scrambled to her feet, picked up his crutches and offered a hand to help him up.

"It's my mess," he protested. "I'll clean it up."

"Tell you what. Let me take care of this one so I can feed you breakfast and the boys lunch. After you're back on your feet, I'll phone you the first time I have another one like it and you can pay me back. Deal?"

Chuckling, David agreed. Using a crutch on one side and Susan's hand on the other for balance, he pulled himself upright and took a seat at the table. Susan brought him a cup of coffee and a doughnut to tide him over until she could cook him another breakfast, then went to work with that quick, amazing efficiency he'd come to admire.

In what seemed like mere seconds, she set a steaming plate of bacon and eggs in front of him and called the boys to the kitchen. David enjoyed their chattering immensely, thinking, *This is what having a family feels like.* He loathed the idea of going back to the bedroom when the meal was over, and Susan set up a lawn chair for him in the backyard, where he spent half an hour tossing around a child-sized football with Timmy and Eric.

The weak October sunshine barely offset a brisk, chilly breeze, but it felt wonderful to see the sky again. Sheba ran back and forth between David and the boys, yapping to let them know she wanted to play, too. He glanced up and saw Susan watching them from the kitchen window, a wistful little smile on her face.

She waved, and David returned the gesture, wishing she would join them and complete the family circle the way she had at lunch. As if she had read his mind, Susan stepped outside a minute later, carrying his navy blue windbreaker over her arm. She gave him his jacket, then participated in the game for another thirty minutes.

He loved watching her enthusiastic, encouraging responses to her sons. He loved hearing her laughter. He loved her teasing and uninhibited pleasure in such a simple activity. He just plain loved her. It was a golden moment, one of those brief, harmonious stretches of time that can't be planned, but will always be remembered with a deep sense of contentment. David savored every second of it.

He nearly protested when she looked at her watch and announced it was time for the weekly trip to the grocery store, but realized she had other things to do besides entertain him. Besides, much as he hated to admit it, he felt ready for a nap. They all trooped inside, and David went into the bedroom.

The house felt like a morgue when the Millers left. David settled back against the pillows and laughed when Sheba jumped onto the bed and curled up at his side without an invitation, as if she knew he needed company. Susan probably wouldn't approve, David thought with a guilty grin, but he let the pup stay, anyway.

Stroking her soft fur, he closed his eyes and exhaled a tired sigh. Unfortunately he couldn't sleep. A subtle yet thoroughly aggravating itching sensation traveled from the center of his cast toward both ends. It didn't help knowing the problem came from his healing incision and his leg hair growing out—he still couldn't get at it for a satisfying scratch.

He glanced at the television, but dismissed it immediately. The Broncos were playing the Raiders on "Monday Night Football" this week, and he'd watched too much TV in the past few days to drum up much interest in anything else. He'd already read everything within reach and he didn't feel like getting up and going out to the living room.

Then his gaze landed on Susan's neatly stacked manuscript to the right of her typewriter. Was she a good writer? he wondered. Although his mother certainly thought Susan had talent, David realized he knew nothing about her hobby.

He'd seen her pour hours of concentration into her current project, and she seemed to enjoy the process of writing, but he didn't have the faintest idea what her book was about.

If he scooted down to the foot of the bed, he could reach her desk with one step. He wouldn't even need his crutches. The idea tempted him but his conscience and previous experience advised against such a move. His mother had scolded him furiously more than once for reading her columns before they were finished. Of course, that hadn't stopped him from doing it again whenever his curiousity got the better of him.

Was Susan that sensitive about her work? Probably. Shaking his head at the insanity of what he was contemplating, David lay back and firmly told himself to sleep. But the itch intensified, and his boredom increased with each passing moment. He opened his eyes, and the manuscript silently called to him like a mythical siren coaxing an ancient mariner toward the rocks.

Promising himself he would only read a few pages, David gave in, grabbed the whole thing and scooted back to his pillows. Sheba gave him a dirty look and woofed, as if complaining about his jostling her out of a nap. He petted her in apology, his eyes already scanning the first page.

By the time he finished the second page, he was so hooked by the main character, Abby Marshall, and her unexpected discovery of a body in her car, there was no turning back. He forgot his itchy leg, forgot Sheba, forgot to listen for the Millers' return. He might have heard a door open and shut, the sound of feet pounding in and out of the house and Sheba's whine of welcome, but they were too far away from the unrelenting action in the story to distract him.

Suddenly a pair of hands flashed before his eyes and snatched the stack of paper from his lap. "Hey," he protested, automatically reaching for it, only to find himself face-to-face with Susan. A stiff, red-faced, enraged Susan.

"Oh. You're back." He attempted a smile, but judging from her furious expression, he figured it was pretty sickly.

"Yeah, I'm back." She grabbed the pages he'd already finished and smacked them on top of the others, then slammed them on her desk. Propping her hands on her hips, she turned back to him. "You've got a lot of damn gall, David Hunter. I never said you could read my manuscript.'

"You didn't say I couldn't."

"You didn't ask."

He looked down at his hands and sighed. "I know. And I know I should have, but—"

"Damn right, you should have."

"I'm sorry, Susan." He glanced up at her, trying for a pitiful expression.

"Don't give me that sad-puppy look. It's cute on Sheba, but not on you. And what's she doing on my bed?"

At the sound of her name spoken in such an angry tone, the pup raised her head and whined softly. David petted her until she flopped back down.

"I was lonesome and bored. And I didn't have anything in here to read."

"And that makes it okay for you to invade my privacy?"

"No, of course it doesn't. But don't be mad at me. It's the best thing I've read in five years."

"Oh, please. Spare me the flattery."

David sat up straighter and looked her right in the eye. "I'm not trying to flatter you, Susan. It's great." He gestured toward the suspense novel lying on the nightstand he'd finished the day before. "It's a helluva lot better than that one. Which publisher are you going to send it to?

"I'm not."

After what he'd just read, her flat statement appalled him. "You can't be serious. It's got bestseller written all over it."

"I'm dead serious. When I finish it, it can keep all the others out in the garage company."

"You've got others? In the garage?" David shook his head, certain he couldn't have heard her correctly. "If the rest of them are as good as this one, you could make big bucks!"

Susan snorted with laughter, the saddest, most derisive laughter David had ever heard. "Get real, Hunter. I haven't even finished college. People like me don't write best-sellers."

"If they can write like you do, I don't know why the hell not," he insisted.

Her expression softened. "Look, David, I'm sure you mean well, but—"

"Sit down, will ya? I don't understand this at all, and I'm getting a crick in my neck looking up at you. Now, why haven't you been submitting your books for publication?"

Studying him intently, as if she couldn't quite believe he was serious, Susan perched on the side of the bed. "I did submit them at first," she said quietly, lacing her fingers together over one knee. "In fact, I sent the first three everywhere I could think of, but all I got was a stack of re-jection letters a foot high."

"Lots of writers go through that. Mom says the ones who get published are the ones who stick with it."

"I'm sure that's true, but some people try for years and never get published. I can't afford the luxury of chasing something that's probably a pipe dream. I have to be prac-tical."

David wanted to shake her. "What's practical about wasting your talent? And why the hell are you slogging away at a nine-to-five bank job?"

"It pays the bills. Besides, I won't be working at the bank much longer.

"What are you going to do?"

"Get a degree in elementary education. I've been taking every class I can here in Cheyenne. If I'm really careful, I'll have enough money saved to commute to Laramie next fall and finish up in the spring."

"I didn't know you wanted to be a teacher."

"I think I'll enjoy it. The hours will be great for me and the boys, and the pay and benefits are better than what I've got now."

"If that's why you're going into teaching, it'll drive you crazy in six months."

"It will not. I love kids."

"In large herds? Like thirty of them in one room all day long?"

Susan shrugged. "I don't know why not."

"I'll tell you why not." David shook his head at her. "I know you've been writing at least since high school, and you're still doing it. I'll bet you've always wanted to be a writer. Haven't you?"

"Yes. I have." She threw up her hands in frustration and glared at him. "I used to dream about seeing my name on the cover of a book. Just like I used to dream about getting married and having kids and living happily ever after. So what? There comes a time when you have to stop dreaming and live in the real world, David. Most writers make less than ten thousand dollars a year. How am I going to support myself and two kids on that?"

"Dammit, Susan, you've got a wonderful, devious imagination and a writing style that's clean and fresh. Your characters grabbed me by the throat by page two, and I'm dying to know how your book will end. I read tons of fiction, and I'm telling you, you're good enough to make a living at this. A better living than you'll ever earn as a teacher."

"It's too risky, and I've had more than enough rejection to last me a lifetime." She jumped off the bed and stalked over to the doorway. "It's a nice dream, but I can't afford it."

"Okay, you don't want to take my word for it? I can understand that. Let my mom take a look when she gets home. She's got an agent, and—"

"No. I don't want to hear another word about this. I have to go start dinner."

David cursed under his breath when she disappeared around the door casing. What was the matter with that stubborn, crazy woman? She probably had thousands of dollars' worth of advances sitting in her garage and she didn't believe in her work enough to send it out? Or was it that she didn't believe in herself? Or in dreams?

She'd compared her writing to getting married and living happily ever after. If she'd given up on one dream, did that mean she'd given up on the other, too? Permanently? That idea jolted him right down to his soul.

Well, he'd just have to see about that. He grabbed the phone from the nightstand and dialed Jason's number.

Chapter Eleven

Susan's heart lurched when she came home from work the next day and saw Jason's Blazer and a huge black Cadillac, the kind funeral directors and television mobsters drive, parked in front of her house. Hoping nothing had happened to David, she rushed the boys inside.

Jason greeted her at the door with a hug and took her coat and purse. Melody poked her nose out of the kitchen and asked Susan how she wanted her steak cooked. With a smug yet excited grin on his handsome face, David sat on the sofa, his cast propped up on a stack of magazines on the coffee table.

He patted the cushion beside him in invitation. Susan gave him a confused smile and turned toward the kitchen to help Melody with dinner and find out what in the world was going on. Jason bluntly informed her that her services were not needed or wanted and told her to "Git on outta here." Feeling as if she'd walked into the wrong house, Susan obeyed his order.

His grin even broader now, David patted the cushion again. Susan shook her head and said, "I'll be right there as soon as I change my clothes." She hurried to her bedroom, opened the door and gasped. A brand-new computer system sporting a huge red bow sat in her old typewriter's place in the middle of her desk.

Mystified, she walked farther into the room, barely hearing the rhythmic thuds of David's crutches moving down the hallway. She reached out hesitantly, then ran her fingertips over the keyboard. A template card surrounding the function keys told her the software was the same brand she used at work.

"What do you think of it?"

Susan started at the sound of David's deep voice coming from right behind her. She whirled around to face him and nearly knocked him over.

Steadying himself, he said, "Hey, take it easy." Nodding at the computer, he rephrased his question. "Do you like it?"

"Of course I do." She glanced at the machine before looking back at David. "But what's it doing here?"

"It's a present, Miller. From me. Didn't anybody ever give you one before?"

"Why did you do this?"

David leaned over and switched on the computer. It set up a soft hum, and, after a few seconds, green letters flashed onto the monitor screen, listing a menu of available options. "Because you deserve it for taking such good care of me. And because you need it to finish your book before I go crazy wondering what's going to happen next."

"It's gorgeous," she murmured. Then she sighed and said firmly, "But I can't accept it."

"Sure, you can." He poked several keys, and the first page of Susan's manuscript appeared as if by magic.

"How did *that* get in there?" she demanded, propping her fists on her hips.

"Rita typed in the first forty pages today. She said to tell you she'll finish the rest later, and that she put each chapter in a separate file so you can just start right in wherever you want. She's as anxious as I am to find out how it ends, by the way."

Susan closed her eyes and inhaled a shaky breath. "I can't accept it David. You'll have to send it back."

"Nope." He turned away from the machine and cupped her cheek with his palm. "I can't do that. It's already been used."

"You have to. It's too expensive and..." She looked down at her shoes. "I don't want it."

"Don't fib, honey," he chided softly, caressing her temple with the backs of his fingers. "You're a writer. This will make your work so much easier, of course you want it. If the expense bothers you that much, you can pay me back out of your first royalty check."

She finally met his gaze and felt her knees go mushy at the warm, loving expression in those big brown eyes of his. When she tried to speak, her voice came out in a husky whisper. "Do you really believe in the book that much?"

Nodding, he lowered his voice to match hers. "I believe in *you* that much."

"What if I still refuse to submit it? Even if I do, there might not be any royalty checks. What if I can't afford to pay you back?"

He shrugged. "I can afford it. The computer's yours whatever you decide, whatever happens. I just want you to have it. Okay?"

Yes, she did want it, Susan admitted to herself. She wasn't sure why David was so determined to give her the computer, but his sincerity melted the last of her resistance. Her throat too tight to utter more than a squeak, she nodded.

"That's my girl."

His delighted smile reminded her of Timmy and Eric on Christmas morning. She felt humbled by his gift, and unutterably touched by the happiness her acceptance of it had obviously given him.

"Thank you," she murmured in a choked voice.

Going up on her tiptoes, she quickly kissed his lips. David dropped a crutch and wrapped his arm around her waist, pulling her close. Susan closed her eyes in anticipation as he lowered his head, then opened them with a start when Jason's voice boomed down the hallway.

"Chow's on! Come and get it while it's hot."

She exchanged a sheepish grin with David, handed him his crutch and turned off the computer. She followed him out of the room, pausing only an instant at the doorway for one last loving glance at that marvelous machine sitting on her desk.

Dinner was a riotous affair. Jason kept everyone giggling by pretending he was a snooty waiter. The prime T-bone steaks had come from Lazy W cattle and were cooked to perfection, although the boys insisted that Jason take their meat back outside to the barbecue and get rid of that "yucky bloody stuff" in the middle. He responded to their criticism by acting even snootier, which made everyone laugh harder.

"You guys are in for it now," Melody warned when the back door closed behind her husband.

"Naw," Eric said, "he's not really mad at us."

Melody leaned closer and lowered her voice to a stage whisper. "Oh, he's not mad, but he's a terrible cook. I'm afraid he'll incinerate it and bring you back a plate of charcoal."

"Hasn't he gotten any better about that?" David asked.

She smiled as if at a fond memory. "Not much, but the microwave has helped some."

David chuckled, then patted his sister's hand in commiseration. "Thanks for bringing the car in."

"Is that yours?" Susan asked in surprise, remembering the black Cadillac parked out front.

"It belonged to Jason's dad. When he died, Jason couldn't bear to sell it. It's been stored in a shed ever since," Melody explained. "We thought it would be big enough to make hauling David around easier for you."

"And they were right," David added. "I can sit in the back seat like King Tut and tell you where I want to go."

"Yeah, well, you'd better tell me nicely, or I might just tell *you* where to go, bub," Susan informed him with a sassy grin.

Jason came back in with a flourish then. Much to the boys' relief, he hadn't incinerated their meat. From the amount of chewing it required them to eat it, however, Susan guessed it had been a close call. The laughter and teasing continued throughout the meal. The Wakefields treated Eric and Timmy as if they were favorite nephews, and David's affection for them couldn't have been any more blatant as he helped them cut their meat and butter their baked potatoes.

We could all be a family, Susan thought wistfully, letting her gaze roam from one person to the next. The kind of family she'd always wanted for herself as a child. The kind she wished she could provide for her sons now. The little devils were certainly enjoying the extra attention.

Eric interrupted her train of thought by spilling his milk. Susan rushed to get the dishrag, but the warm feelings lingered. The Wakefields had to leave when they'd finished eating because Melody needed to study for an exam the next morning. Susan waved away their apologies for leaving her with the dishes, walked them to the door, then went into her bedroom and changed into jeans and a sweater.

She pushed up her sleeves and hurried back to the kitchen, but David blocked her entry. She peeked around him and saw both boys carefully carrying dirty plates from the table to the sink.

"Excuse me," she said, turning sideways as though she would walk past him if he'd only move a few inches.

"Nope." He rested his weight on his crutches and used both hands to turn her around. "You've got the night off to play with your new toy."

She twisted her head and frowned at him over her shoulder. "But the dishes—"

"I can handle them. Go write."

"Not until the boys go to bed," she argued, pulling out of his grasp and pivoting to face him.

David turned her right back around. "I'll play with them, supervise their baths and read to them. You can take a five-minute break to tuck them in bed."

His offer was tempting, but his dictatorial attitude set her teeth on edge. "You don't have to do this," she said, shooting him another frown.

"No, I don't *have* to," he agreed with an easy smile. "I want to. You've been taking care of everybody else for a long time. Now it's time to take care of your own needs for a change."

"Don't be silly. I don't mind taking care of you or my kids," she grumbled.

"We know that." He massaged her shoulders as naturally as if he'd done it every night for years. "But let us feel useful, okay? Go write. Sleep. Take a hot shower. We don't care what you do, as long as it's something just for you."

Susan tipped her head way back and looked up at him. His hands stilled. He leaned down and dropped a sweet, quick kiss on her forehead.

"Please?" he murmured, beguiling her with his deep voice and one of those puppy-dog looks she couldn't resist for long no matter how angry she was with him. "Do it for me?"

"May I have a cup of coffee to take with me?"

"You bet."

"All right. But just for tonight."

He didn't respond to that, but finally let her into the kitchen. She poured herself a cup of coffee, complimented the boys on what a good job they were doing and hurried off to the bedroom when David playfully threatened to whack her with a crutch if she didn't get away from that dishwasher.

Her heart surged with a giddy, joyful sensation as she sat down at the computer. She ran her fingertips gingerly over the keyboard, feeling too excited and overwhelmed to start working just yet. Nobody had ever given her such an expensive or thoughtful gift before. Or cared so much about pleasing her. Or worried about whether her needs were being met.

She reached for her manuscript, and the normal family noises gradually faded from her consciousness as she drifted into the world of her imagination.

Even though she'd used this software program for almost a year at the bank, Susan was amazed at how quickly the pages counted up. No stopping for typos. No stopping to put in a fresh sheet of paper. No waiting for the carriage return. Just freedom. Glorious freedom to let the words flow from her mind onto the monitor screen as fast as her fingers could type them.

It was misery to leave it, even for a few minutes, to tuck the boys in. David came in at eleven o'clock to tell her it was time to quit and unwind so she could get some sleep. Susan knew he was right. She'd accomplished more than enough for one night—at least double what she normally produced—but he still practically had to pry her fingers off the keyboard and drag her away.

He led her into the living room, seated her on the sofa and handed her a glass of blush wine. Suddenly feeling exhausted, Susan sipped the tangy liquid and laid her head back against the cushion. David sat close beside her, propping his leg up on the coffee table. He leaned forward and put some magazines in front of her, then reached down, slipped off her shoes and lifted her feet onto the table beside his cast.

"Who is supposed to be taking care of whom here?" she asked, raising an eyebrow at him.

David laid his arm across the top of the sofa behind her and picked up his wineglass. "Does it really matter? How'd it go in there tonight?"

"It was wonderful," she answered, turning her head to smile at him. "Absolutely wonderful. I can't thank you enough."

"You already have. So, what did Abby do about the threatening letter she got in chapter six?"

"You read the rest of the manuscript? After I yelled at you like that yesterday?"

"Damn right. Didn't you notice I could hardly wait for you to go to bed last night?"

"I thought you were mad at me." She punched his arm affectionately. "You must have been a curious little brat when you were a kid."

"That's what my mom always said. What did Abby do?"

"You can read it tomorrow after I go to work. Just remember this is rough draft, okay?"

"Okay."

They sipped in a comfortable silence until they finished their wine. Then David set their empty glasses on the table. "Hey, Miller," he said, stroking her hair, "I'm having a terrible hug attack."

She turned into his embrace and laid her head on his chest. "That's amazing. Me, too."

His arms enfolded her. His left hand massaged her neck and spine. She rubbed her cheek against the softness of his favorite blue sweatshirt. His heart set up a pleasant, steady thumping beneath her ear. She closed her eyes and inhaled the now-familiar scent of his after-shave. Realizing she hadn't felt this warm, safe and secure in years, she exhaled a heartfelt sigh.

"What was that for?" he asked.

Susan tilted her head back and smiled at him. "I was just thinking you're too good to be real."

"Oh, I'm real, all right." A deep laugh rumbled out of his chest, and he gave her a wicked grin. "But you don't even know how good I *can* be, honey. Yet."

"I mean it, David," she said, poking him in the ribs with her index finger. "How'd you learn to be so thoughtful?"

He squeezed her tighter and rested his cheek against the top of her head. "From my mom, I guess. Maybe from Mel. But with you, it just seems to come naturally for me."

Susan snuggled closer and wrapped her arms around his torso. His heart thumped louder for a moment, then settled back to its normal rhythm.

"Hey, Hunter," she said.

"What?"

"I think I'm about to have a terrible kiss attack."

He tilted her chin up with an index finger and gazed steadily into her eyes, his own eyes sparkling with laughter. "Now, isn't that a coincidence? I was just thinking the same thing. Maybe we're psychic, telepathic—"

"Shut up and kiss me."

"Yes, ma'am. Anything you say."

On a scale from one to ten, Susan would have to rate David's kisses at least a twelve. It wasn't that he did anything particularly different from other men she'd kissed. Oh, he knew what he was doing, all right, but it involved more than which way he tipped his head or how hard he pressed his lips against hers or what he did with his tongue.

He was infinitely gentle, yet she sensed a rigidly leashed passion in him that intrigued, even tempted her to find out if she could make him *un*leash it. He made soft, hungry little noises in his throat that made her feel...well, like a rich, chocolate morsel, the kind you hold on your tongue for as long as possible and savor long after it melts. And his timing...Lord, he could teach Fred Astaire a thing or two about timing.

He kissed as if words such as *hurry* or *impatience* didn't exist, as if kissing her was the only thing on his mind, the only thing that mattered in his universe. He whispered her name between kisses in a husky, aching tone that made her want to give him all that she had, all that she was. With him, she felt unique, cherished and sexy as hell.

She could have gone on kissing him just like this for hours, and yet deep inside she felt itchy and needy and urgent. Whimpering softly, she plunged her fingers into his thick, glossy hair and rubbed herself against his chest, trying to tell him without words that she wanted more of him.

His breathing quickened, his tongue stroked more insistently into her mouth, his palms roved slowly over her back and hips and sides. She shifted, silently begging him to touch her more intimately. His hand moved up her torso and cupped her breast, massaging, caressing, intensifying all the other sensations and emotions already raging within her.

Her head fell back, and she sighed with pleasure. He traced the arched line of her throat with sweet, nibbling kisses that raised goose flesh on her arms and legs one instant, and sent flashes of heat to her fingers and toes the next. Then her arms wrapped around his neck, her mouth sought and found his, and she slid backward to lie flat on the sofa, pulling him down with her.

Groaning, he followed her lead, blocking out the soft lamplight with his broad shoulders. Her hands crept inside the neckline of his sweatshirt, delighting in the warmth of his skin, the smooth, hard contours of his muscles.

She heard a muffled thud and felt David jerk out of her arms. Blinking in surprise, she sat up, then gasped when she saw his face contorted with agony. That thud must have been his left foot slipping off the edge of the coffee table. Good lord, it must have jarred his whole leg.

"How bad is it?" she asked anxiously, struggling to get both of her feet on the floor.

"Don't know," he muttered, clenching his teeth and sucking in short, choppy breaths. "Hurts . . . like . . . hell."

Susan raced around the rectangular table and carefully helped him lift his leg back up. "Did you feel anything tear loose in there? Do you need a pain pill?"

David shook his head. Gradually his breathing evened out and he was able to talk normally. "Let's give it a minute. It's getting better."

"Should I call the doctor?"

"I don't think so. That's why they put a cast on it in the first place." He gave her a crooked smile. "Come on and sit down. You look a little green around the gills."

She felt that way, too, Susan realized. Her knees were shaking so hard, they threatened to give out, but she made it to the sofa before they did. The seat cushions were still warm, and a wave of guilt washed over her. He'd given her such pleasure and received such pain in return.

"I'm sorry, David," she said, brushing back the hair her questing fingers had tumbled onto his forehead.

He raised both eyebrows in surprise. "What for? It wasn't your fault I forgot about my stupid leg." Then he took her hand in his and gave her a devastatingly wicked grin. "Well, that *was* your fault, but I'm not blaming you. I've never had so much fun necking on a couch before."

Susan felt her neck and cheeks grow warm, but refused to give him the satisfaction of looking away. "I haven't, either," she admitted. "You're quite a kisser, Hunter."

"You're pretty hot stuff yourself, Miller." He waggled his eyebrows at her. "Want to see if we can remember where we left off?"

She laughed, half in relief, half in exasperation that he could make light of something that had scared the whey out of her. "You *must* be feeling better. But I think we've had enough excitement for one night. Besides, it's getting late, and we both have to work tomorrow. We've only got three weeks before Melissa's dance."

"I guess you're right," he agreed reluctantly. Then he leaned over and gave her a quick, smacking kiss on her lips. "But we'll have to do it again soon. Real soon."

"We'll see," she said noncommittally. Of course, there wasn't a doubt in her mind that they would do it again at the first opportunity. But for the moment, they needed a time-out.

Ignoring his short of laughter, she handed David his crutches and followed him down the hallway to help him get settled. She turned down the bed and gathered up her things for the night while he was in the bathroom. He looked surprised to find her waiting for him when he came out, and she realized he didn't need her to tuck him in the way Eric and Timmy did. Well, tough. Maybe she needed to tuck him in after he'd been hurt like that.

David stripped down to his shorts without comment and got into the bed. Susan pulled the covers up for him and wished she hadn't noticed there was plenty of room for her beside him. He opened his mouth as if he wanted to say something, hesitated, then closed it again.

"Are you sure you don't need a pain pill?" she asked, moving away to turn out the overhead light before temptation got the better of her.

"I'm fine," he assured her. "Sweet dreams, Susan."

"You, too."

The sofa bed had never seemed quite this lumpy before, Susan thought after twenty minutes of flopping around in a vain search for a comfortable position. She punched her pillow in frustration and finally sat up, pulling her knees close to her chest. The bed wasn't the problem. David was.

If he hadn't hurt himself tonight, she would have made love with him. Despite all of her painful experiences with men, all of her warnings to herself, all of her fears for the boys' future and her own, she would have done it and reveled in every second of the experience. And she didn't even know that he felt anything toward her but lust and gratitude for taking care of him.

That was an admittedly cynical view of the situaton, especially when she thought of the wonderful gift he'd given her and the caring he'd shown her tonight. Ed had never been so considerate and neither had anyone else. Besides, David hadn't started that necking session. She had.

The truth robbed her of sleep. The cynicism she usually protected herself with didn't apply to David. She could have handled their sizzling physical attraction to each other, if that was all there was between them. But he was so warm and giving and fun to be with, she couldn't dismiss him that easily.

In fact, she didn't want to dismiss him at all. No, she wanted to make love with him so badly, her body ached with need. But she wanted to sleep in the security of his arms all night and wake up with him every morning, too. She wanted to know he would always sit at her table and praise her cooking and make her sons giggle with his corny jokes. She wanted to go on watching his eyes light up with pleasure when she walked into the room, hearing him demand the next chapter in her book, having him tell her he believed in her enough to go out and buy a computer system worth thousands of dollars.

She put her hands over her face and exhaled a ragged sigh. "Oh, Susan, you poor damn fool," she whispered. "Now you've done it. You've gone and fallen in love with him."

For the next three days Susan's emotions seesawed as wildly as a teenager's. If it had been a different time of the month, she'd have sworn she had a terminal case of PMS. But as time passed and her relationship with David grew steadily closer and more intimate, a stubborn little seed of hope took root in her heart. Maybe, just maybe, this time would be different.

Suddenly everything started to go right. Susan received a bigger raise than she'd expected at her annual salary review. Donations poured into Melissa Reed's account at the bank in response to David's public-service announcements, and the plans for the benefit dance progressed on schedule. David started going to the station half days, and seemed pleased with the way the staff had carried on in his absence.

Her home life took on a rosy glow for the next two weeks, as well. David would sit in the kitchen and fold laundry or chop vegetables for her while she cooked dinner, eager to hear about her day and tell her about his. Timmy and Eric clearly adored him and insisted on doing the dinner dishes with him every night while she worked at the computer. Even Sheba got into the act by learning to bark at the back door when she needed to go out. When the boys went to bed and Susan finished writing, she and David would sit on the sofa and talk, kiss and simply enjoy each other's company.

They were establishing a mundane, domestic routine, but it didn't feel mundane to Susan. This was the kind of family life, the kind of relationship with a man, she'd always wanted. She feared it wouldn't last, prayed that it would and did her best to put thoughts of the future out of her mind.

Then, after Timmy and Eric were tucked in bed on the Monday night before the big dance, Ed phoned. The mere sound of her ex-husband's voice darkened Susan's good spirits, but she managed to keep her cool during the conversation. Though she dreaded the emotional upheaval that trips to their father's house usually provoked, she agreed to let the boys spend the next weekend with him and promised to have them ready by five-thirty on Friday.

She tried to resume a cheerful expression when she rejoined David, but he took one look at her face and asked, "What's wrong, honey?"

After she had explained the gist of the conversation, Susan sighed and shook her head. "I'm probably making the proverbial mountain out of a molehill. It'll be nice having the boys out of the way while we're setting up for the dance, but I worry about them when they're with Ed."

"Why? Won't he take good care of them?"

"He won't neglect them, exactly." She twisted a lock of hair around her index finger while she organized her thoughts. "I guess he forgets they're kids and treats them like short adults. He doesn't have much patience with them, and he doesn't seem to realize how much he hurts their feelings sometimes. He's convinced I'm spoiling them rotten."

"Timmy and Eric? Spoiled rotten?" David asked, raising his eyebrows as if in astonishment at the idea. "They're not little angels, but I've never met two nicer kids. The guy's nuts if he doesn't appreciate what a great job you've done with them."

At his immediate defense of her sons and her parenting, Susan threw her arms around David's neck and hugged him hard. It felt wonderful having someone so staunchly in her corner for a change. Still, she had to remember her problems with Ed shouldn't involve David.

Unfortunately there were bound to be problems. After the way Ed had reacted when he'd found out she was dating Jason, Susan hated to imagine what he would say when he learned about David. It was funny, in an ironic sort of way, that a man who had left his home and family for another woman should have such rigid moral standards for his ex-wife.

Pulling back and gazing into David's loving eyes, Susan promised herself that no matter what, she wouldn't let Ed spoil what she'd found with this wonderful man in her arms.

Chapter Twelve

Five-thirty came and went the next Friday night with no sign of Ed Miller. Since her ex-husband's phone call on Monday, Susan had grown increasingly edgy and withdrawn, and David couldn't help resenting the unusual tension invading the household. He found himself checking the living-room clock every two minutes, along with Susan, Timmy and Eric, and felt his instinctive dislike of the man grow every time he did it.

The boys had been elated to learn about their planned visit to Denver, but the tense, glum expressions now on their little faces told David they were expecting yet another in a long line of disappointments from their father. By six-fifteen, they quit buying their mother's repeated reassurances that Ed had probably just gotten a late start or had been held up in traffic. When he finally showed up at seven o'clock, David was ready to strangle the SOB.

Ed breezed into the house as if completely unaware that he'd kept four people anxiously waiting for an hour and a half. If the idea did occur to him, David seriously doubted it would bother the guy much. Reminding himself that he shouldn't do or say anything to make the situation more difficult for Susan, David sat back on the sofa, clamped his mouth shut and tried to study the man objectively.

It wasn't easy. Ed Miller stood about six feet tall and carried himself with an arrogant self-confidence that made him seem taller. His brown hair was artfully styled, and his casual, designer clothing and jewelry reeked of wealth and success.

David supposed he could see why Susan had fallen for the guy. He was certainly good-looking enough to attract a woman's attention. And, David also supposed, Ed did have a certain amount of charisma, if you happened to like his smarmy brand of charm. Which David didn't. Not even a little bit. Thank God the jerk wasn't around enough to have much influence over Timmy and Eric.

When Susan introduced the two men, David tolerated Ed's nastily raised eyebrow, which seemed to question his wisdom and morality for staying in her house. He even managed a civil reply and a brief handshake at the appropriate moment. But Ed's condescending attitude toward Susan really graveled David's drawers.

Just about the time David was seriously considering wrapping one of his crutches around the creep's neck, Ed picked up the boys' suitcase and ushered them to the door. Susan knelt down to collect goodbye hugs and kisses. Then she straightened up and faced her ex-husband with a calm dignity David marveled at.

"Don't forget the tubes in Eric's ears are out again. He's had the sniffles for two days, so if he complains about his ears hurting, you've got to get him to a doctor right away."

Ed shook his head at her, as if in disgust. "So you're still babying him about that. Kids get earaches all the time. If you're not careful, you'll turn them both into hypochondriacs."

Obviously struggling for patience, she said, "For God's sake, Ed. Do you want him to lose his hearing?"

"Calm down, Susan. I'll take care of the kids. I'm their father, after all." He opened the door and followed the boys out onto the front porch.

Susan stood in the doorway and called after him. "Yeah, well, just try to remember that."

"I'll have them back by five on Sunday."

David fumed and silently gnashed his teeth while Susan stood on the porch and waved until Ed's BMW drove away from the curb. But when she came back inside and he saw the stricken expression on her face, he pushed his fury aside and held his arms out to her.

"Don't be nice to me," she warned with a crooked grin, sitting beside him on the sofa, "or I'll cry all over you."

"So what?" He put his arm around her, loving it when she rested her head on his shoulder. "I'm not afraid of your tears. That was pretty rough on you."

She shrugged, then snuggled closer. "It always is. But maybe he's right. Maybe I shouldn't be so protective of the boys."

"They're still little. Seems to me somebody's got to protect them. When the time comes, you'll be able to let them go."

"You're good for my ego, Hunter."

He hugged her tightly, and they shared a companionable silence until David's stomach rumbled. They both laughed, and then Susan got up and headed for the kitchen. David grabbed his crutches and went after her.

"I've got a great idea," he announced from the doorway.

"What's that?"

"Let's go out to eat and catch a late movie."

Susan sighed and ran one hand through her hair. "I don't know, David. I'm worn-out and grumpy, and I don't feel like getting dressed up."

"You look fine for pizza and beer. It'll do us both good to get out of here for a while."

"I really should make some calls to the committee chairmen for the dance."

"They'll all be busy with their crews, so let 'em do their jobs. C'mon, Susan. It'll be our first real date."

She laughed at that and wrinkled her nose at him. "I hate first dates."

"Me, too. So let's hurry up and get it over with."

"Okay. But don't say I didn't warn you if I'm lousy company."

"Fair enough."

Fifteen minutes later they arrived at a pizza parlour on Lincolnway. David could tell Susan was trying hard to act cheerful, but as the evening wore on, she became quieter and more distracted. He guessed she was thinking about Timmy and Eric, wondering what they were doing now and how they were getting along with Ed. David didn't blame her. Shoot, he was doing exactly the same thing.

Though it was a critically acclaimed comedy they'd both been anxious to see, the movie didn't help much, either. By the time they got home, David had long since given up any idea of taking advantage of the boys' absence for a romantic tryst with Susan. She locked the front door and turned to him with an apologetic smile.

"I'm sorry, David. I just can't help worrying about them."

He reached out with one hand and massaged the back of her neck. "I understand. Want a glass of wine to help you sleep?"

"No, thanks. I'd rather go right to bed, if you don't mind."

David minded very much. He wanted to share her worries and comfort her if he could. Unfortunately he could see she was struggling to maintain her composure and finally decided to give her the privacy she so obviously craved. He bent down and kissed her cheek.

"All right, Susan. See you in the morning."

"Good night," she murmured, walking toward the living room's picture window.

He went to the hallway and looked back at her for a moment. She stood gazing out into the darkness, her narrow shoulders slumped, arms wrapped around her waist, looking lonely and lost and fragile. His arms aching to hold her instead of his damn crutches, David thumped down the short hall to the bedroom, fervently hoping Eric had gotten carsick and puked his little guts out all over the back seat of Ed's BMW.

The next morning Susan got out of bed and restored the sofa to its daytime position. Next, she went into the kitchen, started the coffee and mixed up some pancake batter. Today would be hectic for her and for David, but she was determined that it would be a good day for both of them. For Melissa Reed, she would concentrate on putting on the best darn dance Cheyenne had ever seen.

David came into the room five minutes later, looking sleepy but more relaxed and cheerful than he had the night before. They discussed last-minute details about the benefit while they ate breakfast, then took turns showering and getting dressed before driving to Frontier Park in Jason's big black Caddie.

Susan let David out close to the exhibition building's back door and went to park the car in the already crowded lot. She hurried inside and was immediately swept up in the jovial atmosphere. Volunteer crews filled the cavernous structure with the sounds of laughter, pounding hammers and shouted directions.

Teenage boys hauled in tables and chairs for the food booths. Teenage girls strung miles of crepe paper and set up gardens of paper flowers. Carpenters built temporary counters, and electricians worked on the wiring and lighting. Members of every women's organization in town carried in tons of food and enough Crockpots to fill a warehouse.

David's crew from KBOY set up the sound system and disc jockey's booth on a stage at the far end of the room, and television crews from as far away as Denver tested their equipment. Trucks from the local soft-drink companies and beer distributors arrived, and the finance committee huddled near the entrance going over the procedure for selling and taking tickets.

Susan started at one side of the building and systematically worked her way around the room, checking on each group, settling minor squabbles and coordinating anything she could find to coordinate. By four o'clock every item on her clipboard had been checked off, and she realized she and David could safely sneak home for an hour and change into their party clothes.

David settled into the back seat of the Cadillac with a tired sigh. Susan shot him a worried look in the rearview mirror. "Is this going to be too much for you?" she asked.

"Heck, no. You think I'd miss the biggest party to hit this town since Frontier Days?"

"No, I don't suppose you would." She chuckled and shook her head, then glanced at him over her shoulder. "But try to take it easy and keep your leg up as much as possible. Okay?"

"Yes, dear."

Susan smiled at his meek, henpecked tone. "All right, Hunter. I'll try not to mother you too much. Do you really think we're going to earn enough money to make all this work worthwhile?"

He leaned forward and patted her shoulder. "Hey, you've got everybody so pumped up, we can't fail. Even the weather's cooperating. At six o'clock we'll have so many people out there buying tickets, I won't be surprised if we have to turn some folks away."

"Lord, I hope you're right."

"I'm always right." He sat back and raked one hand through his hair in frustration. "I just wish we could figure out some way to improve the sound system. That building has the world's worst acoustics. By the time the place fills up, I don't think anyone will be able to hear the music well enough to dance. If they want to hear Wendy Wyoming, everyone will have to be darn quiet."

"For her, they will be," Susan assured him. "At least for a while."

They hurried into the house and took turns showering and dressing again. David wore a white Western shirt with blue flowers embroidered on the yoke and cuffs, a pair of jeans Melody had altered to fit over his cast, a string tie and one cowboy boot. Susan had chosen a peach-colored Western blouse with silver embroidery, silver hoop earrings, jeans and her favorite white Nikes.

David eyed her sneakers for a moment, then said wryly, "You look great, but those shoes sorta spoil the effect, Miller. Don't you have some boots or moccasins?"

Susan laughed and shook her head as she opened the front door for him. "I do, but I'm going for comfort tonight. That cement floor is a killer when you run around on it for hours. Besides, who's gonna look at my feet?"

They teased and bantered all the way back to Frontier Park and were delighted to find a long line of people already waiting to enter the exhibition building, though the doors wouldn't officially open for another forty-five minutes. Rich aromas of chili and barbecued beef greeted them when they stepped inside. They joined the other volunteers in a quick meal, then went to work.

Susan felt a rush of adrenaline as the crowd surged through the doors at six o'clock. Judging from the number of people filing in, she thought the rest of Cheyenne must look like a ghost town. The tables filled up rapidly with family groups, elderly couples, college students and teenagers. Susan's army of workers served food and drinks until their arms and backs ached, then changed shifts so they could take another turn later.

David acted as disc jockey for the first two hours. As he had feared, only the people sitting close to the speakers could hear the music he played, but nobody seemed to mind very much. The crowd was ready to party, and party they did, eating and drinking and hobnobbing from table to table.

At eight-thirty David signaled the lighting crew to dim the lights, and gradually an expectant hush filled the room. Susan leaned back against a pop machine and crossed one foot over the other, as eager as everyone else to learn Wendy Wyoming's true identity. A shiver of delight raced up her spine when David's professional announcer's voice boomed over the sound system.

"Ladies and gentlemen. We'd like to thank you all for coming to our benefit for Melissa Reed tonight, and we hope you're having a good time."

The audience clapped and whistled in response. David smiled and waited patiently for everyone to quiet down. "We have a long list of businesses who have donated food, drinks, and decorations and an unbelievable number of volunteers who have donated their time to make this evening possible. How about giving these folks a big hand of appreciation?"

The crowd's near-deafening reply vibrated the entire building. Susan's flagging energy level received a welcome boost, and she exchanged an excited grin with the man running the pop dispenser behind her.

David finally held up his hands for quiet. "And now, ladies and gentlemen, the moment you've all been waiting for. Please join me in welcoming a very special lady." He paused, drawing every last smidgen of suspense out of the moment. Then he held out one hand toward a table near the stage. "Ms. Wendy Wyoming."

A petite, dark-haired woman wearing a rhinestone-studded, hot pink, Western blouse and slacks raced up the steps to the stage and stepped into the spotlight beside David. Susan gaped at her for a second, then started to laugh and applaud when she recognized Melody Wakefield waving and blowing kisses to the adoring fans giving her a standing ovation.

After giving his sister a quick hug and the microphone, David left the stage and slowly made his way through the tables toward Susan. The applause and whistling went on and on until Melody raised the mike to her lips.

"Hey, all you cowpokes out there," she said in the husky, purring pitch that had been her trademark.

That was all it took to send the audience into another frenzy of applause. Melody raised her free hand and settled everyone down again.

"You know, pardners," she said, using her Wendy Wyoming voice, "I appreciate your warm welcome more than you'll ever know. But I also appreciate your generosity toward little Melissa Reed. It touches me way down deep inside to see so many folks eager and willing to lend a hand at a time of crisis. Now, whaddaya say? Are you ready to boogie?"

"You bet, Wendy honey!" a man down in front yelled.

"Well, then, feel free to write down requests and bring them up to my handsome husband—that mean-looking dude down there in the white hat. Let's get this show on the road!"

With that, Melody took her seat in front of the console and started a record. By stretching up onto her tiptoes, Susan was able to see Jason standing in front of the stage with his arms crossed over his chest, as if he were guarding a priceless treasure. She chuckled at his forbidding expression, then turned to find David approaching her from the left.

"You rat!" she whispered when he leaned back against the pop machine beside her. "You didn't even hint it was Melody."

He grinned at her and gratefully accepted an ice-filled glass of cola from the volunteer. "I thought you'd figured it out for sure the day we went to pick up Sheba."

Susan thought about that for a moment, then shot another glance at Jason. The man definitely did not look like a happy camper. "So that's why he was so mad at you. He didn't want anyone to know."

"That's an understatement. I didn't think he'd like it much, but I never would have guessed he could be so jealous. He darn near took my head off."

"Melody could have said no. Why was he mad at you?"

David laughed softly. "For asking her in the first place. I knew darn well she couldn't refuse. Mel's got a marshmallow heart when it comes to kids, but she gets downright goofy over babies.''

"Look who's talking," Susan murmured with a grin.

"Have any idea how the money's coming in?"

"It's unbelievable. We've taken in fifty-five thousand in ticket sales alone so far." She glanced around the room, noting the steady lines at the food, soft drink and beer booths. "I can't even begin to guess how much we'll clear after expenses with the concessions, but so much was donated, it'll be a lot. Your idea was pure genius, Hunter."

"I know."

She elbowed him in the ribs for his smug grin, then reached up and kissed his cheek. Turning toward her, he put one hand on her waist and leaned down until he could look her in the eye.

"I deserve a better kiss than that, Miller," he whispered, his dark eyes glinting with devilry and determination.

"Wait'll we get home and I'll give you one."

He raised one hand to the back of her neck and pulled her closer. "Nope. I want it right now."

"But there's too many people here," she protested, knowing it wouldn't do her any good, not sure that she cared.

"They're all looking at Wendy Wyoming." His mouth barely brushed hers, teasing, seducing her.

"Think so?" she murmured, returning the gesture.

"I know so."

Then his lips closed over hers, and awareness of the party, the music and the food drifted from her mind and joined the hazy cloud of smoke hovering near the open-beamed ceiling. He tasted of cola and a hint of chili powder. He smelled of soap and his musky cologne. His shirtfront was soft and cool against her exploring palms, but she felt his body heat, ridges of hard muscle and the excited pounding of his heart beneath the cotton fabric.

Wanting more of him, she slid her hands up to frame his face and stroked the sides of his hair with her fingertips. He shuddered and wrapped his arm around her waist, pulling her flush against him. He ignored the clatter when one of his crutches toppled over and hit the floor, and went right on kissing her.

The delicious fire rushing through her body was familiar after all the kisses they had shared. But this time it felt more intense, more ecstatic, more devastating, and she knew that tonight, she would finally find out just how hot it could burn between them. When he pulled away from her, Susan's knees were wobbly and her breath came in short, rapid gasps.

Grasping his shoulders for support, she looked up into his eyes and wanted nothing more than to take him home this instant and make love to him. A slow, sweet smile curved his lips, and she returned it, knowing full well her eyes gave her away. He let out a ragged sigh and reached up to stroke her cheek with the backs of his fingers.

"Are you sure, Susan?" he whispered.

She nodded, then moved back a step and nearly fell over his crutch. A man sitting at the closest table leaped to his feet, picked it up and handed it to David with a sly grin. David accepted it and turned to Susan smiling sheepishly. "I guess they weren't all watching Wendy Wyoming."

Susan darted a glance at the volunteer behind the pop dispenser and received an amused leer in return. "No, I, uh, guess not."

"Are you upset?"

"Not really." She laughed and shook her head. "Just a little surprised at myself. Now I'd better get back to work and you should sit down and put your leg up."

"All right." He gestured toward an empty table in the regular cafeteria area. "How about over there?"

Susan cleared a path for him, helped him get settled and reluctantly went off to check in with her committee chairmen. It was a good thing she had efficient volunteers, because it was almost impossible to keep her mind on business when her lips continually tingled from the memory of David's kiss and her nervous system hummed with anticipation of the night ahead.

They shut down the sound system and concession booths at ten-thirty. The crowd gradually thinned out, and the cleanup crews moved in at high gear. Susan returned to David's table, and her heart lurched when he looked up from a conversation with the Wakefields and held out a hand to her with a welcoming smile. She laced her fingers through his and stood beside him, wishing everyone would hurry up and go home.

Instead, an endless horde of chatty people approached their group. Still holding hands, Susan and David accepted countless compliments on the success of the dance. He tickled her palm with his thumbnail, sending delicious little shivers the length of her spine. She tried to tug her hand away, but he tightened his grip, and the complacent smile on his face told her he'd done it on purpose and had enjoyed her response.

"You'll pay for that when we get home, Hunter," she warned softly when he repeated the action a second later.

"God, I hope so, Miller," he muttered, still refusing to relinquish her hand.

Susan continued to smile and talk to the Wakefields and other people who stopped to visit, and David continued to torment her with sneaky little caresses that nobody else could see. By the time the last stragglers finally left at midnight, Susan wasn't sure whether she wanted to kiss him senseless or beat him with one of his crutches.

Seeming full of good humor, he told her wacky jokes all the way home. But when she parked in the driveway and turned off the ignition, he reached over the seat, touching her shoulder to stop her from getting out. She turned and looked at him, and in the dim illumination from the porch light, saw an intense, uncertain expression in his eyes.

"Have you changed your mind, Susan?" he asked, his voice husky. "If you have, I'd better stay at my own house tonight."

She slowly shook her head and met his gaze without hesitation. "I don't want you to do that, David."

"What do you want?"

"I want you."

"Oh, babe, I want you, too."

Neither of them said anything else until they were inside the house with the door locked against the world outside. Susan hung up their coats and let Sheba out. David headed straight for the bedroom. Susan followed as soon as she could, and found him sitting on the side of the bed, bracing himself with his right foot on the floor while he worked his jeans off over his cast. He cursed under his breath at the stubborn denim.

She paused in the doorway, her stomach suddenly fluttering with nerves. She hadn't slept with anyone since Ed had left her. His caustic remarks about her lack of enthusiasm in bed haunted her for a moment, raising inevitable doubts about her sexuality. Could she satisfy a man like David? Would he still find her attractive when he saw her stretch marks? Would he be patient enough for her to find satisfaction, too?

Then, as if he'd sensed her presence or heard her thoughts, he looked up at her and stopped struggling with his pants. He held out one hand, and she slowly crossed the room to take it.

"Nervous?" he asked softly.

"A little."

"Would a hug help?"

"It might."

He wrapped both arms around her waist, pulled her close and rested the side of his head against her breasts. She held him to her, then combed her fingers through his thick hair, loving the way the glossy strands slid over her fingertips. He sighed contentedly, his warm breath penetrating the fabric of her blouse.

A deep sense of peace flooded into her heart. Being with him like this felt good and right, and she didn't want to waste a precious minute of privacy. She echoed his sigh, put her palm under his chin and tipped his face up, searching his eyes for doubts and finding none.

"Are you protected, honey?" he asked hoarsely, scooting over toward the middle of the bed.

Warmth crept up her neck and into her cheeks as she sat down beside him. "Lord, I hadn't even thought of that. I, uh, haven't needed—"

"It's all right." David grinned, fished three little foil packets out of his shirt pocket and tossed them onto the nightstand. "I thought about it."

Chuckling, Susan put her hands on his shoulders and slowly pushed him flat on his back. She crossed her forearms over his chest and smiled down at him. "Pretty darn sure of yourself, weren't you, Hunter?"

"No, ma'am," he said fervently. "Just mighty damn hopeful. Now, please, come here and kiss me."

She complied willingly, happily, and suddenly the awkwardness between them evaporated like morning dew on a scorching August morning. Their tongues mated while their hands explored and caressed each other's body. Articles of clothing gave way under curious, eager fingers and plopped onto the floor. Whispered love words and giggles mixed with soft sighs and moans of pleasure, breaking the night's stillness.

He made love with the same go-for-it enthusiasm and sense of fun he did everything else. He showed her what he wanted and encouraged her to do the same. He teased and tormented and seduced her with his lips and tongue and hands and trembled in response when she returned the favor.

His touch was gentle, almost reverent one moment, demanding and arousing the next. She burned with wanting him, ached for completion. But just when she thought he'd surely lose patience and consummate the act, he would slow down and start kissing her all over again as if they had nothing more urgent to do.

Finally, unable to wait a moment longer, she took one of the foil packets from the nightstand, opened it and carefully unrolled the contraceptive sheath over his swollen shaft. He groaned at her loving touch, then clamped his hands around her waist and helped her to straddle him.

His cast rubbed the inside of her right thigh, his hard, warm hip brushed against the inside of her left thigh. He laced the fingers of both hands through hers and pulled her up over him until he could lick and suckle her breasts at his leisure. He released her hands and placed them on either side of his head, and used his own hands to caress her most sensitive places.

Her head fell back. Her eyes closed in ecstasy, and with his tender help, she guided him inch by inch into her body until he filled her completely. His hands moved to her hips, guiding her in a slow, rhythmic movement. He shuddered and let out a low groan.

Opening her eyes, she gazed down at him and paused when she saw that his eyes were scrunched shut, his lips pulled back in a grimace.

"Is your knee hurting?" she asked anxiously.

"What knee?" he answered with a choked laugh. He opened his eyes and pushed himself deeper inside her. "It's just...been a long time for me," he assured her. "And you feel so damn good, I don't think I'm gonna last very long."

"Don't worry about it." Leaning down, she kissed him deeply. "I'm so excited, you won't need to."

Then she started moving again, stroking faster and harder. A fine sheen of perspiration coated their bodies as the exquisite sensations intensified and raged out of control. Guiding her hips with his big hands, he praised her, encouraged her, building her excitement and his own to a devastating climax.

Her soul, her spirit, balanced on a pinnacle of sheer, mindless pleasure while her body convulsed with delicious tremors. Then she joined him in crying out her passion and floated back to reality as she collapsed against his chest. His arms closed around her in a fierce embrace, but she'd never felt so free, so adventurous, so sexy, so...loved.

Chapter Thirteen

Despite a chilly, late-October drizzle outside, Susan woke up the next morning feeling as if she'd swallowed a summer's worth of sunshine. Her right arm stretched across David's chest, her head rested next to his on the same pillow and the rest of her hugged as close to his body heat as possible. He lay on his back with his left leg propped up on a stack of pillows, quiet snores escaping his slightly parted lips.

Telling herself David needed all the rest he could get after the night they'd shared, she fought the urge to kiss him awake and contented herself with studying him at close range. Even with his snoring, his thick, bushy hair smashed flat against one side of his head and his lower cheeks and jaw covered with black stubble, he was the most appealing man she'd ever seen.

Last night had been, without doubt, the most wonderful night of her life. She hadn't known she was capable of such uninhibited behavior, of having so much fun making love with a man, of such soul-shattering passion. She wanted to stay right here, snuggled close to him under the blankets, for the rest of the day, the next week, maybe even forever.

David stirred and patted her bare hip and thigh with his right hand, as if assuring himself she was still there, then settled back into sleep with a contented little sigh. Susan's heart contracted at his gesture. Knowing she wouldn't be able to restrain herself much longer from touching him the way she had during the night, she slid carefully from the bed, slipped on her robe and walked into the bathroom.

The woman in the mirror had wild, tangled hair and a whisker burn across her chin, but her eyes glowed with satisfaction. Susan grinned at her for a moment and considered taking a quick shower. Deciding she'd rather take one later with David, she hurriedly brushed her teeth, washed her face and combed out her hair.

In the kitchen she started breakfast. A few minutes later she heard David go into the bathroom. Humming softly to herself, she plugged in the waffle iron, brought in the Sunday paper from the front porch and met him at the kitchen doorway with a smile.

Resting his weight on his crutches, he leaned down and gave her a minty kiss that curled her bare toes against the carpet. He raised his head much too soon and sniffed the air appreciatively.

"Do I smell bacon? And coffee?" he asked eagerly.

She slid her hands inside the lapels of his robe and looked up at him. "If you'll let me in the kitchen, you'll smell waffles, too, in a minute."

"You've got to stop spoiling me," he said without much conviction as he moved aside. "I'll gain forty pounds if you keep feeding me like this."

Susan poured batter into the waffle iron and shot him a naughty, laughing glance over her shoulder. "Well, maybe we can think of a fun way to burn off all those calories."

David came up behind her and wrapped one arm around her waist. He pulled her against him and cupped her breast while he nibbled on her neck. "Have any special activity in mind?"

Turning her head to one side, she guided his lips to hers and kissed him. "What do you think?"

"I think that waffle's gonna burn." His stomach punctuated his statement with a loud rumble.

She chuckled. "Maybe we'd better eat the calories first, before we work them off."

"I think you're right." He kissed the tip of her nose before taking himself off to the table.

Within minutes Susan served the food. She sat at a right angle to David and soon realized that as far as he was concerned, breakfast was simply another form of foreplay. He fed her bites from his plate and stole bites from hers. He repeatedly caressed her knee or her shoulder or her cheek for no reason at all, and gave her sweet, maple-flavored kisses that made her feel as though they must be sitting in some exotic setting rather than her ordinary little kitchen.

She set her fork down on her plate, so beguiled by the heated look in his eyes, she accidentally dipped three fingers in a puddle of syrup. She started at the sticky sensation and reached for a napkin, but David had other ideas.

He grasped her wrist and brought her hand to his mouth. Maintaining constant eye contact, he slowly licked the syrup from her fingertips. He paused between licks, telling her in a deep, gritty tone all the erotic things he'd like to do with her and the bottle of syrup when they went back to bed after breakfast.

Susan feared she might just melt into a sticky puddle where she sat. She couldn't have looked away from those sexy eyes of his if she'd wanted to. The nerve endings in her fingers sizzled a path of excitement straight to the center of her body. The rich, hypnotic sound of his voice made her limbs grow heavy and languid, and she wondered vaguely how they would ever make it to the bedroom to finish what he'd started.

Then the front door crashed open, and an instant later a disgruntled-looking Timmy appeared in the kitchen doorway. Susan blinked in surprise and shook her head, hoping her son would disappear and let her go back to David and the syrup bottle. Instead, the boy walked right into the room, sat in the empty chair across from her and propped his elbows on the table.

David let go of Susan's hand, casually flipped his robe closed over his lap and scooted his chair farther under the table. Susan straightened up in her chair and pushed her plate out of the way, hearing the sound of a car door slamming shut in front of the house. She tugged the lapels of her own robe closer together.

"What's going on, honey?" she asked. "I didn't expect you until this afternoon."

"Dad got tickets to the Bronco game from some guy he knows," Timmy answered. Tears welled up in his eyes, and he angrily scrubbed them away with his fists. "So he brought us home early."

Before Susan could reply, the front door opened again and Eric charged into the kitchen. He ran to his mother, climbed onto her lap and threw his arms around her neck. She automatically cuddled him close and laid her cheek against his forehead. His skin was fever hot and she pulled back, studying his flushed cheeks and misery-filled eyes with concern.

"Well now, isn't this cozy?" Ed drawled from the doorway.

Susan looked over her shoulder at him and felt as if her breakfast had turned into a boulder inside her stomach. Ed slouched aginst the doorjamb, his arms folded over his chest. His gaze flicked contemptuously over the table, lingering for a moment on David's and Susan's bathrobes.

Timmy scooted his chair closer to David as if he wanted protection from his father's angry eyes. David patted his shoulder, then grabbed his crutches from the floor and struggled to his feet. Ed pulled himself up to his full height, obviously disliking the fact that even leaning on his crutches, David was several inches taller.

"I'd like to talk to Susan alone," Ed said to David. "Would you mind taking the boys outside for a while?" His lips curved into a sneer. "Oh. Sorry. I see you're not dressed yet."

David opened his mouth to reply, but Susan cut him off. "Why don't you take them in the bedroom?" she suggested quietly, raising pleading eyes to his.

He hesitated a moment, then nodded abruptly. "Come on, guys. You can watch my TV with me."

Timmy and Eric agreed readily and fled the room. David followed, pausing to give Ed a long, warning glare before joining the boys. Susan waited until she heard the bedroom door snap shut, then rose to confront her ex-husband.

"What do you want, Ed?"

"I want to know what the hell's going on around here. I didn't think you were the kind of mother who flaunts her affairs in front of her kids."

"My personal life is none of your business."

"It is when it involves my children. I can't believe you two, lolling around half-naked in the middle of the day."

"Number one, it's only ten-thirty on a Sunday morning, and number two, you weren't supposed to bring them back until late this afternoon. Have you ever heard of a telephone, or are you just too cheap to waste a buck on a long-distance call?"

"I didn't think it would be necessary. But you've done it again, haven't you?"

"Done what?"

"Fallen in love with a man you'll never be able to satisfy. Can't you see all that guy wants from you is your caretaking and a quick roll in the sack since you're so available? As soon as he's on his feet, he'll be gone."

"Shut up, Ed. Just shut up and get the hell out of here."

He thrust his head forward and loomed over her. Susan stepped to one side and shoved her fists into her pockets to keep from belting him one right in his long, snooty nose.

"Not until I'm finished. I thought you'd finally learned your lesson, but I guess I'll have to spell it out so even you can understand it. You weren't woman enough to hold me or Wakefield. What makes you think you're woman enough to hold a man like David Hunter? I'm telling you, Susan, you'll never be able to do that, so stop filling my sons' heads with the idea that somebody else can take my place.''

Though she felt as if he'd just shredded her guts with a rusty knife, Susan planted her hands on her hips and mocked him with her eyes. "So that's what this is all about. The boys talked about David too much for comfort, did they, Ed?"

"Yeah. They did. And they acted like a couple of spoiled brats all weekend."

"Maybe if you spent more time with them and treated them like human beings, you wouldn't have so much trouble."

Ed ignored her comment and ranted on. "And they told me all about your neat computer and how you're still writing the great American novel. Honestly, don't you know when to give up? Or are you one of those sick masochists who thrives on rejection? If that's the case, maybe I'd better see about getting custody before you wreck my sons completely."

Susan snorted in disgust. "Don't try to threaten me with that, Ed. The boys barely know you. What judge would give you custody?"

"Lots of them would. More divorced fathers are getting their kids every day. Don't forget, I earn a better living than you ever will."

"Well, don't forget I have a record of how many child-support payments you've missed and how many times you've failed to exercise your visitation rights. What makes you think the boys would ever want to live with you?"

"They would if you didn't treat them like babies. God, those two are such whining little sissies—"

"I think you've said just about enough," Susan interrupted. "Why don't you go watch your damn football game? And while you're at it, think about how much having the boys with you would cramp your precious yuppie life-style."

Ed glared at her for a moment, pivoted as if he would stalk out the door, then turned back for one final shot. "This isn't over, Susan. Take my advice and get Hunter out of here now. Today."

"I stopped taking your advice the day you walked out on me, Ed."

He slammed out of the house in a fit of temper. Susan walked into the living room, wrapped her arms around her midriff and watched him drive away. A shiver of dread raced up her spine, and she tried to shrug it off, telling herself she wasn't afraid of her ex-husband or his empty threats. Ed didn't want custody of the boys. Not really. He was simply jealous of their affection for David.

She hugged herself harder, but another shiver ran through her body. This one was much more difficult to dismiss. During their marriage, Ed had had an uncanny ability to find her most vulnerable points and attack them when he felt threatened in some way. It shouldn't surprise her that he had done so again this morning. If she had any sense at all, she would ignore every one of his nasty remarks.

But dear God, what if Ed was right about David? About her relationship with him? Hadn't she warned herself repeatedly about the dangers of getting involved with another man? Especially a man like David?

Somehow he had sneaked past all her fears and defenses and become an important part of her life and the lives of her sons. He'd brought a warm, supportive, masculine presence into their home. They had all come to depend on him for affection and companionship and so much more. Too much more.

Her throat closed up with fear, and her eyes burned with unshed tears as she realized just how devastated she and the boys would feel if he walked out of their lives now.

Staring out the window, she finally saw the bleak, gray sky outside as it really was, instead of the warm, golden sunshine she'd fooled herself into seeing because she'd wanted so damn badly to see it. "Lord, what have I done?" she whispered.

"Susan?"

She turned at the sound of David's voice and found him standing across the room, dressed in the sweatpants and shirt he'd worn home from the hospital. His brow creased with worry, he inclined his head toward the hallway.

"Eric needs you. He says his left ear hurts."

"All right," she said after clearing her throat, then hurried into the bedroom.

Eric lay curled up in the middle of her bed, his right thumb lodged firmly in his mouth, his left hand covering his ear. Susan sat beside him and lifted him onto her lap.

"What's going on, honey?" she asked quietly, stroking his hair out of his eyes.

His little face crumpled up with anguish, and two fat tears plopped onto his cheeks. "My ear hurts, Mom. Daddy said it'd go 'way if I just ignored it, but it still hurts really bad." He sniffed and gulped. "An' he said big boys don't cry, but I can't h-h-help it."

Susan closed her eyes and envisioned Ed being tarred and feathered. When she opened them again, she found David standing next to the bed, his eyes flashing with suppressed fury.

"Well," she said calmly. "I don't think your dad's ever had an ear infection, honey. So he doesn't know how much it hurts."

"Yeah," David agreed, taking a seat beside Susan. "And you know, Eric, maybe your dad doesn't cry, but lots of other guys do. I did when I was in the hospital."

"You did?"

"You bet."

Susan shot David a grateful smile and hugged her son close. "I'll go call the doctor's office and we'll get you fixed up. Okay?"

Eric slid off her lap and climbed onto David's. "Okay, Mom."

Of course, the clinic was closed on Sunday, and the answering service's operator told Susan it would take time to track down the doctor who was on call for the weekend.

Susan rushed around getting dressed and finding her car keys while she waited for the doctor to phone her. Eric clung to David, whimpering softly occasionally.

Susan's nerves wore thinner and thinner as the seemingly endless minutes stretched out. Then Eric screamed and clapped his hand over his ear, and she raced to him with a sick feeling of dread in the pit of her stomach. A stream of bloody liquid poured out of the little boy's ear when she pried his hand away, and she had to bite down hard on her lower lip to hold in the vile curses she wanted to rain down on Ed's head.

"My God, what is that?" David asked, raising appalled eyes to meet hers while his arms tightened protectively around Eric.

"His eardrum ruptured. That stuff builds up behind it when he gets an ear infection, and the pressure causes the pain."

"You mean it's happened before?"

She nodded grimly and reached for a tissue. "Timmy had one do that when he was three. His hearing's fine now, but it's better to avoid it if possible."

The phone on the nightstand finally rang. Susan lunged for the receiver, briefly explained her problem to the doctor and agreed to meet him at the clinic in ten minutes. Eric refused to leave David's arms, stubbornly insisting that he wanted David to come with him to the doctor's office. Susan gritted her teeth and held onto her patience. It wasn't easy when she was so livid with Ed. Boiling the man in oil seemed like far too humane a punishment.

With David's help she finally convinced Eric to come along and bundled him into the car. The doctor confirmed her diagnosis and prescribed the proper medications for Eric. Susan maintained an outward facade of cool competence while she drove to a pharmacy and waited for the prescriptions to be filled. But inside her, a black, bitter rage over what had so needlessly happened to her baby seethed and grew.

Ξ he drove home, chatting amiably with Eric, who was already feeling much better. She gave him his medicine, washed four loads of laundry and cleaned house for the rest of the afternoon. She agreed to David's suggestion of ordering in Chinese food for dinner and joined in the fun of eating with chopsticks as if she hadn't a worry in the world.

By the time she tucked the boys in bed, however, her fury had grown so hot, she felt like a bomb with only seconds left on the timer. She collapsed into one corner of the sofa and dug the heels of both palms into her eyes. David came out of the kitchen on his crutches, dangling five cans of beer by the plastic carrier ring intended for a sixth can from his right index finger.

He sat too close to her for comfort, although yesterday and the day before, she'd happily snuggled a whole lot closer whenever they used the sofa. She shook her head when he plunked a beer down on the coffee table in front of her and popped the top.

"I don't want one, David."

"You'd better have something," he answered, opening another can for himself. "You're so tense, I'm worried about you."

"I'm just fine."

"Sure, you are. That's why you're trying to poke your fingernails right through your hands."

Susan glanced down and saw he was right, but that didn't endear him to her one bit. He laid his arm on the sofa back behind her and cupped his palm around her shoulder, giving it a gentle squeeze. She shrugged him off and moved over to the love seat.

David inhaled a deep breath as if he were struggling with his patience, but his voice remained low and soothing. "Want to go over to my house for a while? You can yell and slam cupboard doors all you want. You can even call Ed on my phone and tell him off. I'll be happy to pay for it."

Though the idea held a certain appeal, David's calm, rational manner fueled her temper. She gave him a distant smile and shook her head. "No, thanks. I told you I'm just fine and I am. Why don't we watch TV?"

"Don't do this to yourself, Susan."

"Do what?"

"Bury all that anger. It'll make you crazy if you don't get it out."

"I didn't know you had a degree in psychology."

"All right, then. Don't do this to me. I'm not the one who hurt Eric."

"Of course you're not. You were a big help today, and I appreciate it. Now if you'll excuse me," she said, climbing to her feet, "I need to go call my boss and sitter and tell them I'll have to stay home with Eric tomorrow."

A deep red flush climbed David's neck and colored his cheeks and ears. "You don't need to do that. I can take care of him. I wasn't planning to go into the office tomorrow, anyway."

"No, thanks. Eric is my responsibility, not yours."

He jerked back as if she'd slapped him, then grabbed his crutches, hobbled around the coffee table and stopped directly in front of her. "Dammit, Susan, don't you dare do this."

"Do what?" she asked, raising her chin defiantly.

"Don't shut me out. Not after everything we've been through together." His voice dropped to a rough whisper. "Not after last night."

"Don't read too much into last night. Sex doesn't solve anything."

"It wasn't just sex and you know it."

The pain in his eyes looked real enough, but Susan felt an icy coat of fear surround her heart and allowed whatever demon was driving her on to have his way.

"Maybe it wasn't," she admitted calmly, "but it still doesn't mean a thing."

"It'll mean plenty if you'll let it."

"David, don't. This isn't the right time—"

"It's exactly the right time. I love you, Susan. Surely you know that."

"You don't know what you're saying."

"Dammit, I do, too! These last few weeks with you have been wonderful for me."

"That's just gratitude and I don't want it. We had enough chaos around here today to convince any sane man he doesn't want a ready-made family."

"Then I must be crazy, because I want to be with you and the boys. I love the chaos around here."

"But how long will you love it?" Susan heard the bitter edge in her voice and hated it, but she couldn't make it go away. "Until it inconveniences you and cramps your style? You'll get tired of the responsibilities that come with family life pretty damn fast once you get that cast off."

"I don't mind being responsible for the boys. I like it. And you sure as hell ought to know by now that you can depend on me to carry my share of the load."

"Depend on you?" she screeched. "You think I *want* to depend on you? Hunter, I wouldn't depend on any man again for a billion bucks. A trillion bucks!"

He rocked back on his heels and stared at her as if he no longer recognized her. "You don't mean that."

"Oh, yes, I do."

"Dear God, what have I ever done to make you feel this way?"

"Nothing. Yet."

"But you're absolutely sure that sooner or later, I'll let you down."

"Yeah, that about covers it."

"It doesn't matter that I love you."

"I've heard it before and it didn't matter. Why should it now?"

Giving his head a sad little shake, David moved back a step. "You know, it's almost funny. All along I've thought you were different from Liz. That you were getting to know the real me and you could love me and trust me some day." His laugh sounded as bitter as Susan's own voice had a moment earlier. "And here you are, telling me to my face that

I'm not one bit different from Ed and you never thought I could ever be any other way."

"Dammit, David, I never said you were like him."

"Sure, you did." With that, he turned and swung himself around her, heading for the hallway.

"Where are you going?" she asked.

"To get my keys. I'm going home."

"Don't be silly. Our relationship or whatever you want to call it may be over, but you still need help and your house will be too cold."

"It won't be any colder than yours, Susan. And for your information, I haven't needed help for days. I could have had my cast cut off last week, but I wanted more time with you. Pretty stupid of me, huh?"

She opened her mouth, but no sound came out, and David left the room without another word. He returned a moment later and went straight to the front door. Susan followed him.

"David, please don't go like this. We can still be friends."

"I don't think so. I'd rather have friends who trust me."

"But—"

His sad smile silenced her. Then he said, "I'll have Jason come get my stuff tomorrow, and I'll stay out of your way as much as I can. But I won't just disappear out of the boys' lives, Susan. I promised Timmy I'd help him with his Cub Scout activities, and I promised both Eric and Timmy they could help me train Sheba. I intend to fulfill those promises whether you like it or not."

The cold shell surrounding her heart cracked and shattered as she gazed into his eyes and realized just how deeply she had wounded him. "I'm sorry, David," she choked out, wishing she had the right words to stop him from leaving. But she didn't.

"So am I." He lifted one hand as if he would caress her cheek, hesitated, then dropped it with a futile-sounding sigh. "If you ever decide you can believe in dreams again, Susan, let me know."

A second later he was gone. Susan stood at the door and watched him cross the street. He unlocked his house, switched on the porch light and waved, letting her know he was safe. She returned the gesture before retreating to the security of her own home.

Only it didn't feel very secure at the moment. It didn't feel much like home, either. Knowing there was no possibility of a long, quiet talk with David, or exciting, stolen kisses, or just a warm, affectionate hug, made the house feel as cold and silent as a tomb.

She grabbed an afghan from the back of the love seat, wrapped it around her and sat down, pulling her knees up to her chest. She wanted the release a good cry usually gave her, but her tears were frozen somewhere deep inside her heart. She justified her actions as best she could, telling herself that David had acted pretty much the way she'd thought he would.

At the first sign of serious trouble, he'd cut and run. Just as her father had done when she was thirteen. Just as Ed had done. Just as Jason had done.

The quiet voice of her conscience argued, *But Jason didn't really do that, Susan. Neither did David. You pushed both of them away as hard as you could.*

"Oh, shut up," she muttered at the quiet voice and went to check on the boys.

They were both sound asleep, of course. Driven by restlessness, she went into her bedroom and felt one sharp stab of regret when she saw the computer, another when she saw the wide, empty expanse of her bed. She gulped, then inhaled a deep, calming breath and grabbed her nightgown and robe from the closet and headed for the living room. Perhaps it was cowardice, but there was no way in hell she would sleep in this room tonight.

Chapter Fourteen

The minute Jason pulled into the driveway at nine o'clock the next morning, David grabbed his coat and crutches and went outside. Jason hurried around the front of his Blazer, opened the rear door, and helped him struggle into the vehicle. David didn't bother trying to hide his bad mood, and shrugging, Jason shut the door and climbed into the driver's seat.

He started the engine and backed out into the street. "You look like hell, Dave," he said with his usual bluntness. "What's goin' on?"

David shot a glance over his shoulder at the little white house across the street and exhaled a disgruntled sigh. "Susan and I broke up last night."

"What?" Jason asked, taking a quick look in the rearview mirror. "You gotta be kiddin' me."

"Nope. It's over. Finished. Kaput. Just get me to the clinic so I can get this damn thing off my leg will ya? Then I'll need your help moving my stuff home."

"Sure, pal. What didja fight about?"

"Take a guess. The woman's even worse than Liz."

"She was jealous? That doesn't make any sense. You've been with her every night and day for weeks."

By the time David finished recounting the previous day's events, Jason had parked in the clinic's lot. He followed David inside and even accompanied him to the casting room. While they were waiting for David's turn with the technician who would remove his cast, the conversation continued.

"Try to look at it from Susan's point of view, Dave," Jason argued quietly. "She took one helluva big step with you Saturday night, and then wham, she runs right into her ex. I only met the guy once, but my impression was that he's the kinda jerk who has to make other people feel lousy about themselves to make himself feel good. Who knows what he laid on her while you were in the bedroom with the kids?"

"Yeah, I thought of that. And I did my damnedest to help her all day. But I resent being lumped with that SOB. Dammit, she just tossed everything we'd built together right out the window at the first opportunity."

"She's always been mighty protective of those boys. Maybe she was too upset about Eric to know what she wanted. Ya know, your timing was pretty rotten. Why don't you give her a few days to cool off and go talk to her again?"

"No way." David sliced his hand under his chin. "I've had it up to here with trying to prove myself to women who can't trust me. I went through enough of that crap with Liz."

"Do you love Susan, Dave? Really love her?"

"Of course I do! I'd have married her in a second. I even felt lucky that Liz had called off our engagement so I was free when Susan came along. I was dreaming about raising Eric and Timmy and having more kids with her. And then she had to go and dump me like that. What the hell did she want from me?"

Jason smiled and slowly shook his head. "I wondered the same thing about Mel. But don't let your wounded pride get in the way like I did. Go to her. Work it out."

"I can't do that, Jase. I wouldn't have any pride left at all." He shot Jason a warning glare. "And don't you dare trot out that old cliché about pride not keeping your bed warm at night."

"Would I do that?"

"Damn right, you would."

Tipping his Stetson farther back on his head, Jason crossed his arms over his chest. "Remember when you called me about getting the computer for her? You told me she'd said something about having enough rejection in her life. I think she's just scared of getting rejected again, so she rejected you first. It was a defensive reaction, pure and simple."

"Well, that's tough. I've had enough rejection too. And I'm not gonna stick my neck out and let her have another whack at it. If she wants to be with me, she can damn well come and tell me so."

"What if she's too scared to do that?"

David lifted his shoulders in a helpless shrug. "I don't think she's really scared. I heard more bitterness in her voice than fear. It was like, any man on earth would let her down. I can't fight that. That's something she'll have to work out for herself. If she wants me, she'll have to trust me."

"You could be right," Jason drawled. "But I think you're makin' a big mistake."

"Yeah? Well, it's my mistake, isn't it?"

"That's a fact."

Later that morning Susan fed Eric an early lunch and tucked him in for a nap. She started when the doorbell rang and felt an instant's wild hope that it was David, coming to talk and work things out. She ran into the bathroom and jerked a comb through her hair, but gave up when she caught sight of her haggard face and raccoon eyes. Nothing short of a good night's sleep and a total make-over would help her look human today.

The bell sounded again. She rushed to the front door and found Jason standing on her porch, wearing a grim expression. Her heart plummeted like a glass of chocolate milk headed for a freshly scrubbed floor.

When she opened the door for him, he stepped inside and studied her face intently. "I've come for David's things."

"They're, uh, in the bedroom. I packed them for him this morning." She returned his scrutiny for a moment. "How is he?"

Jason's face relaxed in a sympathetic smile. "He got his cast off this morning, and he's happy about that. But I've cornered friendlier badgers and he looks almost as bad as you do."

"Thanks, pal. I really needed to hear that."

Susan turned toward the hallway, but he stopped her with a hand on her shoulder. "I'm sorry. I shouldn't have said that. No matter what happened between you and Dave, I'm still your friend, Susan."

She patted his hand and gave him the best smile she could manage. "I appreciate that. Come on, let's get this over with."

He followed her into the bedroom and whistled softly when he saw the mountain of David's possessions piled by the door. "How'd he get all that stuff over here?"

"A piece at a time," she answered with a dry laugh. "He'd think of something he wanted or needed, and either Timmy or I would go get it for him. And don't forget we've got all of Sheba's things here, too."

"Wouldn't it be easier to go make up with him now and save me forty trips across the street?" he asked with a wry smile.

Looking down at the toes of her sneakers, Susan shook her head. "That's not going to happen, Jason."

Jason crooked an index finger under her chin and forced her to meet his eyes. "Why not? You're miserable without him. He's miserable, too, and he's a good guy."

"I know he is." She had to swallow at the lump in her throat before she could continue. "But I'm not right for him, Jason. I've known it all along."

"Do I hear self-pity in your voice? That's not like you Susan."

"Yes it is. More than you know." She wrapped her arms around her waist and looked away. "I found out yesterday that I'm too...damaged. By a lot of things. David deserves somebody who's really whole. Somebody who can appreciate how wonderful he is without always expecting the worst. I can't do that."

"But he wants you."

"He just thinks he does. He's lonely, and he wants a family. He'll find somebody else before long."

"Did my marrying Melody have anything to do with your decision?"

Susan sniffed and shook her head. "No, not really."

"I want you to know something anyway. If I hadn't already been in love with Melody, it wouldn't have taken me long to fall in love with you."

"It's kind of you to say that, but—"

"I'm not bein' kind," he interrupted, scowling at her. "I'm just tryin' to tell you that you're a wonderful woman, damaged or not. Hell, we're all a little damaged in one way or another. People just don't get through life without taking some hard knocks that leave scars and bruises behind. But sometimes those scars and bruises make us stronger and more interesting. So don't sell yourself short because you've got a few."

"That was quite a speech for a cowboy," she answered, furiously blinking back tears.

"But you're not gonna change your mind."

"Nope."

He cursed under his breath. "You're just as stubborn as he is. You know that?"

"I'm afraid so."

"All right." He leaned down, picked up an armload of books and a suitcase, and headed for the door, muttering to himself. "At least I can tell Melody I tried to talk some sense into you idiots."

Susan struggled to maintain her composure while Jason moved the rest of David's belongings out of the room.

"Well, I guess that's about it," he said when he picked up the last load. "You'll call me if you need anything?"

"Sure." She took one last glance around to make sure they hadn't missed anything. "Oh, don't forget the computer."

Jason shook his head and kept on going. "I got strict orders to leave it here."

"But I can't keep it. It's too expensive."

"You'll have to get rid of it yourself, then," he told her grinning at her over his shoulder. "'Cause I'm not gonna touch it."

Susan followed him, sputtering in protest, but he walked out of the house without a backword glance. She slammed the door behind him, then remembered Eric was sleeping held her breath for a moment and finally walked over to the sofa and collapsed. Depression, her old, familiar companion, settled right in beside her.

The house seemed even quieter now than it had the night before. The boys were going to hate her. Telling them David had gone home for the night had been hard enough this morning. How in the world could she explain why all of his things, including their beloved Sheba, were gone for good? And how in the world could she face David and work with him again?

"You'll think of something, Susan," she murmured without much conviction, closing her tired eyes. "You'll just have to."

The next two weeks were even worse than anything Susan had imagined. Timmy and Eric didn't hate her, but they spent as much time visiting David and Sheba as they could whine and wheedle out of her. When she refused permission for them to go across the street, they moped around the house like a couple of sad orphans, fought with each other constantly and refused to participate in any activity she suggested.

Susan reminded herself repeatedly that it was only natural for boys to crave a man's attention. But knowing her sons clearly preferred David's company to hers still hurt. When the boys left, she wandered around her empty living room, peering out the window at David's house, wondering what they were all doing over there and feeling like a child who's been left out of the neighborhood softball game.

Her concentration was too shot to read or watch TV. She rarely slept and couldn't even write. Though she still had the computer, her manuscript had lost all appeal. And every time she walked into her bedroom, she felt as though the damn monitor screen regarded her with disapproval.

As if that weren't bad enough, she couldn't avoid seeing David frequently. For one thing, they left for work at the same time every morning and frequently arrived home at the same time, as well. For another, the steering committee for Melissa Reed's surgery fund met weekly to coordinate the continuing activities and tally up how much more money they needed to raise. And, of course the boys engineered every conceivable excuse to push them together.

David was always courteous and personable when they met, but he didn't waste any of his legendary charm on her. Susan had expected that. What she hadn't expected was how deeply having a purely businesslike relationship with him would hurt and go on hurting, no matter how much time passed or how many times she encountered him.

One night at the end of the second week, she stepped out of her car and saw a sleek gray sedan parked in David's driveway. Her stomach lurched, and her breath caught painfully in her chest at the thought that he'd already found someone else. Without being asked, Timmy informed her that it was David's new car, and suddenly she could breathe again.

After that, Susan found herself compulsively watching David's house for signs of a new woman in his life. Though he was home almost every night and she never saw another female across the street besides Melody and Sheba, Susan couldn't give up her surveillance. She chided herself, silently repeating over and over that David's private life was none of her business. But it didn't help.

He drove her crazy without even trying. The wretch didn't even have the decency to look as if he'd suffered one moment's anguish since they had parted. He moved much more easily now that he wore an orthopedic splint and had graduated to a cane. He walked Sheba around the neighborhood every evening after work.

Susan thought his cane looked rather dashing and, well, sexy, and couldn't help wondering what it would be like to make love with him without a fiberglass cast getting in the way.

She baby-sat for the Reeds the next week, and had to listen to Katie and Tom rave for at least twenty minutes about how David had been faithfully calling or visiting every few days, just to make sure they didn't need anything. He never missed a committee meeting or fund-raising event for Melissa. He fulfilled all of his promises to Eric and Timmy.

Susan missed him desperately as a friend and as a lover. She realized he wasn't anything like Ed. She readily admitted she'd been wrong to end her relationship with him.

But he was so distant, so businesslike, so damn polite, she was terrified to try to change the situation. Every time she thought about approaching David in a personal way, Ed's taunting words reverberated inside her head. Her heart raced, her palms started to sweat and her stomach churned with nausea. If she attempted to reconcile with David and he rejected her, she feared she would shrivel up from the inside out until she looked like an old, dried-out spider carcass.

So she watched him from a distance, listened to the boys continually sing his praises until she thought she'd run screaming into the night and felt more wretched with each passing day for four long, miserable weeks.

The winter's first real snowfall arrived on the Monday before Thanksgiving. David's parents' red Corvette was parked in front of his house when Susan arrived home from work. Wishing she could hear all about their trip to Europe, she hustled the boys inside. They wolfed down a quick snack, then bundled up and went out to build a snowman.

Susan cut up a chicken and put it in the oven with some baking potatoes before changing into her jeans and sweatshirt. Deciding she might as well shovel the driveway and sidewalks while dinner cooked, she tugged on a pair of boots and reached into the coat closet for her old ski jacket. The doorbell rang at that moment.

She peeked through the diamond-shaped window in the front door and saw Karen Hunter standing on the porch, smiling as she said something to the boys. What in the world could David's mother want with her? Susan wondered, opening the door. After stepping inside, Karen gave the living room an appreciative survey, then turned to Susan with one of those friendly Hunter smiles Susan had always found so irresistible.

"Sorry to barge in without phoning first," the older woman said, "but since I was in the neighborhood, I thought I'd stop by and see if you'd finished the books I sent over."

"Oh. Sure. They're in the bedroom," Susan answered, feeling ridiculously flustered, though she wasn't sure why. Karen certainly seemed too cheerful to take her to task for anything that had happened between her and David. "I'll just, uh, get them."

When she returned, Susan found Karen intently studying a grouping of family photographs near the kitchen doorway. David's mother had a soft, wistful expression on her face as she gazed at Timmy and Eric's baby and toddler pictures. Susan felt a twinge of envy, wishing her own mother had shown that much interest in her grandchildren.

"Here they are," she said, holding the books out to Karen. "Thanks for lending them to me. I really enjoyed them."

"Do you have a few minutes to talk about them?" Karen asked. "I'm going to teach a class at the community college next semester, and I'd like to know which one you thought was most helpful."

"Well, uh, sure. Would you like a cup of tea?"

"I'd love one."

Susan hung Karen's coat in the closet, then led the way to the kitchen. Karen sat at the table and chatted about her recent trip like an old friend while Susan brewed a pot of tea. Despite Karen's efforts to put her at ease, however, Susan still felt about as comfortable as a kid facing a disapproving school principal.

When she had taken the chair across from David's mother, Karen chuckled and patted her hand. "Will you please relax? I promise I'm not here to grill you about David. My son is old enough to handle his own love life."

"I'm sorry," Susan said, knowing her cheeks must be flaming. "It just seems a little awkward."

"Don't worry about it. I wouldn't dream of interfering in any of my children's affairs." Karen winked, then confided with a rueful expression, "Not that I'm not tempted, now and then, of course. Just wait'll your boys start dating, and you'll see what I mean."

Susan couldn't help laughing, or liking the woman immensely. "I can appreciate that already. There's a little girl at Eric's pre-school who's always trying to kiss him."

Karen sipped her tea. "I do have a small confession to make," she said in a more serious tone. "I want to talk about the writing books sometime, but I'm really more interested in the one you're working on now. David told me it was wonderful, and I respect his judgment. I'd love to read it, if you wouldn't mind."

The quiet request stunned Susan. In a way she felt flattered and tempted, but it was one thing to let a friend read her manuscript. It was something else entirely to let a professional writer tear it apart. "Oh, well, I don't know."

"I won't give you a critique if you don't want one," Karen said quickly, "but if it's as good as David says it is, I

might be able to help you get it published. Just let me look
at the first chapter. What have you got to lose?''

Sparkling with anticipation and warmth, Karen's vivid
green eyes silently coaxed Susan to agree. Fear rose up inside her, but she was sick and tired of seeing herself as such
a coward. After all, it wasn't *that* big of a risk. And maybe
Karen could tell her what she was doing wrong. After hesi-
tating another moment, Susan gave in and went to get the
manuscript.

Karen took it from her and laid it on the table. ''Why
don't you go find something else to do for a while?'' she
suggested. ''It's awful being in the same room with somebody reading your work.''

Susan couldn't have agreed more. ''I'll go shovel the
driveway.''

''That's fine, dear,'' Karen replied, reaching for the first
page.

The boys called Susan over to their snowman the minute
she stepped out the front door. She duly inspected and
complimented their creation, then got the shovel out of the
garage. Since only four inches of snow had fallen so far, she
enjoyed the work and the cold, refreshing air. The only
problem was, she couldn't get her mind off the woman sitting in her kitchen.

Would Karen like her story? Really, sincerely like it? Or
would she have to scramble around for a diplomatic way to
tell her the book stunk?

Feeling as if she had ants crawling around under her skin,
Susan finished the driveway and started the sidewalks. The
streetlights came on, and the boys went inside, complaining that their hands were getting cold. Finally she couldn't
stand the suspense a minute longer. She put the shovel away,
squared her shoulders and marched into the house.

Timmy and Eric sprawled on the sofa, watching television. After hanging up her coat and kicking off her boots,
Susan padded quietly into the kitchen in her stockinged feet.
Karen reached for her tea cup with one hand and turned
over a page with the other. From the size of the stack of pa-

pers lying facedown on the table, Susan guessed she must be well into chapter three, maybe chapter four.

Susan cleared her throat to attract Karen's attention, but it didn't work. She walked closer to the table and tried again. Karen glanced up, blinking owlishly for a moment. Then she turned to Susan, and a dazzling smile spread over her face.

"Well?" Susan asked, her nerves screaming with anxiety. "What do you think?"

"It's wonderful. Every bit as good as David said it was."

"You're sure?" Susan twined her fingers together in front of her abdomen. "You're not just being nice or anything?"

Karen shook her head emphatically. "I wouldn't do that to any writer, Susan. Come sit down. We have to talk."

Susan obeyed immediately, sitting on the edge of her seat. Karen chuckled, leaned across the table and gently pushed Susan farther onto the chair. "I mean it, Susan. This book is terrific. How much longer will it take you to complete it?"

"Two weeks if I hit it hard."

"Here's what I would like to do. My agent handles lots of fiction writers. Let me phone him and recommend you as a client. He'll probably ask to see the first hundred pages or so. By the time he's read that and gets back to you, you'll have the book all finished and you can send him the rest."

"You really think he'll want to see the rest?"

"If he doesn't, I'll want a new agent."

The utter conviction in Karen's voice convinced Susan of her sincerity. Still, she felt torn by indecision. By letting Karen read her work, she'd taken one small chance. Did she have the guts to take another, bigger chance?

Actually seeing her book in print, having her own name on the cover, was something she'd dreamed of since high school. She'd worked hard at her writing, just as she'd worked hard at her marriage. Neither dream had come true for her, but that didn't necessarily mean one of them *couldn't* come true. Did it?

"You know," Karen said gently a moment later, "writing is like anything else you really want in life. You may have to stick your neck out and risk failing a few times before you succeed. But the failures only make the final success that much sweeter, Susan."

Susan nodded. "I know that. And I'll do it on one condition."

"What's that?" Karen asked, already starting to smile.

"I don't want you to say a word about this to anyone else."

"Especially not David?"

"Especially not David."

"I'll accept your condition as long as I get to read the rest when you're finished and you'll give David your first autographed copy. Deal?"

Karen held out her hand for a handshake. Susan took it with a tentative smile. "Deal."

"All right!" Karen pushed back her chair and stood. "I may not be able to reach Bob until tomorrow morning. I'll call you at the bank when I've talked to him."

Susan walked her to the door, then shut it and hugged herself to make sure she hadn't dreamed the whole thing. One second, her heart expanded with hope; the next second, it contracted with fear. But she'd given her word and she would keep it, no matter how scared she felt. Waiting to hear from Karen's agent would be excruciating, but in the meantime, she had a dinner to put on the table and kids to bathe, read to and tuck into bed. And a book to finish.

David looked out his front window, praying for a glimpse of his mother this time. Oh, God, there she was, and there was Susan in the doorway, but he couldn't see if either of them was smiling. Now his mother had started down the steps....

He grabbed his cane and hurried to the front door, yanking it open when his mother reached the sidewalk. She broke into a trot and came inside with a gust of cold air.

"Well?" he demanded. "Did she let you read it? You were over there long enough."

"I read it," Karen admitted with an excited smile. "And you were right. It's a wonderful novel."

"Did you talk her into submitting it?"

Karen sighed and tucked one side of her chin-length blond hair behind her ear. "I can't tell you anything else."

"But, Mom—"

"No, David. I promised Susan I wouldn't discuss this with anyone, and that includes you."

"It was my idea in the first place," David argued.

"Well, you'll just have to wait and see whether or not it was a good one."

"Mom, you can't *do* this to me! She's already driven me half out of my mind. Are you trying to finish the job for her?"

Karen chuckled and reached up on her tiptoes to ruffle his hair. "Trust me. Okay? Susan will have a wonderful writing career if I have anything to say about it."

"But what about me?" David grumbled. "Will I ever have Susan?"

"I can't answer that, honey," she said, giving him a sympathetic hug. "But I hope so. She's a lovely young woman."

"Yeah," he agreed softly, "she is. And I'm not gonna let her get away."

"Keep thinking that way, son. Why don't you come home with me for dinner? Melody and Jason are coming in. They said they have some exciting news for us."

David shook his head. "Not this time, Mom."

"All right. But don't sit here and mope about Susan all evening."

"I won't. Sheba needs a good walk, and I need to excercise my knee."

She paused in the doorway. "Everything will work out eventually."

"I hope so, Mom. I sure hope so."

Chapter Fifteen

Karen Hunter phoned Susan at work late on Tuesday morning and reported that her agent, Bob Goldstein, was eager to read the first one hundred pages of Susan's manuscript. Susan prepared her submission that night, gritted her teeth and mailed it during her lunch hour on Wednesday. She spent Wednesday evening getting the boys ready for a Thanksgiving trip to Denver with Ed, dreading the thought of seeing her ex-husband again.

Ed arrived on time for a change, acting oddly subdued. He didn't mention David, for which Susan was utterly grateful, and he actually seemed to listen to her instructions about Eric's medication. He promised to return the boys after lunch on Sunday and left without one snide remark.

Susan shook her head in amazement as she closed the front door, then pushed up her sweatshirt sleeves and headed for the bedroom. She hated giving the boys up for any holiday, but reminded herself that this way she would have them home for Christmas. Since Karen's visit had finally ended her writer's block, she spent the entire day at the computer, desperately trying to ignore the empty hole inside her chest that came from knowing her sons were a hundred miles away.

At seven o'clock she stretched her aching shoulders and went out to the kitchen. After making herself a sandwich, she carried it into the living room and turned on the television for company. Then the loneliness she'd held at bay while she was writing set in with a vengeance.

Despite the sound of the laugh track from a popular sitcom playing on the TV, the house seemed bleak and empty. Was this what her life would be like when Eric and Timmy left home for college? she wondered. Of course, there were lots of ways to fill up her time.

She could always take classes in the evenings, spend more time with friends or become more active in her church. But she would still have to come home sometime and face her empty house and empty bed, she thought glumly. There wouldn't be anyone waiting to hear about her activities or share her joys and sorrows.

A car's engine shut down somewhere outside. Susan pulled back a corner of the drapes and peeked out in time to see David step out of his car across the street. He used his cane with one hand and carried a foil-wrapped package, no doubt containing leftovers from the Hunters' Thanksgiving dinner, in the other. She envisioned him sitting at an elegant table with all the members of his family around him, and her heart ached at the thought that she might have been invited to join them, if only...

She dropped the drapes as if they'd burst into flames, snapped off the television and went to bed. There was no use torturing herself over something that could never happen.

On Friday, Susan wrote until five o'clock, then grabbed a quick bite to eat and drove to East High School to sell tickets at another benefit for Melissa Reed.

The boys' basketball team had challenged former players from all of the city's high schools to a game. Since ten of

Cheyenne's all-time best players, including Jason Wakefield, had accepted the challenge, Susan expected an excellent turnout. She met the other three members of her committee and settled in to work.

By the time the game started at seven, the bleachers on both sides of the gym were packed. Susan dismissed her helpers and stayed at the table to take care of any latecomers. When the buzzer signaling the end of the first quarter sounded, she started packing away the tickets and cash box.

Just then, one of the school's front doors whooshed open and she looked up to find David hurrying inside. He paused for an instant when he spotted her and gave her a polite smile.

"Hello, Susan," he said, stopping in front of her. "How'd we do for receipts tonight? Did we make enough to get Melissa on the donor list?"

Her silly heart fluttered at suddenly having him near enough to touch. Her gaze raced over his face, noting automatically that he looked thinner than the last time she'd seen him up close. He looked tired, too, but then who wouldn't after working from eight in the morning until this late in the evening?

"I haven't counted the money yet. It looks good, though," she answered, silently willing him to say something, anything personal.

"Would you like some help?"

"Yes, thank you."

His offer surprised and pleased her, and for a moment she allowed herself to hope that he might be trying to create an opening for a meaningful conversation between them. She led the way down the hall to the school office, her pulse pounding more frantically with every step. Unfortunately, once they were inside the room with the door shut, David was all business.

She flipped through stack after stack of bills, struggling to concentrate on her counting and tally sheet while the scent of his after-shave filled her head with memories and her soul with longing. He worked efficiently alongside her at the counter, seemingly unaffected by her presence. Her spirits sank lower and lower, until he handed over his total.

He stepped close to her side, watching over her shoulder as she added their numbers together. He whooped with delight when he saw the final figure and grabbed her in a rough, exuberant hug. Susan hugged him back, laughing and joining in his happy chant.

"We did it! We did it! We did it!"

Excitement that had nothing to do with Melissa shot through Susan's body. She would have gladly stayed right there in David's arms for the rest of her life and wanted to tell him so. But before she could figure out a way to say what she was feeling, he pulled back and abruptly released her. The ecstatic smile disappeared from his face as quickly as it had appeared, a reserved, businesslike mask replacing it.

"Well, we've got her on the list," he said soberly, "but we still need to raise at least another thirty-five to forty thousand to pay for the rest of the operation and get her through the first year of care."

"We'll get it," Susan assured him. "Donations are pouring in from all over the state now, and even some from Nebraska, Colorado and Utah. We've still got four more fund-raisers planned, too. If they do as well as the others have, we shouldn't have any problems."

David nodded, then headed for the phone. "I've got to call Tom and Katie. You want to talk to them?"

"Uh, sure," she answered, covering her consternation at his abrupt withdrawal by reaching for a deposit slip.

David told the Reeds the good news, chatted with them for a few moments, then handed the receiver over to Susan. As she listened to their repeated thanks, David whispered, "See ya," close to her ear and walked out the door.

Susan hung up a minute later and went back to her deposit slip, feeling as if he'd slapped her in the face with his indifference toward her. The green stacks of currency blurred before her eyes, but she inhaled a deep breath and fiercely blinked back the threatening tears.

If that was the way he wanted to act, it was fine with her. Thank God she hadn't blurted out something stupid, such as "I love you," or "I miss you," or "Can't we try again?" Still, she knew the warmth and security she'd felt during those brief seconds in David's arms would haunt her.

Over the next two weeks, she finished her book—just in case Bob Goldstein did want to see the rest of it. Determined not to spoil the boys' Christmas, she started her shopping and decorated the house. She made new tree ornaments with the boys and baked special goodies after they went to bed.

But no amount of activity could ease the lonely ache deep inside her. Whatever she did, there was always the thought that it would have been more fun doing it with David. She reached for the phone to call him countless times, but could never quite find the courage to punch in his number. Then, just before lunch on Friday, December 15, David phoned her at work.

"Susan? Better sit down. I have unbelievable news."

Her heart quickened at the sound of his voice, but she answered in the same tone she would have used for any other business call. "What's up?"

"They've found a donor for Melissa. Katie and Tom are already on their way to Denver."

"Oh, David. That's wonderful!"

"It sure is. The surgery will take between ten and twelve hours. Katie asked if we could come down and wait with them. Her dad's been sick, so her folks can't go. Can you be ready to leave in an hour?"

"If I can find someone to stay with the boys. Let me call Candy—"

"No need. Jason's already agreed to pick them up and take them to the ranch for the weekend. That is, if you don't mind. I guess I should have checked with you first, but I was so excited—"

"That's great. Don't worry about it. I'll phone my sitter so she'll expect me."

"All right. Go change into something comfortable and pack an overnight bag in case we need to stay over. I'll pick you up at your house."

Susan hung up the receiver, then immediately picked it up again and phoned her sitter. After a quick stop at Hal Baker's office to share the good news, she rushed home, changed, packed and threw some sandwiches, chips and soft drinks into a small cooler. David got there five minutes later, and they took off for Denver.

He talked nonstop for the first thirty miles, filling her in on the details he hadn't taken the time to mention on the phone. Susan listened intently to every word and barely noticed the scenery zipping past the car windows. She desperately wanted to slide over to the middle of the bench seat and sit next to David, but feared he would remember they weren't friends anymore if she did.

Instead, she handed him food while he drove and contented herself with simply enjoying his company. The Reeds greeted them warmly when they arrived at University Hospital. Melissa was already in surgery.

The first three hours, Katie and Tom chatted amiably with Susan and David. But as the afternoon sunshine faded into twilight and the dinner hour came and passed, it became increasingly difficult to come up with a topic of conversation. David gently bullied the Reeds into taking a break, though they both swore they couldn't eat anything.

When they'd left the waiting room, he turned to Susan. "How're you holding up?"

"I'm fine, but it's going to be a long evening, isn't it?"

"I'm afraid so." He paced for a few minutes, then walked over, sat beside her and held her hand in his. "I'm glad we could come, though."

"Me, too." Her hand, her whole arm tingled at his affectionate, if somewhat absentminded, touch. "It would be awful to go through something like this alone."

David leaned his head back against the wall behind the low-slung vinyl sofa they shared and closed his eyes. God, it felt so good to touch her again, he was damn near ready to crumble, get down on his knees and beg her to take another try at their relationship. Since she hadn't jerked her hand away, maybe he should.

That won't solve the problem, a voice inside his head piped up. *She might take you back now, but what'll happen to you the next time she has a run-in with Ed? No, she needs to want you and trust you enough to make the first move. Maybe she'll do it tonight if you just wait her out.*

Unable to sit so close to her any longer without defying that voice of wisdom, David released Susan's hand and forced himself to stand and put some distance between them. He turned on the small television in a corner of the room and pretended to watch the evening news. When Tom and Katie came back, he escorted Susan to the hospital cafeteria and spent a miserable half hour trying to think of something to say that would give her an opening but wouldn't be too obvious.

Unfortunately Susan didn't pick up on any of his hints. If she did, she ignored them. Those big green eyes of hers watched him hopefully one moment, warily the next, until he wanted to shake her and yell at her, "I'm the best man—the *only* man—in this world for you, Susan Miller! Why don't you wake up and see that?"

He couldn't do any such thing, of course, so he finished his chocolate cake in silence, then escorted her back to the waiting room. They found Katie in tears when they arrived, and both stopped dead in their tracks at the doorway.

"What is it?" David asked, feeling his heart jump up into his throat.

"I c-c-can't stop thinking about the d-donor's family," Katie sobbed. "Their baby had to die to give Melissa this chance to l-live."

David crossed the room and hunkered down in front of Katie. "I've thought about them, too. They've given Melissa an incredible gift, haven't they?"

Nodding, Katie sniffled and wiped away her tears with shaky fingertips. "I just wish we could tell them how much it means to us."

"I think they already know," David replied softly, "or they wouldn't have been able to be so generous, Katie."

Susan slipped into the room and sat beside Tom Reed. He grabbed her hand like a man going down for the last time. David kept talking to Katie, comforting her so tenderly, Susan's heart nearly shattered. She bit her lower lip and reminded herself she had to be tough for the Reeds. Like David.

The depth of his caring was too obvious for anyone to miss, yet he maintained his composure and gave all of them a calm anchor to cling to throughout the rest of the hellish wait. By the time an exhausted surgeon came in to report that the surgery was over and Melissa was doing as well as could be expected, Susan could barely find the strength to stand.

All four of them crowded together in a group hug and wept unashamedly at the news. Tension-relieving laughter filled the room when they broke apart and looked at each other. Then Tom Reed stuck out a beefy hand toward David.

"You've been a rock, man," he said. Including Susan in a broad smile, he added, "We can't thank either of you enough for everything you've done for us."

"It's been our pleasure," David assured him.

"Would you like us to stay with you tomorrow?" Susan asked.

Tom and Katie shook their heads in unison. "No, we'll be fine now," Katie promised. "If we can get through this operation, we can get through anything. Go get some rest."

"All right," David agreed. "Call if we can help and don't worry about anything but Melissa."

After a brief conference with Susan, he told the Reeds they had decided to drive back to Cheyenne, and escorted Susan out to his car. She collapsed into the passenger seat and reached across to unlock his door for him.

"Are you sure you're awake enough to drive all the way home?" she asked when he started the engine.

"No sweat. I'm so high right now, I could probably drive ll night. Take a nap if you want to, though."

"You were wonderful in there," she said, stifling a yawn. They really needed you. In fact, I don't think Katie would ave made it half as well without you."

He shrugged. "I like to feel needed."

David turned his head and shot her an intense look, as if e were waiting for her to say something. The words "I need ou" sat on the tip of her tongue, but he glanced away be- ore she could spit them out. A shuttered expression ropped over his face, and her courage failed her. Susan ut her eyes and rested her head against the seat for just a oment.

The next thing she knew, David was parking the car in her riveway and she was slumped against his right side, her eek resting on his shoulder. Blinking, she sat up, groggily ware that the first pale streaks of dawn were pushing at the ight. He ruffled her hair with a low chuckle, then opened s door and walked around the car to help her out.

The frigid air partially cleared her brain by the time they ached her front porch. David took Susan's key from her nd, opened the front door and set her things on the floor side. When he straightened, it seemed so natural to turn to his arms and lift her lips for a kiss, Susan didn't even esitate.

A deep groan rumbled out of his chest as his arms en- lded her and their mouths met in a rush of desperate nger. She gave herself up to the warmth of his embrace, lishing the taste of coffee on his tongue, delighting in his ique scent. God, she never wanted it to end. Never wanted let him go. Never wanted him to leave her again.

"Stay with me," she whispered when he finally pulled ck.

He gazed down at her, his eyes stormy with emotions she uldn't decipher. Then he sighed and sadly shook his head. Not like this, honey."

"What do you mean?"

"Neither one of us is thinking clearly. I can't make lov
to you again unless I'm sure you really know what yc
want."

"I do, David. I want you."

"Yeah, right now I think you do. But I need more tha
that from you, Susan."

"What do you need?"

"Your love. Your complete trust."

"I do love you. And I trust you, too."

"Enough to make a commitment? For a lifetime?"

Stunned by his questions, she pulled away slightly. '
have to answer that now? This minute?"

"That's what I thought," he said dryly, releasing h
completely.

"David, that's not fair," she protested, though her wor
sounded weak to her own ears.

"I didn't think you were ready for that yet." He gave h
a wistful smile. "In any case, you're too exhausted to kno
what you're doing or saying right now. I am, too."

He turned and walked across the porch, pausing at the tc
step. "But there's something I want you to know, honey.

"What's that?"

"If you ever are ready, all you have to do is call me."

Chapter Sixteen

The people of Cheyenne rejoiced at the news that Melissa Reed's transplant surgery had been successful and the baby was recovering well. The Christmas spirit blossomed, and even more donations poured into the bank. With David's parting challenge echoing constantly through the back of her mind during the next four days, however, Susan found it difficult to participate in the celebratory mood.

After what he had said, she didn't honestly believe he would reject her. The only thing that kept her from phoning him and announcing she was ready to make a commitment, was his statement about needing her complete trust. Could she promise him that and mean it for the rest of her life, no matter what happened?

Until she could answer that question with absolute certainty, it wouldn't be fair to either of them for her to contact him. And so she waited, agonizing over the decision she wanted to make but couldn't.

The phone was ringing when she walked in her front door after work on Wednesday. As usual, Timmy raced to answer it and came back a moment later with a puzzled expression on his face.

"It's some guy, Mom. He wants to talk to you, but he sounds funny."

"What do you mean?" Susan asked, hoping it wasn't a heavy breather.

"He says his words weird. Ya know, kinda like that guy we met at Frontier Days last summer? The one from England?"

"You mean he has an accent?"

"Yeah, that's it. Only it's not like the English guy's."

Smiling, Susan hurried to the phone. When the caller introduced himself as Bob Goldstein, the inside of her mouth dried up and her fingers tried to crush the receiver. Until that moment, she hadn't realized how desperately she'd wanted a positive response from Karen's agent.

"I've read your submission, Ms. Miller," he said with an accent that was pure New York City. "I'm happy to tell you I haven't seen anything this good in a long time. When can you send me the rest?"

Susan gulped, then stammered, "Uh, well, tomorrow."

"That's great. Send it overnight-express mail, so I can get it out to an editor I know before the holidays. With any luck she'll read it while she's on vacation, and we'll have an offer by the end of February."

"You really think someone will buy it?" she asked, mortified to hear her voice squeak on the "it."

"Oh, sure. I'm not talking bestseller, here, you understand," Bob cautioned her. "Not with your first book. But I definitely think you've got the potential. There's something that puzzles me, though."

"What's that?" Susan asked, her heart racing as it got the message that this wasn't a rejection.

"Karen told me this isn't the first novel you've written. Why haven't you submitted any of the others? Your writing's good enough. You should have sold something by now."

Susan recounted her earlier attempts at selling her work and the results. Bob was silent for a moment. Then he asked, "Were all of your rejections form letters? You know what I mean? The ones that say, 'Sorry, but this doesn't meet our needs. Good luck placing it elsewhere'?"

"Well, no. The last three or four had some suggestions for revisions, but—"

"Have you got them handy? I want you to read one to me. Don't worry, I'll hold."

Susan charged into her bedroom, dug the file out of her desk drawer with shaking fingers and ran back to the kitchen. She read the most encouraging letter to Bob and could almost hear a smile in his voice when he replied.

"I know that editor. If you'd made the changes he suggested and resubmitted that book, I'll bet you twenty bucks he would have bought it."

"But the letter doesn't say that. It doesn't even say he wants to see it again."

"He probably didn't realize he was dealing with a beginner. How many books have you finished?"

"The one you have is my sixth."

"Send me everything. You don't have to send them all express mail, just the last one. But I want to see every word you've written."

"May I ask a question?" Susan asked.

"Sure."

"I don't have any idea what kind of money is involved here. Do you think I can earn a living at writing?"

"I'll be honest with you. I wouldn't quit your job tomorrow. It takes a long time to get a steady income coming in. And even though I think you've got real potential, you've got to remember, I can't promise you anything."

He named what he called a modest figure, one that nearly gave Susan a coronary, and told her that would be his bottom line in negotiating for her.

"I understand," she answered.

"All right. Any more questions?"

"I don't think so. Not right now, anyway."

"It was great talking to you, Ms. Miller. I'll look forward to receiving the rest of your book."

Susan said goodbye, hung up the receiver and stared at it, immediately wondering if she'd imagined the entire conversation. At that moment, Timmy wandered into the kitchen.

"What did that guy with the accent want, Mom?"

She started at the sound of his voice, then whooped, grabbed him and gave him a big smacking kiss on the lips. He wiped it away with the back of his hand and glared at her in disgust.

"Whadja do *that* for?" he demanded.

"I'm sorry, honey." She laughed and ruffled his hair. "I was just so excited, I didn't realize what I was doing. The man you talked to is going to try to sell my book for me."

"Is that all?"

Susan rolled her eyes at the ceiling and told herself a seven-year-old couldn't possibly understand the implications of that phone call. "I'm afraid so," she answered with a smile. "Would supper at McDonald's help you forgive me?"

"You bet!"

Later that evening Susan boxed up the rest of her manuscript, tucked the boys in bed and found herself wandering through the house like a restless ghost. She wanted to call David and Karen and share her news. When Ed phoned to ask if the boys could visit him for the weekend, she literally had to bite her tongue to stop herself from telling him what a jerk he'd been about her writing.

As always, however, the cautious part of her nature asserted itself. Why tell anyone anything when Bob couldn't promise the book would sell? Why risk looking like an idiot if the whole thing fell through?

Hope was an unfamiliar emotion, one she knew she didn't handle at all well. Since Ed had left her, she'd practically banished it from her life. But had that been such a wise decision on her part?

Dammit, she *shouldn't* have given up trying to publish her writing, no matter what Ed had said or how many times she'd been rejected. At least not without putting up more of a fight. And she shouldn't have given up on David, either. Why on earth had she done such a stupid thing?

That question joined the first one in haunting Susan until Ed arrived on Friday night to pick up Eric and Timmy for the weekend. Again, he seemed subdued, even hesitant. Susan wondered if he had some kind of problem that she should know about. When he asked if he could speak to her privately, her suspicions mushroomed.

She sent the boys off to watch television and led the way into the kitchen. Ed accepted a cup of coffee and sat across from her at the table. The silence between them stretched out unbearably.

"What did you want to talk about?" Susan finally asked.

Ed stared into his mug for a long moment, then met her eyes with a surprisingly wary expression. "I want—" he paused and shook his head, "—no, I need to apologize to you."

"What for?"

"For treating you the way I did when we were married, and since then, too. I acted like a spoiled, selfish jerk, and I'm sorry."

Too stunned by his admission to reply immediately, Susan sipped her coffee. "What brought this on?"

"A couple of things. One was that my boss's son was killed in an accident three weeks ago. He was only six years old, and it made me realize just how important Timmy and Eric are to me. The way I've neglected them since the divorce, you could have made them hate me. But you didn't."

"That wouldn't have done them any good, Ed."

"No, I guess it wouldn't. But I want you to know I appreciate it, and I promise I'll do a better job of being a father to them." He slid a check across the table and gestured at it. "That's all of my missed support payments plus interest. I won't miss any more."

Susan picked up the blue piece of paper, her eyes widening in amazement when she saw the amount. "Thank you." Lord, this whole scene was so unreal, she never could have imagined it in her wildest dreams. "What was the other thing that brought this apology on?"

"Have the boys mentioned my friend Donna?" Ed asked.

"Once or twice. They seemed to like her pretty well."

He smiled at that and nodded his head. "Yeah, they do. I want to marry her, but she was pretty disgusted with me once she found out about the way I've treated you and the kids. She, uh, told me she wouldn't marry anyone who could be so irresponsible and informed me I had a lot of growing up to do."

"And you listened to her?"

"I didn't have much choice," Ed admitted with a shrug. "And I know she's right. When I passed the bar exam, I wanted everything right now—money prestige, all that stuff. I was angry when I didn't get it, and I took it out on you. I'm sorry."

"I can't believe you're really saying this," Susan muttered.

"I don't blame you." He reached across the table and covered her hand with his. "But I am saying it, and I mean it. You were a good wife, Susan. And you're a wonderful mother. I just didn't have the brains to appreciate you when we were married. I know you don't love me anymore, but can you ever forgive me?"

Something cold and hard melted in Susan's heart, and her eyes misted with tears. "I, uh, think so. Eventually."

A slow, sweet smile spread across Ed's handsome features, making him look almost as young as he'd been when Susan had first met him. A faint, warm glow of remembered affection settled in the pit of her stomach. So. She hadn't married a total jerk, after all.

"That's all I can ask." He patted her hand, then pushed back his chair and stood. When Susan followed suit, he asked, "Do you think Timmy and Eric will ever like me as much as they like your friend Hunter?"

"I don't see why not. Most kids want to love their parents, Ed. The boys will come around when they learn they can trust you."

"I hope you're right. Well, I guess we'd better get on the road. I'll have them back by Sunday night." He walked into the living room and helped the boys collect their coats and luggage. They raced outside to his car, and he turned to Susan in the doorway. "Do you have any plans for the weekend?"

Susan glanced across the street, saw David's car parked in the driveway and nodded thoughtfully. "Yeah." she said with a smile. "I think I just might."

Hearing a car door slam across the street, David peeked out his front window, cursing vehemently when he recognized Ed Miller's car pulling away from the curb. What had that creep said to hurt Susan this time? he wondered. The blinking, multicolored lights Susan had strung around her picture window mocked him with their holiday cheer, and he stomped back to his recliner.

After settling his butt into the chair, he supposed he should be grateful he *could* stomp, now that the doctor had finally given him permission to walk without his orthopedic splint. But he didn't feel one damn bit grateful at the moment. As far as he was concerned, Ebenezer Scrooge had the right idea about Christmas. He scowled at the fir tree Jason and Melody had cut and helped to decorate.

Sheba jumped into his lap without waiting for an invitation. Resigning himself to a long, boring evening, he used the remote control to turn on his television and stroked the pup. When his doorbell rang ten minutes later, he muttered another curse, dumped Sheba off his lap and went to answer it.

He yanked open the door without looking first to see who had the gall to bother him on a Friday night and opened his mouth to give the intruder a large piece of what little was left of his mind. Then he stopped and stared when Susan gave him a hesitant smile.

"Are you busy?" she asked softly.

"Uh...no."

Her lips twitched, no doubt because he was still standing there, gaping at her like a beached trout.

"Do you mind if I come in for a while?" she said. "I'd like to talk to you."

"Of course not. Come on in." He stepped back and allowed her to enter, warning himself not to get his hopes up too high. "Would you like some coffee? Wine? A coke?"

"No, thanks. Don't go to any trouble."

"It's no trouble. I was just about to make some popcorn. Would you like some? I've got beer, too."

He cringed inside. Dammit, he knew he was babbling, but was completely helpless to stop himself. From her placid expression, he couldn't get even a flicker of a hint about what she wanted.

"Why don't we talk first?" she suggested.

"All right. Have a seat."

He hung up her coat in the closet and followed her into the living room, his stomach crawling with apprehension. Sheba jumped up beside Susan on the sofa, insisting on washing the woman's face whether it needed it or not.

Laughing, Susan petted the exuberant dog, who promptly curled up and rested her chin on Susan's knee.

Susan turned and looked at David, a sudden, delighted grin crossing her face. "You're not using your cane or your brace anymore!"

Her grin brightened the room better than a hundred-watt light bulb. His tension increasing by the second, David settled into his recliner, gripping the armrests so tightly his knuckles ached. "I got rid of them this week. I'm supposed to use the cane if I walk a long distance, but I don't need it around the house."

"So your knee's all healed now?"

"Pretty much. I still have to exercise it regularly and be careful, but it's coming right along."

"That's wonderful, David."

"Yeah, it's nice to be more mobile."

She folded her hands in her lap and took a deep breath, as if fortifying herself for an ordeal. "Well, I suppose you're wondering why I'm here."

"You might say that," David said, relieved to hear his voice sound calm and rational when his chest suddenly felt too tight for his heart and his gut had tied itself into an excruciating knot.

"All right. I just wanted you to know I'm ready."

He shot forward in his chair. "Are you sure, Susan? Really sure? If you say yes, there won't be any going back," he warned. *You idiot!* his mind screamed. *Why are you giving her a chance to back out?*

A wicked twinkle leaped into her eyes, and she nodded. "I'm absolutely, positively sure. I love you, Hunter, and I'll gladly trust you with my life."

David exhaled a silent sigh of relief, but there was still another question he had to have answered before he could kiss those luscious lips of hers the way he wanted to. "What changed your mind?"

"I finally figured out it wasn't you I didn't trust."

"I'm glad to hear that, but I'm not sure I understand."

"It's kind of hard to explain." She briefly told him about her conversations with Bob Goldstein and Ed.

David whooped triumphantly when she told him about the agent; his eyes bugged out in surprise when she repeated what her ex-husband had said. Then he gave her an encouraging smile. "Go on now, finish the story."

Susan shrugged. "I guess it was a cumulative thing. I believed in my writing at first, and I believed in Ed and our marriage and our family. They were the most important things in my life. When none of them worked out the way I'd expected, I couldn't trust my own judgment anymore. And I just . . . gave up."

Unable to tolerate not touching her for one more second, David bolted across the room, pushed Sheba out of the way and sat down beside her. Wrapping his arms around her, he said "That must have been awful for you."

"It was," she agreed, her words belied by a radiant smile as she turned and laced her fingers behind his neck. "It probably didn't help that my dad walked out on my mom when I was thirteen, either. But it's all over now."

He closed his eyes and rested his forehead against hers. "God, I'm so glad, Susan." His throat tightened, and he had to swallow before he could continue. "I was scared to death when you showed up here tonight. I thought you'd come to tell me it was all over."

Running her fingers through the hair above the back of his collar, Susan pulled back and shook her head at him. "No way, Hunter. Now will you please just shut up and kiss me before I lose my mind?"

David was more than happy to oblige. He pulled Susan onto his lap and, bending her over his arm, fastened his mouth to hers. Her lips parted instantly on a soft sigh of delight, and he drank in the sound and the sweet taste of her mouth, feeling as if he'd finally come home.

His body raged with a need more intense than anything he'd ever felt before, but he was determined to draw every last possible second of pleasure out of making love to her. Her hands dove under the hem of his sweater and tugged the shirt he'd worn under it from the waistband of his jeans.

Her eager, loving exploration of his chest left fingerprints on his heart and made his head spin. Damn. So much for staying in control. If he didn't get them into the bedroom fast, they'd never make it at all.

Breathing raggedly, he pulled his mouth away and captured Susan's hands under his shirt. "Honey, wait a minute."

"Whassa matter?" she murmured, nibbling on his neck.

"Let's do this right."

Eyelids lowered to half-mast, she shot him a teasing glance. "Why? Is there going to be a quiz?"

He pulled her upright and nudged her off his lap, standing beside her an instant later. Chuckling at her quizzical expression, he took her hand and led her into his bedroom. "I just thought we'd be more comfortable in here," he explained, wrapping both arms around her waist. "Besides, I've been fantasizing for weeks about making love with you in my bed."

Susan eyed the king-size waterbed with its mirrored headboard, and remembered a few of her own feverish imaginings about that particular piece of furniture. Talk about room to romp!

"Oh, yeah?" she asked, grinning up at him. "How kinky were your fantasies?"

"Pretty damn kinky." He stripped off her sweater, tossed it onto his dresser and went to work on her belt buckle.

"Why don't you tell me about them?" she suggested, returning the favor.

"Because—" he paused to taste her mouth again, then scooped her up, deposited her on the mattress and lay down beside her "—I'd rather show you."

"Now that sounds interesting."

"Oh, it will be. I promise. And you know, I always keep my promises."

Resting his weight on one elbow, he leaned over her with a leer, making the bed slosh gently and Susan chuckle.

"I've never done this on a waterbed before," she confessed. "What if I get seasick?"

"It won't rock that much."

Sheba wandered into the room and jumped onto the bed, barking as if she ought to be allowed to join in the fun. David rolled his eyes toward heaven and muttered, "Why me?" Susan suffered a fit of giggles as he chased the pup around the bed, grabbed her and hauled her out of the room, closing the door in the animal's face with a loud snap.

Ignoring Sheba's pitiful whines, he shucked off the rest of his clothes on the way back to the bed. Susan propped her head up with one hand and enjoyed watching her own private strip show. Pretending he was an exotic dancer, David swung his tight buns around the room and rippled the impressive muscles in his arms and shoulders for her.

Susan applauded his efforts when he approached her with a cocky yet sheepish grin, then noticed the vivid red scar across his left knee. "Oh, David," she whispered, suddenly wanting to cry as she reached out to trace it with her index finger. "You poor baby."

He sat beside her, dislodging her hand in the process. "It's pretty ugly, isn't it?" he asked, his expression grim as he studied her face. "If it puts you off, we can turn out the light."

She jerked her head up and scowled at him. "You think I'm that shallow?" she demanded, climbing off the bed and stripping off the rest of her clothes while she scolded him. "Good Lord, you got that scar saving my son's life! You may be the most gorgeous man I've ever seen, but I don't love you for your looks."

When she was as naked as he was, Susan grabbed him by the shoulders, pushed him flat on the bed and loomed over him. "I'd love you if you were the ugliest man alive, Hunter, and you'd damn well better believe it. Is that clear?"

His eyes dancing with laughter, David pulled her down on top of him. "Absolutely. And I love you for saying it."

"Been worried about that, have you?"

"It's crossed my mind a time or two," he answered in a more serious tone. "And I've had a few women chase me because of the family name and . . . well, the money."

"Did you worry about me that way?"

He smiled and shook his head. "Nope. Never."

"Why not?"

"Because you let Jason go. And you thought the boys' relationship with their father was more important than getting money out of him. Even money he owed you." He rolled over, pinning her beneath him. Bracing his weight on his elbows, he asked, "Are we done talking yet?"

"I don't know. It's been so long since we really talked, I'm enjoying it."

"Kinda like we had to get to know each other again, huh?"

"Yeah." She ran the heel of one foot from his ankle to his calf. "But I think we're pretty well acquainted now."

Smiling, he lowered his head and effectively cut off any further verbal communication. She reveled in his kiss, delighting in the taste of him, the scent of him, the glorious freedom to touch him wherever she wanted. He shifted to his side, freeing one hand to caress her in return.

This was how making love was supposed to be, she thought. Sharing and laughing and pleasuring each other. Releasing insecurities and inhibitions. Touching vulnerable spots, both physical and emotional, without even wanting to hold back for fear of paying a painful price later.

She tried to tell him how she felt with her lips and her hands, but he pulled away and held her hands at her sides. "Last time you did most of the work," he said in a hoarse whisper. "Now it's my turn."

His dark eyes glowed with a loving intensity that stole her breath. Nodding, she gave herself up to his caressing hands and mouth. Lord, she loved his hands. They were big, strong and bold, and yet infinitely tender. His mouth spread magic wherever it touched—her neck, her breasts, her stomach, her thighs, the backs of her knees, her toes.

She reached for him again, wanting to touch him with a need that was almost painful. He pushed her hands down and straddled her, then patiently went back to stroking and fondling and kissing, making her feel cherished and beautiful and so very, very loved.

Glorious sensations washed over her body in waves, as if echoing the gentle rocking motion of the mattress.

Excitement built within her, layer upon layer, with each moist kiss, each increasingly demanding caress, until she heard her own voice begging him to come inside her. He slid one hand between her thighs and fumbled in a small drawer in the headboard with the other.

A moment later he parted her legs and positioned himself between them. "Open your eyes, honey," he murmured in a husky tone, "I want to see them."

When she obeyed, he joined their bodies together with one strong thrust and placed his hands on either side of her head. Gazing up at him, she felt as if he'd connected himself to her heart as well. She wrapped her legs around his waist and held him close.

"You're so responsive, so wonderful," he whispered, moving slowly inside her.

Her neck arched back at the intense pleasure, and she caught sight of them in the mirror. God, but he was beautiful. The powerful muscles in his arms and shoulders and chest stood out in bold relief. Seeing as well as feeling the smooth, rhythmic motion of his hips was unbelievably erotic.

"Yes, sweetheart. Look at us," he urged, picking up the tempo. "See how incredible we are together."

Her eyes found his reflected gaze, and she couldn't look away. Her hips rose and fell of their own accord, meeting his deep thrusts. His breathing grew ragged, and he praised her in a rough voice that coaxed even greater passion from her. The tension inside her mounted unbearably, and she was grasping, straining, reaching for that sweet, aching release she needed so desperately, she would die if she didn't find it.

Then it happened. That sharp, exquisite instant when time stands still and souls fly in unison. She gasped at the wonder of it, felt his body go rigid, heard his joyful cry of completion. He collapsed on top of her for a moment before rolling to one side, bringing her with him. They lay facing each other while their harsh breathing settled back to normal. She caressed his dear face with trembling fingers. He kissed her fingertips, closed his eyes and sighed with supreme satisfaction.

His smug grin irritated and tickled her at the same time. She tweaked a tuft of his chest hair and whined, "You're not one of those guys who rolls over and starts to snore afterward, are you?"

David's eyes shot open, and he raised up on one elbow. He shook his head at her impish smile, then drawled, "No, ma'am."

"Whew!" She wiped the back of her hand across her forehead in mock relief. "Am I ever glad to hear that."

"Why is that, Miller?"

"Because I have an important question for you."

Draping his free arm over her waist, he eyed her warily for moment. "All right. What is it?"

"Will you marry me, David?"

"Yes."

He laid his head back down and closed his eyes again.

"Yes?" she yelped, poking him in the ribs. "I ask you a estion like that, and that's all you've got to say?"

He opened one eye. "Would you rather I said no?"

"Of course not. But don't you think we should discuss a w things? Like . . . like babies for instance?"

"I vote for at least two more," he answered immediately, ving her a wicked grin. "If we hurry, you can be fat and egnant with Melody."

"She's pregnant?"

"About three months. Wait'll you get a load of Jason's oud papa-act. It's a real hoot."

"And I don't suppose you'll be that way at all," Susan d dryly.

"I'll probably be certifiably nuts. You won't mind, will u?" he asked, nibbling at her earlobe.

"No. I won't mind at all." Laughing, she hunched her oulder up toward her ear to block his access. "Stop that. e need to talk about some other things, too."

Heaving a long-suffering sigh, he sat up and propped his low against the headboard, then helped her do the same, hen he had her settled in the crook of his arm with her ad resting on his chest, he asked, "Okay, what else is on ur mind?"

"Just a few minor details, like when we're going to get rried, what kind of wedding we want, where we're going live. Thank God we don't have to worry about the boys cepting you."

"Yeah, I'm glad about that, too. Now, as for your list, I nk we should get married as soon as possible, like, New ar's Day, so I'll never forget our anniversary."

"But that's only ten days away," she protested.

He went on as if she hadn't spoken. "We can have a kind of wedding you and my mom and sisters can plan a pull off in that amount of time. You'll be amazed what th can accomplish when they put their heads together."

"Are you out of your mind?"

He answered with calm determination. "No, I just wa you to be my wife. Let's see, what else was there? Oh, yea I think we should stay in this neighborhood until school ge out, for Timmy's sake. It'd be easier to move me to yo house than the other way around, so that takes care of tha I'll get Paul Stauffer to start looking for a bigger place can move into this summer. You'll be writing full-time then, so remind me to tell him we'll need lots of bedroo and an office for you with big windows and—"

"Whoa. Stop. Slow down," Susan said, unsuccessfu choking back hysterical laughter.

He raised an affronted eyebrow at her. "What's so dan funny? I'm just trying to get all this stuff off your brain you can concentrate on me."

"And you're doing a wonderful job," she assured hi "but we don't have to rush into this so fast everyone will watching my waistline and counting months. You're stu with me now, buster, whether you want me or not."

He slid down in the bed and turned toward her, meeti her eye to eye as he caged her with his arms. "Oh, I wa you, babe. Don't ever doubt that."

Then he kissed her deeply, reigniting that familiar, s zling excitement.

Several long, delicious kisses later, Susan murmure "Sheba's been howling a long time. Do you think she nee to go outside?"

"She's got a doggy door," he answered, nuzzling her l breast.

"Then why is she carrying on like that? The neighbors a going to start complaining if she keeps it up."

He moved over to give her right breast the same lovi attention. "She's probably lonesome."

She cupped his chin with both hands and forced him to look at her. "Don't tell me. Let me guess. You've been letting her sleep with you."

"Hey, I was lonesome for you," he admitted. "She was a lot of company."

"Do you have any idea how big she's going to get?" Susan scolded him with a laugh. "She's going to want to sleep in your bed for the rest of her life now. There won't be any room for me when she's full grown."

He moved up to meet her eye level again, smiling complacently. "No, she won't. She'll sleep with Timmy and Eric as soon as we're married."

"I can see you've got it all figured out." Susan linked her hands behind his neck and kissed his bristly chin. "You know, it's funny?"

"What's funny?"

"When Jason got married, I thought I'd missed out on the last good man alive."

"So now you think I am?" he asked with a pleased laugh.

"No. There must be quite a few good men around, after all."

His eyebrows drew together in a scowling V. "Well, thanks a whole chunk, Miller. I guess I'll have to be content with being the most gorgeous man you've ever seen, huh?"

"No, silly." She gave his rump a playful swat that got his attention fast. "Now I think you're the best man alive. In every possible way."

"I like the way you think."

"Mmm, I thought you would."

* * * * *

proudly presents
the long-awaited "prequel" volume of

★ LOVE AND GLORY ★

by
LINDSAY McKENNA

Dawn of Valor

In the summer of '89, Silhouette Special Edition premiered three novels celebrating America's men and women in uniform: LOVE AND GLORY, by bestselling author Lindsay McKenna. Featured were the proud Trayherns, a military family as bold and patriotic as the American flag—three siblings valiantly battling the threat of dishonor, determined to triumph... in love and glory.

Now, discover the roots of the Trayhern brand of courage, as parents Chase and Rachel relive their earliest heartstopping experiences of survival and indomitable love, in

Dawn of Valor, Silhouette Special Edition #649.

This February, experience the thrill of LOVE AND GLORY—from the very beginning!

DV-1

Star-crossed lovers?
Or a match made in heaven?

Why are some heroes strong and silent . . . and others charming and cheerful? The answer is WRITTEN IN THE STARS!

Coming each month in 1991, Silhouette Romance presents you with a special love story written by one of your favorite authors—highlighting the hero's astrological sign! From January's sensible Capricorn to December's disarming Sagittarius, you'll meet a dozen dazzling and distinct heroes.

Twelve heavenly heroes . . . twelve wonderful Silhouette Romances destined to delight you. Look for one WRITTEN IN THE STARS title every month throughout 1991—only from Silhouette Romance.

STAR

Silhouette Books®